CalmWaters Entertainment Group, Inc.
*presents*

# The Pussy Whispers

Dean Jéan-Pierre

Library of Congress Cataloging-in-Publication Data
Dean Jéan-Pierre, 1968
ISBN:  978-0-615-35426-2
ISBN:  0615354262
This is a work of fiction. All of the characters, organizations,
and events portrayed either are products of the author's
imagination or used fictitiously.

**The Pussy Whispers**
Copyright 2010 by Dean Jéan-Pierre
CalmWaters Entertainment Group, Inc.
2085 Lynnhaven Parkway
Virginia Beach, VA 23456
www.calmwatersentertainment.com
Dean Jéan-Pierre  www.deanjeanpierre.com

*Book Design:  Cynthia M. Colbert*

# Acknowledgements

*I suppose it would be right, and it is right to thank God first of all like everybody else does. Thank you, God for whatever talent you have blessed me with to this point in my life. Thank you to Pascale Jacques, CalmWaters Entertainment Group, Inc., for all your insights, hard work and dedication to get this project off the ground and finished. Thank you to Rachel Deveaux for your help in editing the stories. I would imagine reading so much erotica over and over would drive one crazy. I appreciate it immensely. Also, a special thanks goes to Ms. Cynthia M. Colbert for her assistance in helping to design the Pussy Whispers vision for the book cover.*

*Everyone who helped bring this project to life or inspired me: Holden Caulfield, J.D. Salinger, Mark Moross, Dewanna Planter, Michelle Brandy, Lesa Gilbert, Billy Pilgrim and Deanny Jean-Pierre. Thank you!*

*To all my English teachers who urged me to write. I don't know if they thought I would be writing erotica...oh well. Thank you!*

*Thank you to everyone who has taken the time out to read my stories and offered their critique and insights.*

# Table of Contents

# The Pussy Whispers

Every woman's pussy has its own distinctive moans, screams, whispers, texture, and flavor. It's as if it has an internal DNA code that is locked safely away in her G spot and inside the deep pool of her honey nectar sweetness. Only the talent of an especially persuasive tongue or dick, with magical depth perception and width expansion, can elicit the whispers that will make her reveal all of her secrets to you in torrents of orgasmic pleasure. The pussy will not just whisper for any old smooth licking tongue that cunnilingus along and demands to taste its most private and treasured secret that has been known to suck men into a honeycomb coma and drive them crazy with desire. Just merely sticking your tongue in a honey pot won't get you any honey. You might get a drip, but what is a drip when you can drink from the entire pot if you are patient, gentle, and deserving of a pussy's entire honey nectar.

A pussy whispers softly like a gentle breeze caressing your face seductively when it finds a man who is worthy of kissing all four of her lips with equal fervor. Even after his thirst has been quenched, a man who relishes a tongue bath in the fountain of nectar passion because his pussy's needs haven't been completely satisfied is a man who understands. He understands that when his pussy whispers for more tongue or dick, he has to quiet that whisper down until all is silent and his pussy smiles with wet content.

The whispers of a pussy is a hushed breath so low that only another pussy in the immediate radius of its throbbing heat of arousal can hear this whisper of its initial attraction to the male species. It is a mating call of a slow drizzle of pussy nectar that moistens her lips and slowly drifts into the air. When it merges with a woman's perfume, any man within the vicinity of this powerful aphrodisiac becomes inebriated from the combination of pussy nectar and the latest perfume created by a myriad of today's music and movie stars. A woman does not have to say her name or even smile at a man; the scent of her honey nectar floating through the air will bring the desired man to her, and when she does smile at him, an extra dosage of nectar is triggered and released into the air. The seduction has begun, and we are powerless to resist the whispers of a pussy in full throbbing mode.

Many men through the years have laid false claims to knowing the secrets that will release the fountain of pussy nectar (cunt, vagina, twat, punani, putang), that would make a woman's pussy sing like an angel or meow like a cat in heat. Truth be told, a pussy is like a combination lock, and without the right sequence of perfect tongue strokes, it is highly unlikely that it will whisper its most intimate wettest secrets to you. It is only an act of patience, a seductive tongue tease, an assortment of deep and shallow probes, combined with aerobic swirls, probing licks, and soft kisses, that will seduce a pussy into releasing the warmth of its nectar unto your tongue. A man can talk a good game of

7

flirtation and seduction that will initially make a woman interested, but his tongue has to be able to do more than just talk a good game; it has to be a seeker of hidden pearls, a treasure finder, and be able to slide in and out of every moist crevice of a woman's nectar pussy to elicit moans of whispered passion that will resonate in his ears and throughout her body long after she has come. A nimble tongue records the sequence or the path of every tongue twist and curl that makes a woman's pussy bloom on your tongue and feed it nature's sweetest nectar passion. The tongue is an amazing instrument, melodically in sync with the brain to create muscle memory that allows it to precisely repeat its tongue strokes. Once the taste buds of the tongue has been aroused, and the first drop of honey nectar dew wets the papillae, the tongue becomes inebriated from the taste; the scent of fevered moist passion sends it on a natural high to extract more honey and incessant pussy whispers to keep it tasting and swallowing sweet nectar all throughout the night. There are times when the nectar of a pussy is so sweet, and the whispers so hypnotic--that men have been known to suck on a woman's quivering lips while she sleeps and wake her with an early morning tonguegasm. Sleep is still in their eyes as they wake up, and they don't even know if they are going—but they do know that they are coming.

The whispers of a pussy can be further enhanced, and taken to a swelling of pleasure, when a man is able to wield the power of his dick in concert with the thirsty hunger of his tongue. Most men often misunderstand the dick as the only tool in their arsenal to bring a woman to her orgasmic peak, but in truth, it should be the last. By the time a man gets down to filling the swollen lips of his woman's pussy, she should be so wet and intoxicated with passion, that all four of her sweet lips are literally quivering to be filled with the throbbing heat of his manhood. Making love to your woman is like a long slow dance. Even if you are not having sex with her, you are laying the foundation for everything that is to come, and the pleasure that both of you will receive. The feel of your body against hers, the scent of your cologne turning her on, whispered words of passion as you fit her body into yours, starts the drizzling of passion between her moist lips that will soon welcome you into her heaven. You have to fuck her mind with your words thus creating the images of passion before you can sexfucklove her body. The tongue is a man's secret weapon to incite a woman's thoughts with erotic images, and those images cause a rippling quivering effect to start the pussy whispering and moaning even before penetration has been achieved.

The pussy will moan for a man before he makes love to a woman or dicks her down to within an inch of her life. Her whispers and moans turn into cries of sheer joy and amazement, but it will not be an audible moan or whisper to let you know that her flower is slowly opening to receive you. The moans will be the yearning look of ravenous passion in her eyes as she silently tries to convey to you that you are fucking her. That she is making love to you. Her lips, when they part slowly, open with moistness. The unchanged look in her eyes is her silent acknowledgment to you that as you continue to arouse her, the sweet ripe lips hidden between her thighs will be yours to taste, fill, and whisper any words that you want it to say. You will hear the fevered whispers of her pussy when you hold her close, and her skin is on fire from the sun throbbing between her thighs. It is a fire so intense that it will enflame everything around you. When you taste her lips with your tongue and kiss her for the first time, her pussy will moan against the throbbing heat of your manhood, and you will know. Her pussy whispers for your touch, your kisses, your tongue, and to be filled with the thickness of your probing manhood.

When a woman's pussy whispers to you, it is a call to action that you must answer with a fervor that will turn her whispers into sweet moanful music. A melody that you will continually hear each time you make love or dick her down because she is happy. She has exposed her truest sexual self to you, and you reveled in her nakedness without a second thought of backing down. Her pussy whispered and the right man stepped forward to do what a woman requires of her man, which is to love her mind, body, and soul. While he is doing all of that, he must also ravish and devour her pussy until all her moans and whispers have lost their voice and all she can do is close her eyes and smile.

2/18/09...1:10pm

# After Office Hours

The flurry of erotic texts flying back and forth all day between them overwhelmed Stacey.  Every time her inbox lit up with Duke's name, a heat would circulate throughout her entire body and her fingers trembled as she read his seductive words of passion, lust and desire. She would slowly trace her fingertips over her blackberry screen and fully absorb the passion of his words, and every syllable felt like his dick was probing the tightness of her moist pretty wings.  Sometimes, she would try to anticipate the next message from him and have her blackberry either between her thighs or against her chest so that the vibration felt like sustained throbs of dick-pounding thrusts invading her sweet pussy.

She had it bad!

If she closed her eyes tightly enough, and cleared her mind of all work distractions, Stacey could feel his warm breath tickling her ears and making her pussy wet like an early morning May shower.  Sometimes her pussy became so wet that she had now taken to bringing an extra pair of panties to work just in case she had another unexpected orgasm.  Last week, while texting Duke and speaking to a client at the same time, he made her come in her panties so hard that she had forgotten that she was on the phone with a client and moaned loudly.  An awkward silence had ensued before they got back to business.

*This is the kind of power he held over her that no man had before—not her ex-husband, nor previous boyfriends.* None of them had been able to release the true submissive woman in her. It had always been there; anxiously waiting to be released, but they didn't know how to set it free and thus make her into the passionate woman she yearned to be. Surprisingly, Duke had been able to do, in a short time, what men before him could not accomplish. Maybe it was his smile or his casual manner that threw her off guard, and she lowered her defenses to allow him inside her sanctuary.

They had met a few weeks ago when Duke worked in her building on a temporary assignment. He stopped by to introduce himself and it all seemed innocent to Stacey. She appreciated him saying hello without the requisite come on that most men approach women with before they even know their names, whether they're married, or even interested in becoming involved. He was attractive enough but nothing to get your panties wet, or to fantasize about. His head was clean-shaven, thick eyebrows, sensual brown eyes, and lips that looked like they had made a few women scream his name during his lifetime. He was a shade darker than her light complexion, and at 5'11 stood three inches taller than Stacey. It always starts innocently enough, and before you can catch your breath, you are riding the dick of a man and calling him names that you swore you would never call any man.

Today, her mind had wandered to him a few times and lingered on what he might be doing and to whom he might be talking. Every orifice in her body screamed to have him inside of her aching pussy and etching his name permanently inside her pink walls. Two weeks without having him inside of her had been pure torture for Stacey. She had laughed when she heard her girlfriends talk about worshipping some guy's dick as if it was an erectile god that could cure the ails of any woman and could feed the countless hungry pussies all around the world, with a nut or two still to spare for anyone who wanted seconds. Now she had quickly become addicted to his kisses, the way he set her body on fire so easily, and the constant insane cravings she had to suck his dick and having him stretch her pussy walls with his thickness. Days after they had first made love, Stacey could still feel his fat dick pulsating inside of her as he laid claim to her body and mind. It was only Tuesday, and Saturday seemed so far away until they would meet again for the second time. Her body craved for a taste of his flesh or anything that was attached to him that could satiate her hunger until he could dick her down again. When a woman is incessantly craving a dick, it becomes a lifeline to the next moment, the next day. Until you can feel that same intense feeling again, everything you do doesn't seem to hold the same importance as it once did. Only when you can come again with the same fervor and intensity, will the haziness dissipate and glorious sunshine make its triumphant return to prominence.

There is sometimes no rhyme or reason why certain women have the ability to inspire a man's desires, making him crave her constantly. Duke had craved others before Stacey. He had indulged in the feathery sweetness of full lips and pussies that could make a grown man weep like a baby as he begged to be let back into the sanctuary of her heavenly wetness. With Stacey, she intoxicated his senses with just the sensuality of her laughter, how she would blush furiously whenever he said something naughty. He would imagine her pussy lips blushing with the same pink hue as her cheeks. The good girl image that she had carefully cultivated over the years was under intense attack from Duke with every conversation, every word, every kiss and every time he was in Stacey's presence; he was infiltrating her defenses and was now settling deep inside of her. Duke knew he had her. He knew that she would do anything he asked of her because she did not want to disappoint him.

Stacey felt alive as if she was living on the edge, and for the very first time, embracing her true sexual self without having to apologize to anyone for craving her sexual desires to be completely satisfied. Saturday could not come fast enough for her to let Duke hurt her pussy ever so sweetly with his beautiful long dick strokes. She shivered as she closed her eyes and imagined him inside of her.

At 5 p.m., the office was ghost town as everyone tried to beat the traffic getting out of Virginia and into D.C. and Maryland. There is usually no way around traffic during rush hour therefore Stacey usually left an hour later and spent that time catching up on emails while listening to the Michael Baisden Show on WHUR. Although Stacey thought Baisden to be an arrogant SOB, she still thought his show topics were timely and always informative for his audience. Today's show was about addicted women who were damn near losing their ever-loving horny minds with constant cravings for the dick, and everything else that came with it. Stacey almost spit out her Kiwi-Strawberry juice drink when she heard the topic. Was the universe trying to tell her something? Were her moon and stars aligning for a perfect storm of monsoon cum weather? Baisden read a recent survey conducted in a popular women's magazine about the five signs to know when your pussy has been whipped more than a black child's ass by his parents:

### You Know You Are Addickted When:

1) The sound of his voice sends your already turned on body into shivers and just sucking his dick can give you an orgasm. You have never relished sucking a dick as much as you do now because every suck of his throbbing head can make you come without him even penetrating you.

2) You wake up screaming his name in a pool of your own cum and you masturbate multiple times while enjoying a picture of his dick on your

computer or cell phone while sitting at your desk at work. You also made sure to send his dick pictures to your multiple e-mail accounts—just in case they somehow were accidentally deleted from one account—you will have extra copies.

3) You find yourself doing and saying things that at first make you cringe that you have become this person who allows her desires to overwhelm her senses. The words that come from your mouth shocks you but you can no longer help yourself because your body and mind are constantly on fire for his touch, his kisses…his dick that you want to mold so it can always be with you.

4) You know in your heart that you are heading down a one-way street and you can't turn back but you are powerless to resist what you are feeling. Addictions by their very nature usually don't end well but you don't care—just this one time, you will throw caution to the wind as the sensual pleasure that has invaded your life makes you do so.

5) You neglect your friends just on the off
chance that he might drop by or call
you.  You want to be ready just in case
he decides to come by for a few minutes.

Stacey shook her head in amazement as she walked down the hall past the cleaning crew on the way to the bathroom and nodded hello to them.  Was she really dick whipped?  Was her pussy now on a short leash for Duke?  She suspected that the cleaning men would sneak glances at her thick frame when she walked by but she could never prove it.  The roar of the vacuum cleaners masked their words, but men will be men.  They can't help sneaking a peek at every reasonably decent woman that walks by, and by the time she has walked away, every hole on her body has been filled in a man's imagination.

Stacey's sweet holes ached to be filled by Duke as she stepped into the bathroom.  For a moment, she wished he was hiding in the bathroom waiting to devour her.  Yeah...she was whipped and loving every minute of it!  Her laughter resounded in the bathroom and was drowned out by the vacuuming noises outside of the door.  The face staring back at her from the bathroom window was beautiful according to what men had always told her.  If pressed, she would have to admit that she was a beautiful woman according to the standards of society.  Her light complexion and unblemished skin were decorated with amber colored eyes, soft pink lips that were always glossy and ready to be kissed.  There was an approachable warmth to her smile that gave men

17

confidence when they approached her, that she would not laugh in their faces and send running away with their limp dicks between their legs. They could not possibly know that beneath her confident exterior was a woman so shy that hearing herself moan during sex made her blush profusely.

She peered in closer to the mirror to apply her cherry lip gloss, and she licked her lips as she imagined his manhood trapped between its warmth. It wasn't something a lady was supposed to brag about but she loved giving head. The reaction she received in the past confirmed that she was quite good at it and she loved doing it because it gave her pleasure. Feeling a man's erection pulsating like a heart beat between her lips turned her on and made her so wet that if she relaxed her pussy muscles, cum would gush from between her pretty wings like a fire hydrant in the middle of summer. The fact that her man became a moaning, groaning, screaming idiot when her soft lips strangled his dick was a bonus.

The cleaning guys pretended to be busy as she walked by but Stacey felt their eyes on her ample bottom. The men gave each other knowing looks and simulated spanking her ass as they rode her hard and deep without any mercy. Stacey consciously slowed her steps down but with the black skirt she was wearing, her ass had a mind of its own as it sashayed back and forth in search of attention. She heard the elevator door open behind her as she opened the office door and locked it without turning back. A few seconds later, the tapping of fingers against the glass door made her turn around, her eyes opened wide and a look of shock was etched across her face.

*It was him.* It was Duke.

Stacey stood there dumbfounded as if unsure of what to do as she stared at his dark frame through the glass door. The lettering of the company's logo on the glass fragmented his face like a jigsaw puzzle. She stared directly through the O in Operations and his sensual pussy sucking lips teased her, sending her mind racing again to the first time he sucked on her lips and clit and buried the girth of his gauntlet inside of her moistness. She could still feel him throbbing and sliding deep inside of her days after they had made love. It was as if his deep probing had opened a secret portal inside of her pussy and she craved to have him inside of her again so she could drown his dick in the sweetness of her rosewater. A spring of wetness bubbled furiously inside of her panties as she watched him and she pierced her lips to swallow her moans. Her pussy was conveying to her in urgent Morse code what her mind and body were craving.

Duke stood there, unmoving, staring intently at her, fucking her with his eyes and daring her not to let him in. Her body quivered with desire and it felt like a thousand needles pierced in every pore of her body. However, there were only two pores she desired something deep inside of at the moment. A sudden naughty thought of lifting up her skirt and bending over her desk to let him fuck his pussy flashed across her mind.  Her clit throbbed in compliance of her thoughts. The intensity of that thought made her blush.  Looking at her suddenly blushing through the closed door, he knew what she was thinking.  He had come for the same reasons that were written all over her face and danced in her amber eyes.

Duke wasn't sure if Stacey would still be in her office, but he decided that being spontaneous and catching her off guard would work in his favor.  After today, she would always wonder if maybe today would be the day that he would come by again unannounced. He would always be on her mind even when she wasn't totally conscious of his presence.  Years of experience had taught him that the mind was the biggest sexual organ. If you are able to infiltrate it and fill it with erotic thoughts and images that will remain even in your absence, then you are able to make love to a woman and dick a woman down from thousands of miles away.  The seeds of passion are not planted with the sweet strokes of your dick, but laid with the foundation of the gentle deep probing of the words you say to wet her imagination. When the imagination is wet, the pussy is never too far behind to join in the cum shower.

"What are you doing here?"  Stacey stammered as she opened the door to let Duke in.

His body barely touched hers as he brushed by her but it was enough to make her nipples hard against the silky fabric of her bra.  She tried to subtly inhale the scent of his *Eternity* cologne as he walked by, but then he pressed her up against the wall next to the receptionist desk and his growing erection pressed hard into the soft flesh between her thighs.

"I came for you. I felt you thinking about me, wanting me, and I needed to kiss you again," he said boldly.

"You came all this way for a kiss?" Stacey asked as the heat in her body rose and he slipped his hand around her waist then cupped her ass. "Here's a peck on the check," she said jokingly as she stared deep into his eyes. She felt weak as if she was going to pass out. His fingers stroked her pink cheeks, his erection pulsated throughout her skirt against her clit; and if her clit could speak right now; it would speak in multiple languages of orgasmic ecstasy. The bristly hairs of his goatee rubbed against her chin and tickled it as he leaned in to suck her bottom lip with a kiss. Her lips parted open and her hot breath escaped in a rush to ignite the skin on his face. "Oooooh," she moaned as he sucked her bottom lip into the heat of his mouth. *It was beginning all over again.* She was flying off to places unknown without a seat belt, and her façade of being in control of her feelings was as see-through as a negligee from Victoria's Secret or a man pretending not to stare at a beautiful woman when she walked by because he is with his woman. All men look, it is like breathing to them. The absence of not doing it would render their eyes useless to them.

"You know what I want, don't you?" His husky voice filled the tiny hole of her ear. She knew what he wanted but she loved hearing the words. The words would ripple through her body and they would make her feel...submissive.

"Tell me what you want?"

His hands were gliding effortlessly around her breasts, teasing her sensitive nipples and the heat felt between both of them loosened the top two buttons of her orange blouse. Sweat trickled down her cleavage even though the air in the office was cool. She was on fire and ready to explode with the slightest provocation. The low humming of the vacuum cleaner momentarily brought her back to her senses. Even though the office lights were turned off, they could still be seen through the glass door. Sensing her sudden shyness, Duke said, "Let's go somewhere more private so I can really have my way with you." Stacey took Duke's hand and led him to an empty office that wasn't being used by anyone in her law firm. The only furniture in the office was a desk and chair when she flicked the lights on.

Stacey had never in all her thirty-five years, done anything so daring as bringing a man into her work place after office hours. Concern flashed in her amber eyes as she turned to face Duke and he did what he always seemed to do to her; he calmed her fears and brought her back to the moment before she allowed her thoughts to sabotage the pleasure that was in store for both of them.

"It's just me and you here. Leave everything outside and just enjoy us being here together." His voice soothed her nerves and he kissed her again. He was such a sweet talker without sounding cheesy. This time, he kissed her more urgently and forcefully pulled her body into his. It felt good to have him so close. The scent of his manliness and cologne ignited an already smoldering fire. His hands and fingers hungrily searched her body as he kissed her lips, shoulders; her closed eyelids; and he used his tongue to trace small circles all around her neck. Stacey moaned uncontrollably. *What was this man doing to her?* Even if she wanted to stop moaning—she couldn't. Her body was so aroused and her mind was slowly being mind fucked by his words. Stacey was so turned on that she didn't realize Duke had slipped his hands into her skirt and yellow boy shorts. She tried to pull away in mock protest at his boldness for thinking he could have her anywhere and anytime he wanted. He was supremely confident, bordering on almost arrogant but a confident man who could back up his words with dick pounding action turned Stacey on. She liked knowing that someone was in control in the bedroom and she didn't want it to be her. She wanted to be told what to do, how to do it, how deep to take and suck it, and if she dared to refuse; a little subtle pressure to coerce her should be applied. That shit made her pussy tingle like a crazy car alarm that wouldn't stop buzzing. She wanted Duke to ring her alarm until she damn near lost her mind.

Before she could protest any further, his soft pussy sucking lips were on her nipples trying to suck the erectness out of them. The more he licked and sucked them, the harder they got. "You're making me crazy," she managed to moan in between a free breath. "You're making me do things I've never done before in my life and corrupting me." It wasn't a complaint from Stacey but more of a sudden realization of where she was and what she was doing. If her girlfriends could see her now; hair disheveled, blouse open, a man's hands all over her ass and pussy, and she was loving every minute of her newly found sexual awareness.

"You know you love it," Duke breathed on her neck as he gently bit her. Her body collapsed into his arms and there was no denying that she was caught up and completely hooked on the adrenaline rush of being enraptured and devoured by this man.

Duke stepped a few inches away from Stacey to continue teasing her. Her body was on the brink of exploding and he was galloping right behind her. The fatness of his dick bulged against his pants and Stacey's eyes cast downward to sneak a peek. She unconsciously licked her lips in throaty hunger.

"I know you want to feel that fat dick on your lips—*come here*."

Stacey did as she was told and Duke placed her hand on the pulsating bulge in his pants. He closed her fingers around his erection and she squeezed it carefully as if not to hurt it.

"Feels good," he breathed hotly in her ears. Her nipples were pressed into his chest; his erection throbbed through her skirt like the soft wrapping of knuckles on a door. Stacey wanted to fling her pretty wings wide open to let Duke fill her completely again as he had done two weeks ago. She shivered as she recalled the depth of his penetration. Duke's hands curled around her neck and she stared into his eyes. She felt weak. Her face was flushed with light perspiration and her mind was spinning. *"On your knees."* She gulped wanting to defy Duke's command but his stare was so intense that it made her large amber eyes blink repeatedly as if she was staring into the sun. He repeated his command again. This time a little firmer to let her know that it wasn't a request but an order.

"I can't."

"Don't tell me you can't! You will do as I say," he increased the pressure around her neck to let her know he was serious. Stacey was used to being in control in her everyday life but she didn't mind relinquishing control to a man who knew what to do with so much power.

Duke unbuckled his pants, pulled his zipper down and watched Stacey's eyes and lips as his pants fell into a heap around his feet. His erection poked through the open flap of his boxers and swayed back and forth as it waited for her lips to engulf it in its warmth. Stacey's eyes followed the hypnotic swaying of Duke's anaconda like thick black dick. She didn't have a choice to do anything else but to drop to her knees, spread her lips apart and sigh deeply as the hot flesh of his dick landed smoothly on her lips. She slid his boxers down to his feet while keeping a firm lock on his dick with her lips. The flap to his boxers said, *"Caution! Enter at your risk!"* She had been cautious all her life; today—she would just say fuck it and do what she wanted to do for once.

Duke stood rigid waiting to see if her lips were as sweet as they looked. Usually if a woman was an excellent kisser, then her dick sucking skills will be equally pleasing. She took the first few inches of his manhood between her lips and massaged his shaft with her right hand. He exhaled sharply as the pleasure he was receiving made his knees buckle and he grabbed her hair to steady himself. Damn! She had sucked the air completely out of him and she hadn't yet taken the entire length of his shaft into her mouth and down her throat. Her lips felt soft and fluffy like a cloud. He felt like a tree caught in a gentle seductive breeze that was blowing both his heads at the same time. The deeper she took him into her mouth, the louder his moans became. She was now in control. Her hands moved down to his balls, cupped them and gave them a few squeezes as if she was squeezing one of those stress balls at work. He leaned back, dug his fingers deep into her scalp and fed every inch of his dick to her lips and mouth.

Stacey gagged and tried to pull away, but his hold was unrelenting as the thick veins of his dick slid across her tongue to cut off her air passage. Just as she thought she was about to black out stuffed with dick; he pulled her head away and she was both scared and exhilarated at the same time. She wanted it again but didn't want to ask for it. She was still trying to be a good girl even though she was down on her knees sucking a man's dick in her office after hours. She looked up at him from her knees hoping that her eyes would tell him that he should do it again. Her eyes said, *Feed me that dick again*!

Duke stared down at her and looking into her innocent eyes made his dick throb even harder. The moans that came from her lips as he slid down her throat were the moans of a woman whose hunger for dick had never been fully satisfied—until now. He knew she wanted him to force it down her throat again, but he wanted her to ask him to do it. Hearing a beautiful woman say naughty things had always been a turn-on for him. There was just something about making a good girl do things that took her completely out of her element as she embraced her inner erotic self.

"Tell me what you want?" He urged her as his right hand still grasped behind her neck.

"You know what I want. Don't make me say it."

"If you want it that badly—then you will have to ask for it," Duke told a thirsty Stacey. Her lips quivered as she watched his dick bobbing up and down. *She had to have that feeling again*. Knowing that a dick could make her feel so good and was only a few inches away from her lips, was almost too good to be true.

"Feed my throat, baby. Ram that fat dick down my throat again!" she cried out.

Hearing those words sent a fire racing through Duke's dick like a log being set on fire, and it made Stacey's nipples and clit ache for deliverance from the sweet pain of torture engulfing her body and mind. It didn't sound like her voice saying those words coming from her mouth; but she recognized the guttural moans as hers when his dick pierced the warmth of her lips, rattled against her teeth and filled the space in her throat.

This time, she was ready, and curled her tongue around his erection to bend it to her will.

Duke stood there as if he had been electrified on a fence as Stacey deftly swallowed every delicious inch of his black dick. In an effort to regain control, Duke slowly withdrew his glistening manhood from Stacey's lips but not without resistance from her. She tightened her lip hold on his dick and she moaned in defiant anger when the last few inches plopped out of her mouth.

Saliva dripped seductively from Duke's dick like a slow leaking faucet and he wanted every drop to splash into Stacey's wet pond. He didn't have to say anything to her. She knew what she had to do. Her face flushed with excitement, eyes wide open in wonderment, Stacey felt as if she was in a trance as she removed her blouse and bra. She had never thought to do something like this before Duke, and now, here she was on her knees being submissive and loving it.

"Lay down and let me take those panties off for you."

Stacey lay down on her back without a word of protest and Duke followed her to the floor. Her pussy throbbed with fevered arousal and her legs trembled uncontrollably when Duke grazed her legs and thighs with his fingertips. "Damn," Stacey said to herself as he slid her skirt and yellow boy shorts down her legs. Her entire body was shaking and he hadn't even entered her as yet. Before sleeping with Duke, she thought that she had enjoyed great sex. After their first time together, Stacey would never admit this to Duke, but he made her feel and say things that sent her mind into orbit. Her body went into a state of orgasmic shock and constant craving for his touch. Her heart was beating so fast every time she came; she would cry into Duke's chest as orgasm after orgasm hurtled through her pussy walls and whispered sweetly from her moist lips.

Duke's bald head glistened with perspiration between Stacey's legs and she could almost see her reflection on his shiny scalp. The look of ecstasy on her face was undeniable as his tongue flicked across her tender pussy lips. Stacey cried out in ecstasy when Duke clamped his lips around her clit, which resembled a mini thumb. He sucked her clit so hard that her screams were caught in her throat and came out sounding like a cat meowing in heat.

"Pleasssse stop...I...I can't take anymore," Stacey squealed as Duke continued to suck hard on her clit as if he was sucking a string of spaghetti. His arms were wrapped around her upper thighs as he pulled her pussy back and forth into the hunger of his lips. Duke relished the taste of warm pussy nectar on his lips. Hearing a woman beg for mercy and cry for him to stop because the pleasure of what he was doing to her was too overwhelming, only made him want to suck her clit harder. Just when it seemed as if she was going to go over the brink, he stopped and slid his body on top of hers. Their clothes were strewn under their bodies as some sort of makeshift blanket to make it more comfortable. The carpet hummed with renewed energy as Duke teased Stacey's clit with slow circular licks around her clit and wet lips. Stacey shivered in anticipation of Duke's penetration when the soft flesh of his thick head kissed her fat clit. Her hands moved involuntarily and she grabbed his ass to pull his Magnum covered dick into the sweltering heat of her pussy.

"I'm in charge here," Duke growled into Stacey's ear as he balanced his body on top of hers.

*Then handle your business Black man,* Stacey thought to herself. *This pussy is here; served for you on a platter, so go to work.* Shock reverberated through Stacey's body as Duke gently probed the tight opening of her pretty waxed wings. She was wet like a rain forest and ready to be fucked. Her pussy screamed the hallelujah song as the heat of his dick merged with the warmth of the wetness dripping from between her pink lips. His dick felt like a boomerang curving to find every pleasure spot nestled inside the fleshy moisture of her pussy. Beneath her fingers, the muscles in his back moved in unison with the stroking poetry of his sweet dick as he dipped his manhood into the warm pool of bubbling nectar waiting to welcome him inside. Shudders of sweet delicious pain rippled inside of Stacey's pussy as Duke penetrated and withdrew his erection into the tight confines of her pussy. Every time he withdrew his manhood from inside of her, he would then dive deeper inside of her and her soft wings fluttered with quivering moans to accept all of his thick black strength. This was the most dick that Stacey had ever been fed in her life, and even though it was their second time together; she was still amazed at how big he was and how deep he could go inside of her. He teased her, toyed with her, and reveled in knowing that he had discovered the secrets to her eternal wetness.

"You know you're mine now," he said in between deep plunges into her pussy. She hesitated and his next thrust was his show of strength to fuck her into compliance.

"Yesssssss...it's yours—it's all yours!"

Another orgasm flooded her pussy walls and she fought back her tears of joy, sadness, and embarrassment. She didn't want him to see her crying. She didn't want him to know yet how much power he had over her so soon after they became intimate. When men think their dick game is God's gift to women, they become insufferable ego maniacs. They wanted to lay claim to everything on a woman right down to her last pubic hair.

The pursuit of ultimate pleasure is what Duke lived for. He wanted to know he was the best at everything he did. He needed confirmation and the only way to get it was to have Stacey scream with abandon as she came again.

All pussies aren't the same. They might go by the same name, but Duke was a pussy connoisseur and he understood the delicate intricacies of treating each pussy like a pussy queen. When a woman feels special, when a pussy feels the tender lickings of a tongue and sweet penetrations; they are more open to trying new things to please you; and along the way discover secrets about themselves they didn't know existed.

Duke got to his feet to stretch his legs and streams of Stacey's honey come dripped from his dick and onto their wrinkled clothes. Stacey crawled across the clothes, sat up on her knees, grabbed his ass cheeks and sucked the sweet nectar of her cum from his condom-covered dick. After several licks, satisfied that there was nothing else for her lips to lick—Stacey assumed the doggy style position. A low whistle came from Duke's lips.

"Damn...look at all that ass for me to handle."

"Are you man enough to tame this fat ass," Stacey teased him again.

Duke laughed that laugh letting her know that he had more than enough dick to fill all her holes whenever she was ready. He surveyed the terrain of her ample fleshy bottom, spanked it a few times to warm her up and spread her reddened cheeks wide open. The small eye of her anus winked at him as if to say, *It's my turn next time.* He lightly touched her tightest orifice with his thumb and a shiver ran up and down Stacey's inner thighs. Her body was still in revolt from having her virgin anus touched; so when Duke penetrated her dripping pussy, her back dropped lower to the floor and her ass rose into the air to receive the blessings she had been praying for. He pounded her ass relentlessly and with each penetration, Stacey's fleshy walls buckled against his unrelenting assault.

"Fuck your pussy baby! Don't stop! Don't fuccccccking stop even if I beg!"

Duke had no intention of stopping with or without her permission. He knew what his pussy needed and he planned on delivering.

Stacey heard the delirium in her voice but she didn't care. Duke's dick felt like it was made for her pussy and every deep stroke of his magic wand had her name written all over its thick deliciousness. Three months ago, she could never have imagined herself in this kind of position and saying those words. Those were words that *other women said and not her*. Other women became hypnotized with sweet dick strokes—but not her. Her body didn't care about the past. Right now. Right here. The only thing that mattered was satisfying the cravings clawing at her insides to burst out of her pussy with a next orgasm. Her fingers dug into the carpet, her face was twisted to the side under her armpits and another orgasm came screaming out of her tender lips.

Before she could recover, Duke was ready to have his way with her again.

"Get up," Duke ordered. He walked over to the wall next to the door with sweat dripping down his face and back, and waited for Stacey to follow him. "Assume the position," he told her as she looked at him from the floor. She got up without protest, walked over to him, raised her hands up against the wall, placed her palms against the white walls and spread her legs. Duke stood behind her as he drank in the fullness of her ass with his eyes before grabbing a handful of ass and slowly easing his dick inside of her sweet warmth again. When he was fully buried inside of her, he released her ass from his hands, covered her body with his and intertwined their fingers together.

They found each other's tempo and a slow grinding rhythm followed. It felt as if they were conducting their own personal orchestra, and every deep plunge of Duke's dick into Stacey's throbbing pussy elicited an almost pained sweet note of ecstasy from her throat. Just when it felt that he might be going off key, she would bring him back by squeezing her inner pussy muscles around his dick to slow down his rhythm. His head rested against the back of her shoulders, his hands caressed her breasts and squeezed her nipples hard in an effort to make her come before he did. He didn't have to wait too long. He bit deeply into the right side of her neck, and she thrashed about like a kitten caught in a bear trap. His teeth pierced her skin, triggering another orgasm that zapped the strength from her legs and she fell to the floor before he came.

On her knees again, Stacey ripped off the Magnum condom, took his dick between her hands and fed it to her hungry throat. Furiously, she pumped Duke's dick as if she was drilling for oil and the next gush would make her a millionaire. Just as a flood of cum worked its way steadily through the full length of Duke's throbbing dick—the door next to them flew open. One of the cleaning men walked in with his vacuum cleaner humming, didn't notice Duke and Stacey until he looked up and stood there transfixed—in complete shock. Stacey was too far gone to get off her feet and gather her clothes. She was thirsty to have a drink of

Duke's sweet cum.  Duke stood there grinning, head tossed back and exploded deep into Stacey's virgin throat.  His body lurched forward as if in the throes of multiple orgasms and Stacey didn't release him from her lips until she was sure that he had nothing else for her to drink.  Sweat poured down Duke's face into her hair and he dropped to his knees beside her.  The cleaning guy retreated hastily without saying a word but not before getting an eyeful.

"You have completely corrupted me.  What if he tells everyone in the building that he caught us having sex?"

"They will wish they had been you and enjoying this fat dick," Duke answered back with a smirk on his face.

Stacey couldn't help but smile.  He had an answer for everything to quickly disarm her.  He swept away a few strands of wet hair sticking to her face and basked in the glow of her beautiful smile.  She smiled as beautifully and as easily as she came when she had an orgasm. Listening to her cumming was like closing your eyes and hearing beautiful poetry being spoken, but her prose was written in the sensual moans, murmurs and sighs that whispered from deep within the sweet walls of her pussy and gave birth through her pretty wings.

5/12/09…10:09pm

# Fruit Salad Dessert

Everything was prepared for when Anna came out the shower. Nicholas lit candles all around the bed and the red sheets looked as if they had been set ablaze in flames of orange fire. He then perfumed the air with the scent of roses and waited for her to finish showering so he could begin eating his fruit salad dessert. Dinner had consisted of shrimp, oysters, scallops, and chunks of crabmeat, and washed down with a bottle of white wine. Nicholas had insisted that Anna take a shower while he washed the dishes and took out the garbage. It was only a ploy to prepare his special fruit salad, which consisted of small grape tomatoes, slices of pineapple, mangoes, strawberries, kiwi, green and red seedless grapes, apples, bananas, pears, peaches, and slices of tangerine. He mixed his special concoction into a green salad bowl and placed it on the floor on his side of the bed while he waited for her to come out of the shower.

He loved at times to lay in bed as she took a shower, and let the wonderful aroma of one of her many body scrubs and lotions arouse his senses. By the time she came to bed, he would be fully aroused and ready to ravish her from her toes all the way to the top of her head; but not before taking the scenic route between the sweet pond of nectar bubbling sweetly between her moist lips. He would bury his nose in every orifice of her warm skin as he inhaled and sniffed how delicious she smelled. Even after five years together, it still turned him on every time without fail. Nicholas was a scent addict for Anna's seductive fragrances.

The falling water in the shower came to a stop and he could hear her humming an old tune by Al Green. On cue, he turned on the stereo and quickly found the song she was humming, "Let's Stay Together." Anticipating a long night of lovemaking, Nicholas put the stereo on repeat to that one song.

"You know just what I like to hear, huh," Anna stepped out the bathroom still dripping wet and swayed her waist hypnotically to Al's impassioned plea of forever love. "Come here Daddy. Come dance with your sexy woman," she giggled as she said it. "Show me what you can do." The lithe of her singsong Caribbean accent filled the bedroom as it accompanied the soulful sounds of Al Green.

Nicholas propped up his naked body on the bed and his face beamed with love for his wife. The orange flames from the candle cast a shadow over her body as she danced. Her dreadlocks bounced in rhythm to her hips, her perfect perky breasts joined in the jam session and she turned around to give Nicholas a view of her behind. It was a sight he never grew tired of seeing. It was always beautiful. The sun rises and sets every day, and its beauty always amazing though you have seen it a thousand times; and every time it fills your eyes with its amazing beauty, you are left in awe. Nicholas was in awe of his wife. Her honey colored skin bronzed by countless weekends sitting out on the beaches of Antigua just contemplating life. She was a free spirit and it was what drew Nicholas to her. He didn't want to own her, keep her captive, but instead, he wanted to watch her fly as high as she could and always be the man that she came back home to when she closed her wings and landed back on earth.

He jumped over the bed to keep her from coming to his side so she wouldn't see the surprise he had in store for her. "Come here sweetpork," their bodies were already touching in a slow soca grind. "This is what I can do to you."

"You're a bad man, bad man," she laughed. "Trying to corrupt an innocent island girl. What you have to say for yourself, mister?"

"Guilty as charged," Nicholas breathed in her left ear as his wet tongue licked inside of her ear, and she moaned while holding on to him tighter. Her hair was still wet and strands of her wet hair clung to his eyes as he bit into her neck as if it was a peach.

"Don't start anything you cannot finish," she warned him playfully.

"Come here let me show how hungry I am for you," he said as he led her to bed. "Lie down and let your husband have some dessert."

The red sheets felt warm against her back as she did what she was told and propped her head against the pillow. "Show me then."

Nicholas walked around to the other side of the bed, picked up the green salad bowl with two hands and rested it on the bed next to Anna.

"You're going to feed me fruit, mister man?"

"No, I'm going to feed myself," Nicholas said with a sly look on his face that caused Anna's clit to peek out from its safe place of hiding. It was as intrigued as she was in anticipation of what Nicholas had in store for both of them. His hand reached into the fruit bowl and produced a chunk of mango, which he rubbed across his lips and swallowed. He did the same thing to her with a piece of pineapple.

"You like that, sweetpork?"

It was his pet name for her pussy. He had renamed it after the first time they made love and his tongue had become inebriated from her juices. "Your pussy is the sweetest meat I have ever tasted in my life," he exclaimed as he went back for numerous helpings. She was unable to walk the next day and every time she peed, it felt as if his tongue was still licking her swollen clit and lips. The sensation was so intense that she came again as pee flowed from her aching pussy.

"Let me see what else my wife has for me to taste tonight," he said as he slid between her open legs. He lifted her feet one at a time from the bed and kissed and licked her soles. His tongue swirled around her arches and Anna twisted back and forth in sweet pleasure. "Do it again...again baby," she squealed like a little girl not accustomed to having all her desires fulfilled. She did not have to ask him to please her again. Giving his wife pleasure brought Nicholas more pleasure than his own immediate gratification. Pleasing your partner is the silent whisper of true lovemaking, a sustainable joy that lasts longer than all your screams of passion combined. He lived to please his wife.

Nicholas twisted his wife's body like a pretzel until she was lying on her stomach and his face positioned right between the sweet space of her ass. Without prompting, Anna spread her legs open to give Nicholas a preview of the volcano of bubbling sweet juices that was waiting to engulf his tongue and keep his dick wet. "Mmmmmm," he sighed deeply as his tongue dove right into the center of her sweetest ache and rode the first releases of her orgasmic wave. He reached into the fruit bowl and closed his fingers around half of a banana. He swirled his tongue around it to make it warmer, rubbed it against his wife's puffy pussy lips and fed it slowly into her sweetpork.

The sensation of having something inside of her, other than her husband's tongue and dick, made Anna's inner muscles contract in protest to expel this intruder from her pussy. The protest was short-lived when she felt the grooves of the banana stimulating her already sensitive lips, and when she turned around from her doggy style position; the sight she saw made her say, "Oh shit!" The banana was dripping with her warm caramel nectar and Nicholas brushed it against his lips before inserting it into his mouth, but he didn't eat it. He licked it clean as he closed his eyes to savor the taste, and smiled broadly as if he had just discovered the secret to everlasting happiness.

"You have to taste this. It's like a mixture of sinful thoughts and realized expectations."

This time he plunged the banana deeper into the core of her heated center to get to that third degree heat burn which was waiting impatiently to be released from the prison of her tight walls. It felt too good for her to be silent, and her screams released an extra dosage of heat that made the banana even softer. "Taste your dessert, baby." A few drops spilled onto her back as Nicholas reached over to feed her lips the sweet delicacy brewed from her garden. The spillage felt like hot candle wax against her soft brown skin and Anna winced and moaned loudly. Nicholas dangled the dripping fruit a few inches above her lips and Anna stuck out her long tongue to steal a taste. It felt warm against her lips and the added flavor of the banana created an interesting pussy concoction that made her salivate for more. She licked it clean and sucked it hard for good measure to ensure she had gotten everything before Nicholas dipped it between her moist lips again. They fed on her juices a few more times until she stopped. She laid her head on the pillow, repositioned her ass in the air, and waited for him to continue.

Nicholas rummaged around in the green salad bowl and finally found what he was looking for, the other half of the banana. With a piece in each hand, he mashed them together hoping to make them fuse together as he plunged the entire banana into Anna's unsuspecting pussy. The swift depth of penetration caught her off guard and her legs quivered; her inner muscles clenched and unclenched as she tried in vain to expel the fully-grown banana from her sweetpork. It was lodged inside of her and Nicholas covered her entire pussy with his right palm. Every time she tried to push it out, he would push it back in deeper. Her pussy was being fucked by a banana!

"I can't take anymore baby!" Anna pounded the pillow like a crazy woman as another orgasm exploded through her sugar walls. Nicholas placed his lips around her pussy completely encircling it, sliding his tongue between her wet lips to set her clit free from its hooded shelter. Her pussy muscles went weak and he used his hands to spread her ass wide open. He squeezed both ass cheeks as if to check the buoyancy of its bounce ability and with every squeeze, a piece of banana was expelled from her pussy dripping with the warm release of her Caribbean passion. Nicholas took deep bites and swallows of potassium, delicately dipped in pussy juice, until every tender morsel disappeared and all that remained was the tiny moist smiling hole of Anna's pussy. He took one more lick before coming up for air and she fell onto the bed in a quivering heap.

Nicholas slapped her ass playfully and it quivered like red Jell-O in a bowl. "I'm not done with your sweet ass yet. When I'm finished with you, all that chat you have will be quiet."

"You trying to tame this wild island pussy," Anna playfully taunted him. "Yankee man like you from New York gon' drown in these deep sweet waters," she laughed her melodic laughter as she turned around with her legs spread and feet up.

"In five years, I haven't drowned once," he verbally sparred with her.

"Well tonight might be that night. It's been nice knowing you Yankee boy."

They enjoyed the back and forth trash talking. It intensified their bedroom aerobics. Anna usually got the better of Nicholas because island women naturally just have chatty mouths and can wear a man down; and if a man wins an argument what is the benefit in that for him? He will have bragging rights, a pouty sore lover, and the loss of pussy. Losing has its rewards sometimes.

Eyes closed, Nicholas stuck his hand into the fruit bowl and grabbed a handful of assorted fruits, which he placed on the sheets alongside Anna's backside. He placed the first piece in his mouth. Strawberry. It felt cold inside his mouth, but within a few seconds, it had warmed up after being sucked by his lips. There was no other place Nicholas enjoyed being than between his wife's legs. His dick hadn't gotten hard for another woman since the first time he laid eyes on her. For once, his dick, mind, and heart were in complete agreement about a woman. She was the one that all three of them wanted to fuck and make love to for the rest of his life.

Expertly, he balanced the strawberry between his lips and rubbed it around her swollen lips, then the tip of her clit; and her back arched from the bed as the strawberry penetrated the warm pool of her moistness. Her nails dug into the sheets, she spread her legs wider, and every time he dunked the fruit inside of her, she would clinch her muscles to repel it back in his mouth.

"Best strawberry dessert I've ever had," he mumbled in between sucks and licks, and finally he swallowed the nectar-covered fruit.

"You haven't seen anything yet," she said as she released her grip from the sheets. Her body relaxed momentarily, but not for long.

He was fully laid out in-between her legs, and tossed both of them over his shoulders to have a better view of the fruit salad dessert he was creating. She tried to guess which fruit he was putting inside of her, and after four different fruits, she had gotten all of them wrong. Funny thing, peaches, apples, kiwi, and seedless grapes all feel the same when they entered her sweetpork. She could only guess which fruit was inside of her when they gave birth through her lips and found the warmth of his lips. The smaller fruits: grapes and small tomatoes, required less effort to pop out of her pussy. The other fruits needed greater suction from his lips before they would leave the warmth of passion, and she enjoyed those better inside of her.

"Are you ready for your special treat, darling?" His voice rose from between her legs and kissed her face.

"More for me?" She feigned surprise. "You're too good to me baby."

"You deserve my best always baby," he said as his hands slid under her ass and his middle finger found the tightness of her anus.

"Oooooh shhhhit baby," she moaned.

He couldn't resist the obvious comeback and said, "Not right now, honey. It would be a bad time to do that." It cracked both of them up, and she didn't even realize that he had coated four grapes with her come and plopped them one by one into her ass. Her anus tightened and it tried to spit out the invading green and red grapes, but he placed his thumb over the tiny opening to keep her stuffed.

"Hold them in there until I tell you to feed me."

Her non-response was her answer that she would comply with his request. He then took pieces of mango, strawberries, pineapple, and tangerine in his palm and stuffed them into her dripping pussy. Both her holes were stuffed to capacity, but Nicholas was determined that she could take more. He kept his thumb on her anus and crawled on top of her.

"Let me stir your fruit salad dessert with my spoon." Without waiting for her to respond, Nicholas penetrated Anna's overflowing fruit filled pussy with his dick, but was met with resistance from chunks of mango, tangerine, and strawberries lodged inside of her. Undaunted, he stroked his dick in and out like a car weaving back and forth through a congested highway. Finally, he found an open space big enough to accommodate his erection and slid smoothly in between slices of mangoes and strawberries and every sweet piece of fruit was swirling around and stimulating Anna's fleshy walls until she burst open with a Starburst flavored fruit filled orgasm.

"You're killing your pussy, baby," Anna moaned aloud as if she was having an out of body experience. It was just her and Nicholas' dick bonding, fucking...making love. He loved when she got like this. It made him feel as if his dick had mystical powers and he was the commander in chief of the pussy universe. In the pussy universe, he came in and out as he pleased and there were no rules of behavior. The only thing that mattered was the pursuit of pleasure and finding that ultimate mind-blowing orgasm hiding in a secret pocket in the pussy. The man who finds the path to this giant O orgasm will be able to give simultaneous orgasms to every woman in the world. The men who are in touch with their feminine side will also experience these orgasms. The men who will be unable to have these giant masturbatory orgasms will wish they had been more in touch with their dormant feminine side.

"Ohhhh...ohhhh—God—I'm coming again all over the fruit." Slow, steady deep strokes of Nicholas' dick into his wife's fruit salad dessert pussy brought her to a sudden orgasm that threatened to spew all the fruit from her pussy and anus, but Nicholas withdrew quickly, laid down on his back between her legs and palmed her ass in the air directly over his lips. He licked her swollen lips, and Anna's entire body trembled and slowly pieces of fruit oozed out of her pussy mixed with her sweet come. With every piece of fruit that Anna fed to Nicholas, he rewarded her with quick flicks of his tongue that sent her pussy into quivering spasms of moanful profanity. She was unconsciously channeling Bernie Mac's most famous comedic bit. Every word from her lips was motherfucker this and motherfucker that, and she used it colorfully as an adjective, noun, adverb, pronoun, and verb. The last piece of the come-soaked strawberry slipped out from between Anna's pussy lips and Nicholas savored its taste on his lips before swallowing it.

"Now give me the rest of my salad."

She loved it when her husband took over and demanded she obey, but Anna also enjoyed making him work for the pussy. "No—you can't have it." Her ass still covered her husband's face like a full moon. He grabbed her roughly behind her upper thighs, forced his tongue deep into her ass and then bit both cheeks deeply as Anna screamed and moaned her pleasure.

"You dirty mother—"

Another bite of her plump ass and Anna lost her will to fight her husband. She gave him what he wanted, and even after her salad dish was empty; he probed her anus deeply looking for one last piece. Satisfied that she had given him everything she had, Nicholas released his wife's ass from his grip, rubbed his full belly and smiled at Anna as he wrapped her naked body in his arms.

"Are you happy now?"

"I'm always happy after eating my wife."

The Reverend Al Green was still pleading in the background telling everyone that they had to stay together for sake of love. Nicholas wrapped his arms around his wife's body and kissed her forehead. Anna smiled as she buried her face in his chest. They sang the chorus of "Let's Stay Together" slightly off-key, but everything else about them was perfect.

3/22/09...8:42pm

## Every Time We Make Love

Everything is still
It is as if the silence is listening to us as we make love
Exhaling in unison as we express our passion
You are barely breathing now
We just made love again
Soft whispers of your warm breath kiss my lips
Slowly they part open and you are inside of me once
again
Strands of your hair cling to your face
Your body is still flushed and sensitive to my touch
I saw your heart in your eyes as you came in all colors of
the rainbow
Your eyes said they would love me forever
Mine said the same as we lay together completely
exhausted
Your body now nestles softly into mine
I inhale the heated scent of our passion
Remnants of our love cling to your body wet
Whispers of our passion still echo in the air
You are always amazing, a lover born of another time
Who understands that making love is about giving
A giving lover who gives with his heart receives love
back from the soul
The way you make love to my body cannot be taught by
anyone
It is an innate understanding of touch and feel of what
gives pleasure

The power you possess over my body in your fingertips
makes me quiver with delight
Making love to you has no definition
I have run out of adjectives to describe the depth of your
passion
You are the sun, the moon and the stars all wrapped up
in one
Making love to you is like simultaneously watching a
beautiful sunrise,
Then watching it set in all its beautiful splendor
We have not taken a breath yet
And along comes a breathtaking full moon gracing us
with its presence
Accompanied by millions of stars illuminating the sky
Imagine experiencing all these glorious things all at once
That is how I feel every time we make love.
12/06/08...12:43pm

# Twenty Fingers, Two Tongues And Something Hard

It wasn't even lunch time yet and Mariah was already stressed the fuck out. Everyone at Delicious Scents believed that she slept her way into being President of the company after only three short years on the job. It never occurred to them that perhaps she was qualified for the job that she had been working for her entire life, or that having an MBA from Yale put her ahead of the pack. It was a world of survivors out there and no one will just hand you a job of a lifetime unless you are qualified. Business people don't mess around when it comes to their money so she had to be on her best game at all times. One slip up and it was back to the end of the line for her. At thirty-three, she was more than qualified and doing the damn thing; so she ignored all the evil eyes from the other women and the grumblings of angry men behind her back. Since she had taken over Delicious Scents in the past six months, they had moved up from tenth to third place behind of Victoria's Secret and Bath and Body Works. It was no surprise that because of her seven day work schedule, her personal life had suffered. There was no time to meet any available men, so she tried to block out the cravings of her body and keep her eyes on the prize. At some point though, the body has to be fed or it would start feeding on itself. There were a few brothers at the office that Mariah wouldn't mind slipping off her panties for and letting them get a whiff of her waxed goodies, but she knew that men were worse gossipers than women. You smile at a brother and he would tell his friends that you wanted that dick. *Imagine what would happen if you actually let them get their dicks wet?* It would be all over BET before their dicks could dry off.

There was no way that Mariah could concentrate on work today. Her mind was tired, her body was starving for a good old-fashioned dick down, and she had gotten wind of a website called www.mariahisawhore.com that was set up to trash her character. There were photos of her cut and pasted together that made her look like a porn star on steroids. She had to get away for at least an hour to clear her mind and then deal with this shit before it completely undermined her authority. Her first rule was that an angry mind made stupid rash decisions, so Mariah called her favorite masseuse, Angelo, to massage her aching muscles and give her time to formulate a plan of action. She summoned her secretary into her office to dictate a few instructions before leaving.

Janet Myers took a deep breath before entering Mariah William's office with her notepad and plastered on her best fake movie star smile. Everyone knew that Mariah was fucking old man Johnson, and she walked around the office as if she had earned the promotion on her own merits. She had earned it alright—with her ass in the air and the old man's wrinkled old penis shoved down her pretty little mouth. Janet had to give it up to Mariah though, she was beautiful and smart. Her long brown hair was shoulder length and perfectly done to accentuate her pecan brown complexion. Her eyes were piercing and always made Janet feel as if she was being undressed, not that she minded at all. Mariah always wore business suits to hide her figure, but Janet had seen her working out at the gym downstairs and knew that she had an apple bottom that needed to be bitten by a set of hungry lips. If Mariah could read her eyes, she would know instantly the craving thoughts in Janet's heart that was making her wet, but Mariah was far too distracted to notice anything but her life right now.

"Janet please cancel my appointment with the Sampson sisters and reschedule it for tomorrow. Call up the distributor in our South Carolina warehouse and make sure that all the supplies were shipped for the showcase next week. Make sure to get a tracking number from Herb. We can't have anything going wrong next week at the convention. If everything goes according to plan then we could be number two by next week."

Janet's head bopped up and down furiously as she wrote down Mariah's instructions and repeated them out loud to her just to be certain she had written down everything. Mariah nodded in agreement and turned her back to get her bag to leave. Her black business suit snugly fit her thick shape and defined the contours of her ass. She was only 5'6, wore a size fourteen and was blessed with 38DD breasts that announced themselves before she got into a room. Society classified her shape as BBW (big beautiful woman), but everything on her body was well portioned and equally pleasing to the eye. She was a delicious chocolate sister that men and women wanted to lick cleanly like an ice cream cone.

Janet leaned back in her chair, licked her lips, felt her pussy quiver and drank in the full beauty that filled her eyes. Every man and woman in the office wanted a taste of Mariah, and though she dressed conservatively, it was obvious that the girl was packing a dynamite body that was ready to explode. She despised Mariah's uppity elitist entitled attitude, but she couldn't help wanting to slide her skirt down to inhale the fragrance of Mariah's sweet nectar and feed on it for breakfast, lunch, and dinner; with a few snacks in between. Janet was sprung and she didn't even know it. The fantasy of the moment transported Janet and she didn't avert her eyes in time when Mariah spun around. Janet lifted her eyes to meet Mariah's stare and the hunger in Mariah's eyes made her wet.

Mariah felt the electricity in the room and it made her feel uncomfortable that her secretary had seen her so vulnerable and needy. She quickly excused herself and brushed past Janet to meet Angelo. Janet held the scent of Mariah's perfume, a new scent by Beyonce and inhaled it deeply. Janet would spend her lunchtime dreaming of ways to get Mariah into bed and turning her out. It was all she could think about the rest of the afternoon.

Angelo had better work his magic today Mariah thought to herself. She was about to explode with the stress she was under with work and no sex; and now the heated exchange of lust between her and Janet had worked her libido into a frenzy. Something had to give—and fast. She hoped she wouldn't have to fire Janet. The last thing she needed to deal with were rumors that she was fucking her secretary. The idea didn't repulse her, but you can't mix pussy and business. There's nothing worse than having an angry woman lover scorned at the office. Life would be hell.

The Day Spa was on the first floor of her building so Mariah took the escalator down ten floors and walked into a whole mess of foolishness between Angelo and his sometimes boyfriend, Juan Manuel. Angelo was a pretty boy on the light side of black and he made no excuses for loving him some dark chocolate like Juan who was from Santo Domingo. Seeing them together was something to be seen and not believed. Angelo was a slight man with braids, high cheek bones, gray cat eyes, and lips so full, that Mariah was certain that Juan had no complaints for pleasure. Juan was a straight up thug from the streets; short and buffed, bald-headed, with tattoos covering him like a second skin.

"I'm tired of your sorry ass coming into my place of business and embarrassing me by flirting with my customers," Angelo was near tears. Everyone in the spa pretended not to be listening, but every ear was tuned in to their weekly soap opera show.

"You can be on your way then. If you leave another one just like you will come along and be better than your sorry ass and can have all of this." He grabbed his crotch crudely like a rap star in a video but everyone knew that Angelo was under the power of the dick. He always went back to Juan, begging him not to leave. This time would be no different. When you are under the power of the dick, it can rule your life like an iron fist. Mariah had known women who had lost their minds for some good dick, but she had never been one of them. The right man hasn't fucked you yet, her friends would always say. Maybe they were right. Right place, right time, right dick, and she could be the female version of Angelo.

Mariah had seen enough of this drama to know that she was about to get screwed by Angelo. It wasn't the kind of screwing that she needed right now. "Listen, girl," Angelo whined in his most apologetic voice, "Juan needs me at home right now and you know how men can be when they want their pussy."

"Angelo, what the hell am I supposed to do now? I need this massage. I feel like I'm about to fucking explode. Just tell Juan you will meet him in an hour after you're done with me. Your loyal customer of three years comes first."

Mariah tried to sound menacing but she knew that when dick called Juan's lips would answer. He grabbed her hands and brought her over to a new masseuse named Marcus who had only started yesterday.

"Marcus meet Mariah. Mariah meet Marcus," and with that introduction, Angelo was gone before Mariah could protest.

"Follow me," Marcus' baritone voice ordered Mariah. It angered Mariah that he just ordered her to follow him and assumed that she would do so. Marcus was a huge man with hands that could probably wrap around Mariah's waist and twirl her like a yo-yo. She stood there unsure of whether or not to follow this stranger into the massaging room, but her muscles ached so much and needed to be worked over good. She hoped that he was at least half as good as Angelo.

Mariah had been in this massaging room dozens of times before with Angelo, but today, it was a completely different room. She felt as if she was on one of those design makeover shows on HGTV. The lights were dimmed so she had to squint until it came into focus. Candles surrounded the massaging table and the sound of thunder and rain poured in from the sound system. The walls were painted to resemble that of an early morning sunrise and a glass of Merlot was waiting for her. The customary white bathrobe was strewn across the massaging table, but Mariah had no intentions of getting undressed in this sexified atmosphere.

Marcus walked back inside massaging his hands to get them warmed up for the job at hand. The entire room smelled of strawberry and almond massage oil which was her favorite. "You can go ahead and hop on the table," he said calmly as if he had known her for a long time and not just met five minutes ago.

"You expect me to take off my clothes, here, now, in this Playboy sex room?" Mariah said as her eyes swept around the room to make her point.

"Listen, I am a professional. I have seen hundreds of naked bodies before, so there's no reason to be shy. Go ahead, relax. You're in good hands."

She detected the confidence of a man who got what he wanted from women and wasn't used to hearing the word no. There was an ease to him that made Mariah feel comfortable enough to begin undressing. He had turned his back to give her a moment of privacy. She took two quick gulps of wine and then took everything off except her black thongs. She then quickly jumped on the table to lie on her stomach with her robe still on. If this man thought he would be seeing her coochie, he had another thing coming. He would need more than this atmosphere and a glass of Merlot to get that privilege.

Marcus turned around just as Mariah lay down on the massage table. He knew women like her. They were successful, motivated, highly intelligent, and their success usually threatened a lesser man who felt unworthy of someone like Mariah because he didn't have his own shit together. Women like Mariah often went home alone to do more work and sleep in an empty cold bed. Unbeknownst to Mariah, Marcus was known on the masseuse circuit as "Tongue". She had no idea what was in store for her this afternoon.

Marcus licked his fingers to make sure they were warm and ready to perform. His first rule was never to touch a woman with cold hands or else her entire body shuts down and becomes unreceptive to anything that comes after.

He gently pulled down her robe and felt her muscles tighten as it slid down her shoulders, below her ass, and down her legs to lie in a heap on the floor. Mariah was fully exposed on her stomach with nothing but a floss-like thong going up the crack of her ample ass to hide her private parts. A smile of recognition of great beauty danced on Marcus' face and he licked his lips like an animal about to feast on a succulent meal. He was the hunter and his prey was laid out before him, naked and defenseless.

Mariah was mortified but too embarrassed to even speak for fear of making the situation even worse. Her hands dangled over the sides of the massaging table and her 38DD breasts pressed into the cotton fabric beneath her. Without warning, Marcus' hands touched her shoulders and she felt as if she had been electrocuted. Tremors of hot flashes raced all throughout her body without any direction or destination in mind. His fingers gently massaged away her stress and worked deeper into her muscles to find the source of her pain. He worked his way down to the small of her back and pressed deeper into her flesh. A soft moan of pleasure pain escaped Mariah's lips but went unheard by Marcus. He was in the zone. The rain forest music had stopped suddenly to disrupt the moment; but just as quickly, the sweet seducing sounds of Marvin Gaye filled the tiny room. It got hotter as Marvin wailed to no one in particular, "I Want You".

With expertise, Marcus worked the tight muscles of Mariah's body and he began to feel some of her tension slowly dissipate under his fingers. He avoided her ass for now and let his hands slide down to her calves. Her muscles felt good in his hands and he could feel the temperature between her inner thighs starting to rise to the surface. These were the moments that he enjoyed the most; the moment when women allowed themselves to give in to him and let the moment just take over and deliver them to the promise land. It was a non-verbal exchange of power which made it easier for them to submit and feed their bodies the pleasure of sensual release. He walked around to the end of the table, lifted her feet and placed them against his chest.

Her feet felt like they were suspended in air and just flying through space. Mariah held her breath, afraid to move because her feet were planted firmly on Marcus' chest. It felt as if her feet were touching the hot concrete on a corner street on a summer day. This man was ripped and she briefly wondered what his chest would feel like beneath her small hands. She heard about nerves in your feet that, when massaged the right way, felt like you were about to lose your mind. The pleasure could be so intense that some women actually had orgasms. Marcus wrapped his two hands around Mariah's left foot which measured a size seven and proceeded to work his fingers into the soles of her feet. He inserted his fingers between her toes and wriggled and pulled them to release some built up stress. Mariah's right foot slid down Marcus' chest and inadvertently brushed against his thick shaft. Shocked at feeling his dick against her feet, Mariah quickly pulled it back up, but the damage was done. The gentle touch of her foot against his erection aroused Marcus' hunger to taste a part of Mariah. He needed something in his mouth to quench his building hunger.

Mariah knew that she was in the danger zone and she could either walk out now to stop anything from happening or stick around and hope she would have the strength to resist Marcus' advances. All her life she had done the right things, said the right things, and had been the perfect child that any parent could be proud to show off to their friends. She didn't know how to be bad or just enjoy the moment without worrying about the consequences. Her father constantly preached to his only daughter to think before you act; but right now, Mariah didn't want to think, all she wanted to do was feel like a woman. She went against her natural instinct and allowed Marcus to explore every inch of her body.

The sensation of having her toes sucked for the first time sent spasms of excitement shooting throughout her ten toes and fingers, and she struggled for a moment to free herself from Marcus' mouth, but it was a fruitless struggle. He sucked each toe like a man who hadn't had a toe dinner for months. This brother knew what he was doing. There was no excess saliva running down Mariah's legs or excessive smacking of the lips. Marcus was a connoisseur of women and he knew where to touch, how to touch and when to let a moment just build itself up until it exploded like firecrackers on the Fourth of July.

"Stop it. *Please* stop," Mariah heard the words come out of her mouth. She didn't know how she was able to form words to speak because her body was running a high fever, and Marcus had the thermometer she needed to make her hotter and drive her to the brink of madness. He screeched to a stop as if he had approached a stop sign. He shifted into gear again when he heard her say, *"Please don't stop."*

This man was doing everything to her body that a man is supposed to do to make a woman go crazy. Without prompting, Mariah laid her palms flat on the table, arched her back into the air and raised her ass like a full moon rising. She had given Marcus the green light to go to work on her body and hold nothing back. Watching Mariah's ass rise slowly as she wiggled it slowly hypnotized Marcus. Her pussy lips were so plump that the back strip of her thong got lost between its plumpness. With one swift motion, Marcus removed Mariah's thongs and lifted it to his nose and inhaled the delicious strawberry scent of her wet dripping pussy. He sensually licked a few drops of moisture from it and dropped it to the floor. Mariah heard him inhale and assumed the rest when she didn't hear her thong immediately fall to the floor. She couldn't recall any man ever inhaling the scent of her moist panties and then proceeding to lick her juices from it. That shit turned her on even more. Whoever this man was, she was thankful that Angelo had to leave and Marcus had taken over. If she was lucky, both she and Angelo would be getting their pussies fucked for lunch.

Even though she hadn't been getting any for a few months, Mariah was thankful that she kept on going to get her weekly Brazilian wax. Her coochie shone like a bald man's head, and she wanted Marcus to polish her pussy off with his dick. Droplets of her sweet juice dripped seductively from her swollen pussy lips like a busted pipe dripping water. Marcus gently rubbed her throbbing lips in a circular motion and honey nectar flowed sweetly down his fingers. The natural thing to do when you find sugar on your fingers is to lick them clean and get some more. The sugar factory was ready and willing to dispense more of its sweetness at the slightest touch.

Guttural moans of built up stress and needing a dick down made Mariah meow like a pussycat being stroked. "What the fuck are you doing to me?" He didn't answer her. He let his actions speak for him. Talk is cheap. A woman won't remember your sex talk if you can't make her pussy scream for mercy. Marcus intended to make her pussy scream as if it had seen a horror movie and it was the first black pussy to be killed. He licked the back of her calves, bit each one deeply and worked his way up to her voluptuous ass. Marcus smiled to himself. He enjoyed being Marcus Smith especially during times like these. He palmed her ass, spread both cheeks open and admired the beauty that lay in front of him. The heat fast escaping between her throbbing lips felt like the heat of sun warming his face. He wanted to kiss the sun and taste its sweetness.

Mariah tried in vain to control the shivers that ran through her body. It had been too long since she had been touched like this. Her body shivered and quivered and was rejecting what it was feeling, but soon it would comply and give in to its innermost desires. Feeling Marcus spread her ass cheeks open, as if he knew her like that, again embarrassed her to be so wide open to a stranger, but damn--it felt good to have a man take control instead of asking permission to be a man. She was the boss all day at work and for once, she wanted to submit to somebody else. The heat of his tongue made slow deep circles around her clit then he licked right up the center of her ass and stopped at her tight virgin hole. She shut her eyes tighter but it only made her feel weaker as if she was about to black out. Everywhere felt wet as if she was in an ocean of warm passion. Marcus dove back in with a tongue that knew tricks other men before him didn't seem to know. Without even thinking, Mariah reached back, placed her hands on his bald head and pressed his face deep into her pussy.

"Taste this pussy. Don't let a drop go to waste," she was breathing so heavily that it sounded like gibberish to Marcus. He was occupied so he groaned his approval of how sweet her nectar tasted on his face and lips. Her pussy was giving him a face bath of strawberry nectar. He wanted to taste all of her and reluctantly separated himself from her quivering lips. Nothing made sense to Mariah. Her mind was gone. Her body was floating on a journey of pleasure. She put herself completely in the hands of Marcus.

She was now on her back and her full figured body covered the massaging table. Her nipples hurt and yearned to be sucked and licked. She started to lick them herself, but Marcus stopped her because he wanted to give her that pleasure. He inserted the middle finger of his right hand between her full lips and she sucked it like she was dying of thirst. He then used his thumb on his right hand to massage her clit and then inserted it between her pussy lips. Then without warning, he probed her anus with his middle finger. Mariah felt it slip deep inside of her ass until it couldn't go any further. She gasped, and then shuddered so hard that she came again. The sensation of having all her sweet holes simultaneously filled sent her into a temporary shock, but it felt so good that she wished his fingers were about five inches longer. He was all over her like a gigantic octopus with his fingers all inside of her and now his lips were making love to her nipples. Mariah didn't know if she was coming or going; well, she did know she was coming. The dam was now open and all her juices were flowing out all over the table.

Marcus didn't remember ever making a woman come so much without actually penetrating her. How would she react if he was actually able to enter the depths of her tightest sweetness? The thought of her losing her mind intensified his already hardened erection. Mariah wanted more than Marcus' thumb filling her mouth. She slowly dismounted the massaging table, placed both hands against the firmness of his chest, and lowered herself closer to where her lips ached to taste. As her knees reached the carpet, she hooked her fingers into the waistband of his black biker shorts and slid it down to his knees. His tree trunk Mandingo eleven inch erection popped out firm and fully developed and ready to do some deep sea pussy diving. Instinctively, Marcus spread his legs slightly open and Mariah lowered her head and turned her neck upward. She popped one of his balls into her mouth while slowly working his thick shaft with her right hand. She felt out of control. Even if she could stop herself, she didn't want to right now. Her body was on fire and Marcus was squirming like a snake caught in a trap. Mariah came up for air and held Marcus' throbbing erection in her two hands and seductively licked off some pre-cum from his fat dick head. "Suck it already," was the only thought on Marcus' mind, but he didn't want to rush the moment because he knew how quickly it could be lost if the wrong thing was said.

"Damn baby, I don't know if I can take all of this in my mouth."

"I bet you can," Marcus urged as he gently guided her head towards his erection. "Take it slowly inch by inch." He was damn near losing his mind and just wanted to ram it down her sweet throat.

The intense heat of Marcus' dick felt good on Mariah's lips, so she gently rubbed her lips all around it. She hadn't done much dick sucking in her life, but she had a natural affinity for it. An ex-boyfriend had told her that it's a waste of full sensual lips if a woman who has them can't suck a dick worth a damn. Needless to say, her ex had never received the pleasure of her using them on him. If all she was good for was to suck his dick then she didn't need him around.

Marcus decided that Mariah was going too slow and took matters into his own hands. He put his left hand around her neck and grabbed some hair with his right and fed her a full meal of eleven inches of dark meat. She gagged at first, but didn't resist him taking control. Sometimes, a man just needs to say fuck it, take over a situation, and deal with the consequences afterwards. In the bedroom, a woman doesn't want a man who is in touch with his feminine side. She wants a man who can tame her pussy and make her scream bloody murder like a fucking cat in heat. Mariah licked, slurped and got her mouth fucked like a tight pussy. Her jaws were aching from his jackhammer pummeling of her mouth, and she wanted to feel the same sensation inside her throbbing wetness.

Marcus didn't have to be told that it was time to do some serious work. He didn't understand how people who can have sex anytime they wanted would choose not to have it. Mariah obviously could have any man that she wanted and probably any woman also, but she had chosen to be celibate. He was about to rock her celibate ass into an orgasmic coma. Two strong hands lifted Mariah from the floor and palmed her ass like Kobe toying with a basketball; and quicker than her clit could twitch, her legs were wrapped about Marcus' muscled back and her breasts pressed against his hairy chest. The gentle friction of his hairy pubic area against her clit and his hairy chest against her nipples made Mariah grind into Marcus' body even harder. She couldn't help herself.

"Damn, I'm about to come again. Shit!"

"Hold on baby. Let me get some of that sweet pussy before your ass bust another nut again," and without missing a beat, Marcus reached under the massaging table and whipped out a XX Magnum condom. He had strategically placed them all over the room just in case something popped off. Something was definitely about to pop off in here. He was going to ride her sweet black ass like she was a ride at Disney World.

Their faces were inches apart and the heat radiating from his body scorched her breasts. His eyes stared hungrily into hers and it made Mariah even wetter to see the lustful cravings living in them. This brother had to be doing some serious bench pressing at the gym because Mariah wasn't exactly the size of a skinny model, but Marcus effortlessly raised her body a little higher until his lips were attached to her hardened nipples. He now only had one hand spread between her two ass cheeks and used the other one to maneuver her nipples into his mouth. Somehow he had managed to get both breasts together and was sucking both nipples at the same time. Her entire being was on fire: the air around her was suffocating, her senses had been lit by a torch of passion and she could feel warm cum escaping her throbbing lips. Each sweet drop landed on Marcus' pulsating dick which was like a black spear just waiting to penetrate her deeply. She wanted to feel him so badly inside her tightness that a physical pain of desire rippled through her body making Mariah hold on tighter and kiss him more deeply. Their lips met in a heated embrace of lust, passion, and desire. Marcus sucked on Mariah's bottom lips and trailed his tongue back and forth and in circles around it. She moaned in appreciation and sucked on his even harder.

Marcus felt the scorching heat of passion that was breathing from Mariah's plump pussy lips and wanted to bask in its glory. With his hands palming her ass, he lowered her gently onto the thickness of his erection and she did the rest.

"Oh, oh, oh damn...that shit feels so fucking good baby," Mariah wrapped her arms around Marcus' neck even tighter and allowed her weight to descend slowly on his pulsating shaft. With every inch that he fed her famished pussy, Mariah wanted more until she was stuffed with dick meat. She had always had a tight pussy, but the lack of sex had made it even tighter. Marcus was gentle and didn't try to fuck her and rip her open like an overexcited teenager. He allowed her to dictate the pace of his entry into her swollen sugar walls, and he would know when she was ready to be fucked sweetly and deeply.

Mariah sucked on Marcus' neck as if she was a vampire thirsting for blood. His dark-brown complexion would show no proof of her attack. The men she had been with before would have flinched by now at the force of her bite, but Marcus enjoyed it so much that Mariah bit deeper, and it made her thirstier and ready to be devoured. She was ready to be fucked. Marcus' muscles tightened as he got set to launch his stealth attack on her thirsty pussy. The thick head of his shaft teased her sensitive walls, and then without warning, Marcus deep stroked her with quick rapid dick ram shots that pierced her so deeply that she almost forgot to scream. His dick was like a crazy ass jackhammer that kept on pounding deeper and deeper as if in search of finding her loudest orgasm. Mariah bounced up and down on Marcus' black pole as if it was on a horse galloping at break neck speed. This ride was closed and everyone else would just have to wait their turn to jump on it. Dick like this didn't come around too often, and when you find it, you have to ride it until you are all dicked out; and even then, you should ride it until you pass the fuck out. A woman never knows when platinum dick will come around again so she has to enjoy it as if it's going out of fashion.

The patrons at the spa knew all about Marcus' reputation of being a pussy killer, so some of his clients smiled knowingly when Mariah's screams and moans resounded through the halls and blended into the music that was playing. Marcus lifted Mariah a little higher and allowed his cum soaked dick to slip from the tender walls of her sweetness. His condom covered dick glistened like a sword fresh from battle and dripping with the honey nectar of his conquest. She levitated above his shaft quivering with anticipation to feel him inside of her again. Sweat was pouring from every available orifice on their bodies and Mariah needed him to fill her up again. He didn't move to pleasure her again and his dick continued to tease her; rigid and ready to launch at his command. Their eyes locked and she silently begged him to do his worst damage, but he didn't relent. That's when she knew what he wanted her to do. He wanted her to beg for it like a common whore. Mariah had never begged for dick in her life and wasn't about to start now. Her body had other ideas and it was feening something crazy for some more of Marcus' deep stroking pussy stirring sexing. Mariah swallowed her pride and did what it would take to get some more of his sweet dick.

"Marcus baby please fuck me. I need to feel that fat dick of yours inside of my tight pussy again. Make it yours baby…make me scream your name and come all over your dick. Make me your bitch," Mariah almost choked on saying that word but her body was still hungry for what he had to give.

Mariah cringed at those words but sometimes you have to soothe a man's ego to get what you wanted. It was a small price to pay for dick this good. It was like having the Black American Express card. It's a privilege that few ever get to experience but always dream about.

The last words were music to Marcus' ears and an aphrodisiac for his erection. He launched his erection upward and this time Mariah was ready for its onslaught. Her inner muscles gripped his shaft, and she slid up and down it like it was a greased pole. With every penetration, Mariah felt something inside of her give way. She was being opened and fucked by a master dick slinger. The sensation of feeling eleven inches of hard black meat sliding in and out her sweet pussy was more than Mariah could bear. Marcus' dick was pulsating, growing and she knew he was about to shoot his load. She had to get hers before he exploded inside of her. Who knew how long it would take him to get it back up.

"Is that all you got, Mr. Dickman. I thought you were going to make my pretty pussy scream. I thought you were going to make me your slut," she whispered seductively in his ears. She was taunting him, giving him every reason to show no mercy.

He would show her who the boss was. No one questioned his dick game. It was now a personal challenge to Marcus to fuck her into submission. He released his magnetic hold on her ass and her feet slid back down to the floor. The insistent erotic sounds of "Sexual Healing" infused him with more energy and Mariah urged him on with her prodding. They were both standing straight and he turned her around and marveled at the size of her ass. She had been given more than enough to feed a village. He grabbed both of her arms slightly above her elbows and thrust her full weight forward. She was bent over and ready to be fucked.

Mariah didn't like being so vulnerable. What if she slipped from his grasp and went crashing to the floor and fucked up her face? Marcus didn't give her much time to ponder this any further. He was pounding her pussy hard. Her hair was flying all over the place, breasts jumping around like fish in the sea, and his balls

71

were smacking against her clit making her even more turned on. Mariah let herself go and trusted that she wouldn't fall. It felt like a ball of fire was building deep inside of her and about to explode and wreck havoc. With a final deep thrust, she felt Marcus explode like a bomb inside of her and her knees buckled, but she held on. An explosion of electric energy shook her body to the core and she moaned with the ecstasy of orgasmic bliss. Her ass rocked backwards on his erection, and she released all of her sexual frustrations on his dick. She couldn't stop coming. There were numerous aftershocks of tiny orgasms that sent her body in spasmic overload. She braced her body against the massaging table, and Marcus' dick now flaccid, slipped limply out of her cum soaked lips.

They were both breathing heavily, sweating profusely as if they had just run a marathon. Marcus would never admit it but he was tired and dehydrated. As soon as Mariah left, he would turn off the lights and go to sleep. Mariah was exhilarated, on a natural high and she knew that Marcus wouldn't be ready to fuck her again like he just did. Her clit was still tingling and her body was still hungry for something more.

"That was hot, baby. We will have to do it again."

"Yeah, we will," Mariah responded. They both smiled. It was a smile of understanding, knowing that they were only being polite. It was an intense encounter but it wouldn't happen again. The room smelled of their sexual encounter and Mariah needed a shower before she could go back to her office. She would take one at work.

The last thing she needed was more gossiping in the office about her sex life. They chitchatted as they both got dressed and Mariah tried to sneak through the spa without making eye contact. She could hear a few women snickering and some were even imitating her moans of passion. Mariah shook her head and laughed as she headed back upstairs to take a shower. The entire episode was still surreal to her and she couldn't believe what she had just done with Marcus. She would have to thank Angelo for the gift of Marcus later on. Her mind was still on Marcus as she rode the elevator back to work.

Lunch time was almost over and the women who were using the gym had already taken their showers. Mariah was left alone with her thoughts and enjoyed the sensual touch of warm water cascading over her body. Her mind was lost in deep thought and she was unconsciously massaging her soapy breasts and wished that Marcus' lips were still sucking them. She moaned in appreciation at the sensations still running rampant through her sensitized body and inserted her manicured fingers one by one into her tight hole. If she hadn't been so engrossed in pleasuring herself, she would have heard someone come in.

Janet, forever the nosey person had seen Mariah walk by the office and head straight to the showers. She found it curious that she would go there and not come right to the office; so after a few minutes, she walked into the showers and heard Mariah's moans of release. There was a haze of fog from the hot water and Mariah's intense passion that made it almost impossible to see, but her moans were like a trail of honey drops that Janet couldn't help but to follow.

The shower door must have somehow come open and right before her eyes was a scene being played out that made Janet's moist pussy tingle with an ache that made her crazy. Mariah stood under the shower with her eyes closed and facing Janet. Water cascaded down her face, sliding off her firm breasts then made a momentary detour between the heat rising between her thighs before finally sliding down her legs. Janet slid her hand into the waistband of her skirt and started to gently rub her clitoris and squeeze her breasts. The entire scene was surreal to her and without thinking about it; she quickly removed her clothes and walked towards the shower to join Mariah. She was unsure of what Mariah's reaction would be, but she was past the point of caring. She wanted to taste the warmth of Mariah's pussy on her lips even if it might cost her, her job.

The sudden awareness that someone else was with her in the shower came too late for Mariah to do anything about it. Before she could open her eyes, the intruder had entered the shower and kissed her wetly on her lips. The shock of being kissed interrupted her self pleasure. She was now face to face with Janet who now seemed so much taller, even though Janet was only a few inches taller than her. Mariah didn't know if she should smack her assistant or ask her to leave, so she hesitated on her response. Janet emboldened by Mariah's confusion took it as a sign to continue her seduction. She slipped her hands around Mariah's waist and drew her soapy heated body closer to her. Their bodies touched and the heat of arousal sent a jolt of excitement through both of them. Her hands massaged Mariah's round ass, slowly working their way up her back and then pulled her in for a deeper kiss.

*"Who does this bitch think she is?"* Mariah thought to herself, but didn't resist or pull away. She found herself excited and scared all at that the same time. Adrenaline of desire was running through her body at being caught and being aroused at the hands of a woman. She had thought about being with a woman before, but was always too scared that she might like it too much and become a lesbian. Now she was wondering what the hell had taken her so long to try this.

There was no need for words because they both knew what they wanted. Janet took control of the situation and tenderly massaged Mariah's sensitive clit as they kissed. A heat engulfed Mariah's body and her moans of pleasure reverberated throughout her entire body. The softness of Janet's lips against hers was a pleasure that went beyond anything she had ever felt, and she wanted more. They were both oblivious to everything else around them as they continued to kiss hungrily and touch every sensitive place on each other's body. Janet seemingly read Mariah's mind and knew what her body wanted. She dropped to her knees and used her face to slowly nudge Mariah's quivering thighs open. Mariah thrust forward with her pelvis and Janet's tongue was erect and ready to be buried inside of Mariah's aching pussy.

Marcus had devoured and ravished her so thoroughly that her pussy was still leaking cum as she came back to work, but it had only made Mariah hungrier. She couldn't understand this craving; to be consumed until she was left virtually exhausted. She didn't know how to put the brakes on her desires once they were lit and it made her feel out of control. There was no in between for her; either she went on a dick-less diet, or she indulged to gluttony. She remembered her Bible studies as a child that gluttony was one of the seven deadly sins, but sometimes gluttony does the body good.

Janet felt like she was submerged in the ocean between Mariah's thick thighs. Water merged with the warm nectar flowing from Mariah's sweet lips was coming from every direction, and she couldn't lick and suck fast enough to satisfy her hunger. She was drowning in a sea of water and pussy nectar, but she didn't want to be saved. She tilted her head backwards, stuck her tongue out as far as it could reach, braced her back against the wall and let Mariah ride her tongue into the sweet land of pleasure. Janet was in heaven as Mariah's warm nectar flowed down her tongue and she greedily swallowed every drop. She had died and gone to pussy heaven. She felt like a wino on a pussy nectar binge, and she was drunk with passion.

Watching the pleasure that Janet got from tasting her sweet goodies reminded Mariah of Mr. Johnson, the CEO of the company. She had been spurning his advances for years until the last few months when he told her that he would be retiring. He had made it clear that if he didn't get what he wanted from her, he would bring in an outsider to run the firm. Mariah hadn't busted her ass for the last three years to be second in command to anyone. So she considered her options: quitting, suing for sexual harassment, or just giving the old man what he wanted from her. Neither quitting nor suing would get her what she wanted, so she opted to give him what he wanted—a taste of the goodies.

The night that she was supposed to sleep with him; he sent over a black slinky dress that hugged her ass and breasts like an over excited uncle at a picnic and the company car to drive her to his penthouse downtown. She felt like a trick as she waited for him to open the door of his apartment. She could feel his eyes raping her as she walked into the living room. Before they got down to business, she whipped out an air tight contract stipulating that the job would be hers. The old man was so excited that he would be sniffing her pussy that he signed it without reading it. He could have signed over his entire life's savings to her and he wouldn't have cared. It always amazed Mariah how stupid men became at the prospect of getting pussy. They would literally put everything they worked hard for in jeopardy if the possibility of getting between the legs of a beautiful woman became a reality. They were worse than dogs. They were rabid dogs in need of tranquilization.

The old man took off his clothes faster than he had ever done anything in the last twenty years and he stood naked in the bedroom. Mariah's eyes gazed down at his manhood—which was putting it loosely—and knew that there was no way that he was going to get an erection. He had already taken a 100mg of Viagra and still his penis dangled lifelessly between his legs. They waited for another hour and still nothing. The old man wasn't going to go away empty handed so he ordered Mariah to take off all her clothes. She hadn't worn any panties or bra in order to hurry the evening along. The sight of her naked body caused the old man to breathe heavily. For a minute, she thought that he might have a heart attack. Mariah caught a glimpse of herself in the mirror and she had to admit that her body was banging. She almost wished that she could fuck herself into submission.

Still unable to get aroused, the old man started stroking his limp penis and had Mariah lay down on the bed. He parted her thighs with one hand and continued to play with himself. "All of this for some pussy," Mariah thought, but in the same breath; she realized she was being hypocritical since she was doing all of this for a job. He licked her wetness a few times while continuing to play with himself. She moaned as if she was enjoying it, but was already thinking about her new office and how she would decorate it. The old man was enjoying himself; his limp penis squirted all over the bed, and a few drops spilled on Mariah's legs. He went into the bedroom to clean himself up, and by the time he came back, Mariah was in the elevator and on her way home. She had gotten what she came for and her contract was safely in her purse.

Replaying the entire incident in her mind made her angry that even though she was qualified for the position, she had to sleep with the boss to get what should have been hers. Looking down at Janet between her thighs, lapping at her pussy like a puppy dog, infuriated Mariah even more because she was the one responsible for spreading rumors around the office. Even if it was true – it was still malicious and uncalled for in a place of business. She would make Janet pay for making her look bad in front of her employees.

Mariah reached up and positioned the shower head directly over her right shoulder so that the water would stream directly down into Janet's face to blind her. She angrily grabbed a hold of Janet's hair with her right hand, and Janet looked up with half-closed eyes to avoid being blinded. There was anger in Mariah's eyes and her full lips were curled up into a snare. The transformation was sudden and it left Janet bewildered as to what caused it, but before she had time to wonder any further, the full force of Mariah's right hand descended through the streams of water; the sound of flesh meeting flesh resounded through the shower. The force of the slap literally spun Janet's head around and Mariah's grip on her hair and scalp had tightened. She slapped her three times in succession without provocation.

"What the fuck is wrong with you?" Janet screamed from her knees with streams of hot water in her eyes and mouth.

"That's for spreading those fucking rumors around the office about me bitch."

Mariah bitch slapped Janet again then forced her face deep into her pussy's heat. Between getting slapped

79

around like a hooker being beaten by her pimp, and having her face forced down into Mariah's pussy, Janet's body was in shock. Her fear had turned into excitement and she wanted more of this punishment. The sweet warmth of Mariah's pussy nectar flowed between her lips and she eagerly swallowed it as if she was dying of thirst. She wanted more but Mariah pulled her face away, and her anger had now turned to amusement.

"You like that huh bitch? You love me slapping your ass around like a hoe?"

Janet tried to answer but all that came from her mouth was a weak yes and she nodded her head in agreement. She was so turned on and visibly shaking from the experience. Mariah felt empowered as if Janet was hers to do with as she wished.

You want more of this don't you?"

Janet didn't care if it made her look weak in Mariah's eyes. She loved being woman-handled by another woman. Yes, she wanted more. She didn't have to answer. Mariah could see the lust in her eyes.

"This is what I want you to do. After I'm finished here with you, I want you to go back to office and tell everyone that you lied about me and that you were just jealous. Okay?"

Janet hesitated and Mariah slapped her across her face again. The pain was so severe that for a moment Mariah regretted hitting her that hard, but Janet looked at her and smiled. She would do as Mariah wished if it meant that she would continue to abuse her like this and allow her enjoy the pleasures of her pussy.

It was another full hour before Janet and Mariah were finished in the shower. Her face and tongue were sore with sweet pain, but she enjoyed every second of it. The entire day had been a whirlwind for Mariah and she couldn't wait to go home and rest her body and process everything that had happened.

Janet would be coming over the next night to continue what they had started in the shower and Mariah couldn't wait. She was the master and Janet was the slave so she couldn't allow Janet to know how much she enjoyed what they were doing. It was new sexual territory for her, but she was a fast learner and there was nothing she couldn't do once she set her mind to it. She was the new CEO of Delicious Scents and had a submissive slave to do her sexual bidding. Life was good.

10/21/08… 12:02pm

# Floor 6...9

The threat of rain loomed ominously all day behind the dark-grayish clouds, and like an orgasm seeking a place to release its rainfall; showers of warm rain would soon burst through the weakened clouds to fertilize the earth. Sara O' Reilly enjoyed running through Central Park at this time of morning. Summer's heat hadn't as yet laid claim to the city, but it was still humid enough that the mere act of walking could work up a full body sweat.

A few early morning joggers would occasionally run past her, nod their heads in greeting and continue on their way. A cool gust of wind crept up behind her to kiss her ass cheeks under her blue running shorts. It sent shivers between her sweaty thighs, clung to her wet white wife-beater and rustled through her long red hair which went airborne making her look as if she was flying. An electric feeling of arousal ran through her body, and it only served to remind her of how long she had been without sex or the touch of a man.

She enjoyed the anonymity of the city since moving from Boston six months ago to pursue her dreams on Broadway, but lately loneliness seemed to be her constant companion. She was a month shy of her 30th birthday; no kids, no man, and a pussy that seemed to throb every time the wind changed directions. Her girlfriends couldn't understand why she was still without a man in a city that was notoriously filled with men randomly flirting with women on every street corner. Without even trying, any woman could get laid everyday if she wanted. Even women who were beauty challenged were getting laid with an alarming frequency. Sara, with Angelina Jolie-like lips, perfectly toned body, legs that could crack a man's skull like a walnut, and breasts the size of perfectly ripe cantaloupes hadn't been laid in almost eight months. There are some mysteries that have no answers. Everyone was at a loss explaining Sara's long sexless drought. If she didn't get laid fast and soon, her pussy would be on the endangered species list and eventually declared extinct.

Patrick took a quick peek around the corner, temporarily leaving his doorman duties. Just as he hoped, Sara came sprinting around the corner and was drenched in sweat from her daily morning run. This was the highlight of Patrick's day to watch Sara finish her run at the top of the stairs that led down into the front door of the apartment building. She was like a contortionist bending her legs and body at will. Sara was unaware that Patrick would watch her through the surveillance cameras perched a few feet above her head. From that angle, he could see every trickle of sweat rolling down her face and thighs as he zoomed in repeatedly to get a closer look.

Completely out of breath, Sara sat down on the stairs for a few minutes. She couldn't have sat down in a worse place, but it was perfect for Patrick's ogling eyes. He knew he didn't stand a chance in hell of ever seeing her naked so this was as good as it got for him. The camera lens zoomed in on her and came to rest between her open thighs. She never wore panties and her running shorts had ridden up her thighs leaving her cleanly shaven pussy exposed to his deviant imagination. Sara was the sexiest white girl that Patrick had ever laid eyes on, and it was because of her that he had a perfect work attendance. She was always cordial and smiled his way whenever they met in the building, but she had no idea just how familiar he was with her body. She always found it curious that he was never around when she entered the building and waited for the elevator, but didn't give it much thought. She barely understood a word he said whenever he attempted to engage her in conversation. His thick Caribbean accent left her at a loss to understand what he was trying to say so she would smile, wave and walk away. She pressed the up button and waited for the elevator to come down.

Shirtless and looking like a black chiseled god, Hunter sprinted to the front door of the apartment building with a last burst of energy but was too late to catch a view of the girl with the beautiful body. He received a lot of attention from women and some men when he ran through the park shirtless. No one had to tell him that he was a good looking black man. He told himself that everyday without provocation. The image in the mirror staring back at him a few times a day confirmed that fact. Believing himself to be a god among men, Hunter didn't smoke, drink, or eat meat. He didn't eat pussy either because, as he so eloquently put it to the last woman he slept with, "pussy was meat that was uncooked." His body was his temple of purity and he basked in the adoration it brought him. The reflection staring back at him through the mirror next to the elevator made Hunter strike a pose of a bodybuilder. He was 6'4, 240 rock hard pounds of muscle, a smile that could light up New York during a blackout, and a dick that didn't discriminate. His male friends referred to him as Mr. United Nation. Hunter hadn't met a pussy that he said no to. His vanity led him to believe he was offering a contribution by allowing women the pleasure of his body and a dick that was too thick to quit.

There was only one elevator in the building and when it came back down; Hunter was pleasantly surprised to see Sara in it since she had already gone up. It was the first of the month, so she came back down to drop her rent check in the outgoing mailbox. She couldn't help but notice the shirtless black man waiting for the elevator when she walked by, and Sara felt like a little Catholic school girl in heat when she walked by him. A musky scent of sweat with a faint hint of cologne caressed her nostrils. An image of him ravaging her body flashed through her mind quickly, and it made her blush that a stranger could have this much of an effect on her. She hoped that he hadn't seen her reaction to his physique, but Hunter was the consummate predator of flesh and he noted how red the back of her neck and ears had gotten when she walked away.

"Game on." he thought to himself.

Hunter, always the phony gentleman, held the elevator door open and Sara reluctantly got in with him. She noticed him holding the elevator door as she walked by and didn't want to insult him or his kind gesture, so she got on. She pressed the sixth floor and he pressed the ninth floor; both lit up at the same time—69. Maybe if she was having sex on a regular basis then it wouldn't have mattered much, but seeing the numbers 6 and 9, lit up like an invitation, sent a wave of arousal spiraling through her body. She gulped hard in hopes that she wouldn't blush, but it was too late. Her body reacted to the image of her and Hunter in a 69 position. Her nipples grew in size and protruded through her white wife beater t-shirt, and trickles of sweat dripped down the small of her back. The heat of arousal blazed hot between her thighs. She gulped again but there was no air in the elevator, so she stared off in space hoping that Hunter wasn't looking at her. Sara had never been so mortified in all her life. There might as well have been a sign on her forehead saying FUCK ME PLEASE!

Patrick sat at his station in his office with the cameras zoomed to within inches of Sara's face and chest. He instantly noticed how hard her nipples had gotten and how her face had become flushed with excitement. He couldn't figure it out for a second until he zoomed back and noticed Hunter. He despised Hunter's arrogance, but had to admit that he was an attractive man and he understood why the ladies threw themselves at him. Patrick rationalized that if he was a woman that he would probably do the same thing. That thought repulsed him and he quickly zoomed back to Sara.

"Are you alright?" Hunter innocently asked Sara. He knew how to play the game and she was in his arena now.

Sara was startled to hear his voice and that he had noticed the change in her face. She hoped that he didn't think that she was scared because it was the last thing in the world she was feeling.

"I'm okay," she turned to him and smiled. It was one of those smiles that you give when you're trying to mask your true feelings in hopes of deflecting attention. Hunter was a true predator and he noticed everything. "Maybe I ran a bit too far today. I'll be okay," she said to him, hoping the words coming from her lips were believable.

"I'm Hunter Strength by the way. You're a strong runner. I've seen you a few times in the park."

His voice hummed like a deep baritone and it electrified Sara's body. Her clit jumped so suddenly that she almost jumped back in shock, but she was able to contain herself.

"I'm Sara, Sara O'Reilly."

Knowing that he had seen her running made her blush even harder. Hunter extended his right hand and she shook it. The smallness of her tiny white hand disappearing into his large black hand made her feel small. She was only 5'5 and looking up at him was like looking into a beautiful dark sky. She felt woozy and that's when the elevator lurched suddenly and came to a stop. Everything went black for a few seconds, and they stood there unsure of what had just happened.

"Are you okay?" Hunter asked.

"I'm fine. This is the second time this has happened to me since I moved in."

"How long were you stuck the first time?"

"It was about ten minutes so it wasn't that bad."

Rays of light streamed in through the cracks in the elevator door and their eyes adjusted to their surroundings. He was looking right at her and she held his stare. Patrick's voice streamed in through the intercom system that help was on the way. He was still able to see their shadows in the elevator and hear everything they were saying through his monitor.

Hunter wasn't sure if he was reading Sara's body language correctly. Her eyes told him that she was hungry and her nipples and body betrayed that hunger. If he was wrong—then there might be hell to pay. He prided himself on never thinking with his dick first but instead with his other head. The air in the elevator had gotten thicker with heat, and within minutes they were both sweating profusely. Trickles of sweat dripped down Sara's face, and she unconsciously licked her lips to taste the saltiness. She wanted Hunter, but she knew he wouldn't make the first move. She knew he had too much to lose if he guessed wrong and made unwanted advances to her. It had been eighth months without having a man inside of her, eight months without a man kissing her, eight months without losing control and feeling the passion of an orgasm raging uncontrollably through her pussy. She wanted to feel that sensation again. She wanted Hunter Strength to fuck her with reckless abandon. A voice that didn't sound like hers spoke from her full lips. It was the hunger in her body speaking.

"So what are you waiting for? Do I have to beg you to fuck me?"

Sara couldn't believe what she had just said and neither could Patrick and Hunter. Their dicks throbbed in unison of anticipation of what was about to happen. Sara had no idea she was turning on two men at the same time.

Hunter slowly approached Sara. Her words had emboldened him and given him permission to handle his business. He enjoyed all kinds of women, but there was something about white women that really got him stirred up. He enjoyed watching his dark skin tone merge into the hue of the pale skin of a white woman. It drove him literally insane to watch the thickness of his shaft stretch and fill the soft pink folds of skin. He could often feel the stares of some angry black women and white men who seemed to wish him death for crossing over to the other side. It seemed like it was a battle between good and evil for the salvation of the universe. He also received the jealous stares of black men who wished it were them, and white women who yearned to taste his chocolate thunder as he enjoyed the company of a beautiful young white woman. He was oblivious to it all. It was his life and he could do whatever the fuck Hunter Strength wanted to do with his life.

"You're gonna get it," he smiled at her devilishly as he bent his head down to kiss her.

"I sure hope so, Mr. Strength."

She breathed his last name with the intense heat of desire and it made Hunter even harder. He couldn't wait to part the wet folds of her pink flower and hear her moan for him. He wanted to fuck her like one of those women in the porn movies. Moans of passion were an adrenaline rush for him and his erection would get so hard that it was painful. It was a sweet kind of pain that he relished and wanted. Lately, sex for him didn't hold the same challenges and passion anymore. When you've had something way too much, it loses its appeal; but now, he felt his blood racing hot and he was fully engaged in enjoying the sweet flesh of Sara O'Reilly.

Sara tilted her head forward and her red hair covered her face and stuck to his. They were both blissfully sweaty. Hunter brushed her hair aside as he pulled her small body into his. She felt fragile as if she could be easily dominated. Their lips met. It felt like two balls of fire raging for dominance. His hands were on the small of her back and quickly eased down to her ass. His hands were huge as they firmly squeezed both her cheeks. She moaned her approval as she planted herself against his chest. Her small hands massaged his bald head then wandered to his face, then his chest. Just touching him was making her wetter and she tightened her muscles to keep her moisture from escaping. Their tongues danced and spoke to each other exchanging the secrets of passion they hoped to discover. Hunter's hands disappeared into Sara's shorts and the warmth of her flesh greeted his touch. Her moist lips were thick.

They were extra sweet and filled with the sweet nectar of passion with which he wanted to coat his dick.

Patrick sat at his desk both shocked and jealous at what he was seeing and hearing. Little Miss Boston was going to get fucked in his elevator and he wasn't the one doing it. His erection thrashed about angrily in his pants and he released it from its prison.

Sara was beyond the point of no return. She wanted this. She needed it right now as much as anything she had ever needed in her life. She enjoyed feeling powerless in Hunter's embrace. The strength of his erection thumped repeatedly against the front of her shorts. It wanted inside of her in the worst possible way. Her hands slid down his chest and into the front of his black shorts. His pubic hair tickled her palm as she wrapped her hands around the heat of his thick shaft. She squeezed it and felt its heat kiss her fingers. He moaned in appreciation. She squeezed it again and this time his moan was that of the sweet pain of pleasure. Her right hand wandered further down to massage his balls. They felt like golf balls in her hands and she couldn't wait to see the size of the club that he was swinging. He would definitely be hitting a home run today. Hunter was fully loaded and could quench her thirst with a full glass of passion cum juice. Sara squeezed the base of Hunter's balls and his erection stiffened as if saluting her passion. It was primed and ready to dive deep into her sweetest and wettest ache nestled between her quivering thighs. Slowly she lowered herself onto the elevator floor until she was on her knees and her face was mere inches away from Hunter's crotch. She was not herself anymore. Her suppressed desires had manifested into pure lust and her body felt as it had been set on fire by passion. That's when Sara heard two distinctly different sounds of heavy breathing. At first, it confused her because she thought it was her breathing so heavily, but then she realized that the speaker was directly next to her ear. It was that pervert Patrick getting his jollies off viewing them from the screen above her. She didn't care. It excited her even more that she was turning on two men at the same time.

Hunter looked down at Sara who was on her knees in a praying position. Her red hair was matted against her face. He could still see her eyes and her full lips which he hoped would soon be filled with the darkness of his pulsating erection. He was ready to anoint her and forgive her of all her sins. All she had to do was deep throat him until he squealed like a pig in mud heaven. He closed his eyes, leaned back against the cold metal wall and felt his black shorts being slipped off until he was completely naked. He didn't allow himself to think of what would happen if the power suddenly came back on and his mostly white neighbors caught a glimpse of his naked black body in the elevator. There are some things in life that are worth the risk. A beautiful woman who had now undressed herself and was on her knees about to pleasure him in an elevator was a risk well worth taking every time.

Patrick was in porn heaven. He felt as if he was watching his favorite porn actor, Lexington Steele, in action.  Instinctively, he begun to massage his crotch and now his pants and underwear were on the floor in a heap around his shoes.  He was in full masturbating mode and was in awe of how perfect Hunter's body was sculpted.  His eyes lingered on Hunter's body and then back to Sara's, and he continued to masturbate.  He closed his eyes for a few seconds and imagined that she was on her knees for him.  A surge of energy pulsated through his body, and he struggled mightily to hold off spewing his pleasure all over his hands.

Sara had never had a black man before and her body ached with curiosity as to whether she had been missing anything.  Black men had always been a fascination to her, but the opportunity had never presented itself – until now.  If there was a chance that she was missing out on something so wonderful that it would blow her mind, then she had to find out for herself instead of always wondering.  Hunter's erection merged in the dimly lit elevator and a sliver of light shone on its magnificence as it swayed slowly in front of Sara's lips.  It reminded her of an elephant's trunk.  The sheer girth of it was magnificent.  A rush of adrenaline shot through her body and she felt as if she was already having an orgasm.  Her lips parted and Hunter slowly thrust forward and there seemed to be no end in sight to the depths of her mouth and throat.  He had completely disappeared between her lips and she gagged as if struggling for breath but then found her wind again.  There was something soothing about sucking a man's dick that Sara thoroughly enjoyed.

She didn't do it to please him.

She did it to please herself.

The heat of a man's erection throbbing uncontrollably in her mouth and sliding effortlessly down her throat made her feel powerful. She enjoyed knowing that while a man was in her mouth he was powerless, and he would do and say basically anything to continue experiencing a mind bending blowjob. The thickness of Hunter's dick slipped in and out her swollen lips and the sensation of having it rub against her bottom lip stimulated her even more.

His intense excitement led him to grab two fistfuls of her red hair and force it deeper down her throat. She hungrily took it. Hunter had never heard of anyone choking while giving a deep throated blowjob. It was something he enjoyed having done to him to get maximum pleasure.

Hunter and Sara had seemingly forgotten where they were and were oblivious to everything but their pleasure. If the elevator door opened and she was suddenly on stage performing—there was no way she was stopping. She would take her bow and cheers for the encore that would surely be requested and granted by her. It would be a story she would have to tell her girlfriends and maybe even put in her memoirs if she ever became a famous Broadway star.

Hunter reached down and wrapped his hands around Sara's upper arms in an attempt to get her to stand up, but she was resistant. She wanted to continue sucking on his black thick elephant trunk. Normally,

Hunter didn't mind having a hot mouth suck him like a Hoover vacuum cleaner, but something told him that this would be a one time thing. He wanted to make sure he made use of every available sweet tight hole she was offering him to fill. Beautiful women like Sara just don't fuck guys in elevators without their being in such a state of extreme horniness, that with every step they took, their engorged clit rubbing against their clothes felt as if someone was licking their clit with a long snake tongue. Finally, she released his swollen dick from her pink lips, and she licked the sweat off his chest as she stood up to face him.

"I am going to fuck you now," he growled at her in a husky voice that gave away his arousal. He had already forgotten her name but could easily pick her pussy out from a lineup if he had to. Funny how men can easily remember the dimensions and texture of a woman's pussy, but remembering a name takes too much brain power.

"You need to fuck me. I need you to fuck me until this tight pussy aches and stretches around your dick like you own it. Can you do that?" Her voice quivered as she spoke those words.

He nodded his head weakly as she caressed and massaged his engorged erection almost to the point of him coming then she would stop. It was like hitting the brakes on a car going a hundred miles an hour and suddenly stopping. The pain building in his balls and dick was excruciating, but it turned him on even more. The feel of his thickness in her hands aroused her, and she eagerly anticipated having him fill her tight box. Her entire body ached as if she had been exercising and lifting weights for hours. It was the kind of deep aching hunger that had to be fed immediately or bad things could happen to the man who left her unsatisfied. When a woman wants to be fucked this badly; nothing less than being fucked with abandonment will suffice. Conversation is inappropriate unless it's the language of passion being moaned...screamed. Orgasms coming together like a jazz band hitting their high notes, one after the other, until all the lines of pleasure and pain are blurred and all that's left is the sweetness of passion's release.

Sweat dripped down Hunter's bald head and face as he pulled her into his embrace. The heat emanating from her body felt like someone had lit a match to his flesh and he was ignited. Her erect nipples poked him in his chest and he lowered his head to suck on them. They were a nice full size; not too big or too small—just enough to leave your lips satisfied. He wanted the taste of her flesh in his mouth. The sweet heat of her nipples between his lips made him crave even more to be inside of her pink sweetness.

Watching them together; black and white, night and day, Patrick enjoyed the beauty of their skin merging into each other like a mixture of paint blending together to create a beautiful picture. They reminded him of a cup of strong hot black coffee and cream poured into the black steaming liquid to slowly change it into warm creamy brown—not as potent but almost as good.

Watching Sara give Hunter head made the imagery even stronger as his dark thickness disappeared between her pink lips. A shudder of arousal ran through Patrick's body and his manhood began to rise again.

Hunter couldn't wait any longer, and Sara felt this slow ticking explosion inside of her pussy that would detonate without her permission. She wanted to be filled with dick meat when her orgasm exploded. She reluctantly pulled herself from Hunter's embrace and walked over to the hand rail next to the elevator doors. Hunter's eyes drank in her naked body and his erection slowly swung in her direction. Sara grabbed on to the hand rail, bent over and turned to face Hunter.

"Can you handle all this pussy?" Her right hand slipped off the rail to smack her ass then spread it open to give Hunter a better view of what was waiting for him. "Can you fuck me so hard that I cry for more?"

Hunter followed his throbbing erection and stood directly behind Sara and admired the plumpness of her ass. He caressed its smoothness lovingly as if it was the first white ass he had ever seen, although he had already been dick deep in quite a few. Most white women didn't have that much of an ass to warrant a second look, but Sara definitely had a little black in her, and in a few seconds she would be filled with ten inches of black meat.

The lights in the elevator flickered for a moment and bathed their naked bodies in its bright light. As quickly as it came, it got dark again. Patrick's mouth dropped wide open when he had a clear view of Sara's white cheeks spread open in anticipation of Hunter filling her tight pussy.  It was an image that he would replay over and over in his mind.

The full weight of his erection slid up and down between the smooth cracks of her ass.  She wanted him inside of her and tried to wriggle her hips so his thick shaft could slide into her.  His hands tightened around her waist.  His fingers dug deep into her skin. A soft cry of pain, but not of resistance, escaped her lips. She would feel the pain for days to come every time she ran, but right now, none of that mattered.  He pushed his way inside of her without any finesse or regard for probing foreplay.  She didn't want foreplay.  She wanted rough, mindless sex fucking.  He groaned as his erection was engulfed by the tightness of her moist pink lips.

Shit, was all his brain was able to mutter.  There weren't too many thoughts occupying his mind except to get the pussy.

A shot of fear raced through Sara's mind as she thought that she would be unable to accommodate his thickness.  Her fears were soon laid to rest.  Hunter knew what to do. He eased out halfway from her quivering lips, used both hands to spread her ass open so that a tiny shadow of darkness from inside of her stared back at him where he quickly filled with his own darkness. Darkness engulfed inside of darkness; the symmetry was beautiful.  Her body shuddered as he repeatedly slammed deep inside of her.  Her head slammed against the elevator and all her thoughts became scrambled like rice being shaken in a bag.

Every stroke from Hunter became more intense as if he was trying to bore a hole beyond the depths of her pussy. Sweat poured down his black skin and dripped down her back to merge into the juices that were flowing from her pussy. After a succession of about ten pummeling strokes, he would ease his manhood all the way out of her throbbing lips and would massage her clitoris with his fingertips while slowly feeding her the head of his shaft. It drove her crazy; so crazy that she had a fleeting thought of letting him analize her, but she had just met him and something like that was for someone special. Sara almost laughed out loud at her sudden sense of decorum. She was buck naked with the dick of stranger pummeling her pussy, and she was worried about saving the rest of herself for someone special. She would let him have anything he wanted.

They heard voices coming up through the elevator shaft asking if they were okay. Someone shouted to them that they would be out in a few minutes. They didn't answer and continued to be lost in their own world of sexual pleasure.

Hunter pulled Sara away from the hand rails into the middle of the elevator and held her right above her elbows. She was suspended in mid-air and if his grip came loose, she would crash to the cold metal floor. The potential danger excited her, and with every pounding of his shaft deep into her moist abyss, it made her hunger even more obvious. Hunter was giving her a first class dick down and she took it like a Playboy champ. He was surprised but impressed at how much dick she could take without begging him to stop. He prided himself in having women beg him to stop because they were unable to take all he had to offer. She got off on it, and the way her ass perked up in the air let him know that she wanted more of the same.

Patrick was exhausted watching this sexual marathon, and if he masturbated one more time; he might find himself in a masturbatory coma. He sat back and enjoyed the show. There was no way the other doormen would believe this. It was a good thing that he would have the tape to prove it.

"Turn around," Hunter ordered Sara. He wanted to see the passion in her eyes when she came. Her muscles were contracting faster around his shaft so he knew that she was close to an explosion. Her response surprised him.

"Make me turn around," she answered without even looking at him. He knew what she wanted to him do as her ass gyrated hard against his firm dick. She hoped that she would be able to withstand that depth of penetration.

Hunter stood up a little bit straighter and the natural curve of his erection rested against Sara's tight anal hole. He smiled in anticipation of filling her anal cavity and started to gently massage the head of his shaft against it. She relaxed when she felt him beginning to stretch her open. He was gentle and that allowed her to relax even more, but he was huge. It was like trying to thread a tree trunk into the eye of a needle. Inch by inch, he slowly eased into her tightness until his manhood had completely disappeared inside of her. They both felt as if they had taken part in performing the greatest magic trick ever.

"Awwwwww damn...damn...damn..." Sara groaned deeply when she felt Hunter touch down inside of her like an airplane touching down safely. He had nowhere else to go and could still push in about two more inches. Hunter tried to relax, he even took some deep breathes; but there was no stopping it. He was about to blow like a geyser out of control. Sara was right there with him as tremors ran up and down her legs and it felt like thousands of tiny orgasms exploding simultaneously inside of her vagina. A surge of hot cum flooded her anal cavity as Hunter released his passion inside of her. His entire body was jerking as if he was having a seizure, but it was only the aftershocks of numerous tiny orgasms.

Even after he came, Hunter's erection was still hard and he continued to slide in and out of Sara's extremely lubricated anal cavity. She urged him to go deeper, to feed her those two extra inches. An extra two inches sometimes can make all the difference in the world. Every nerve in her body screamed. She felt as if she was floating on air and didn't even realize that Hunter had released her arms and was only holding on to her hair.

From Patrick's vantage point, Hunter looked like a rider on one of those electronic bulls as he and Sara swung back and forth.

Everything seemed to go black at the same time. Sara felt as if she was careening down a ski slope with no way to stop, and in mid-flight; her orgasm rippled throughout her entire body. Her screams of passion could be heard on every floor as months of pent-up sexual frustrations reverberated through every floor. It sounded as if a cat was being slaughtered. Children who heard her screams were instantly scared, but adults looked at each other knowingly as if wishing they were the ones who were having their kitty cats slaughtered. A woman who screams like that is a woman who has had every cavity filled to maximum capacity.

Sara collapsed in a heap on the cold floor, but her body was so enflamed that she might as well have been laying on a bed of coals. Hunter held on to the railing as if he might pass out from sheer exhaustion. They were both quiet, lost in their own thoughts about what had just happened.

"I can't believe what we just did. I don't know what came over me," Sara said almost apologetically.

"We did what our bodies wanted to do. We fed each other and it was beautiful."

The sounds of cables grinding alerted them that the problem had been fixed. The lights flickered back on and stayed on this time. Under the glaring light of the elevator; they were clearly able to see other each other naked for the first time. They both drank in each other's bodies and were happy with what they saw. Sara's eyes cast downwards between Hunter's legs and she was shocked that she was able to accommodate the size of his manhood inside of her. Hunter smiled as he read her thoughts.

"You shocked the shit out of me too," Hunter confessed, and they both laughed.

The elevator jerked and started to go back down to the lobby. They quickly got dressed and waited for the elevator to open. As the doors slid open, Hunter gazed at Sara and saw her nipples protruding through her t-shirt. His dick stiffened and he suddenly realized that she had forgotten her bra. It was dangling from the hand rails behind them. Sara realized it and looked around in a panic just as the doors slid open. Hunter stretched his right hand backwards to reach it and stuffed it into his pocket.

The lobby was filled with residents waiting for the elevator to be fixed. The men and women who had heard Sara's piercing scream gave her a knowing look of admiration. She had done what many of them wished they had the courage to do, and her body was still feeling the afterglows of her passionate encounter.

"Are you guys okay?"

They both turned in the direction of the voice. It was Patrick. The smirk on his face confirmed what they both already knew. They played along with his little charade.

"It was good to have Hunter there to keep me company. He was a perfect gentleman and a night in shining armor."

"Yes, a knight in shining black armor."

They laughed at that joke, but Patrick wasn't amused and walked away.

"I think this is yours," Hunter reached into his pocket and discreetly handed her back her bra.

They stepped back into the elevator and pressed their respective floors, six and nine. This time they would make it to their apartments without any further incident.

9/18/08...10:39pm

# Cinnamon Strawberry

It had only been three days since Lennox tasted his favorite flavor Cinnamon Strawberry, but it might as well have been a year. He felt as if he was going through withdrawals; although he didn't know what that felt like, he imagined that it had to be something like this. It was an awful feeling of constant neediness that supplanted everything else in his life. He ached to taste her on his lips again. Before this day was through, he would be face and tongue deep in the sweetest flavor in the world, Cinnamon Strawberry, made fresh daily from the sweet throbbing lips of his woman.

Destiny knew that she missed him tasting her Cinnamon Strawberry because every time her mind wandered to him, all she could think of was his tongue snaking in and out of her plump lips. The thought so aroused her that her plump lips strained the corners of her pink panties and threatened to spill out. She didn't envision his body or the thickness of his manhood. To her, his tongue had become this living entity that licked her entire body as she lay naked in bed at nights trying to touch herself in places that only his tongue could reach to make her body quiver and moan with orgasmic joy. The sounds of her moans would merge with the night air and disappear out of her open window into the sky.

He was the first man she had dated who took intense pleasure in licking the wet space between her legs. He used his tongue in the same fashion as Van

Gogh used his paint brush to uncover something beautiful. It seemed to her that others before him did it only to have her wrap the fullness of her pink lips around their manhood. They didn't relish being down between her legs and couldn't wait to escape and lay on their backs so she could pleasure them. Pleasure is derived by giving and receiving. Most men didn't seem to know that, but Lennox was different. He didn't do it because she asked him to or because he couldn't satisfy her sexually.

Knowing that Lennox enjoyed the taste and scent of her Cinnamon Strawberry pussy made her want to please him even more. Destiny would make sure that everything was extra fresh and met his tongue tasting requirements. He enjoyed licking her until she was no longer able to produce anymore of her Cinnamon Strawberry juices. His tongue would continue to slide inside of her thick lips in a quest for that last Cinnamon Strawberry nectar drop to quench his thirst. Just thinking about him licking her like an ice cream cone on a hot summer's day made her clit throb, and the slow trickles of moisture began to wet the insides of her tender lips. He would be here in an hour. She ran a bath and added drops of fragrances in it that would fill his nostrils with an aroma that would make him even thirstier for her and lick her wet rose flower.

The air was thick with the smell of summer, the seductive sounds of birds making love in the trees, and the undercurrent of sexual energy as women and men engaged in the time honored tradition of flirting. The winter had been surprisingly brutal. For the occupants of the city, it felt as if they were escaping the prison of their apartments and the multi-layers of clothing they had worn to keep warm. Flashes of female flesh could be seen on every corner basking in the heat of summer's long sensual kiss. Legs that had been covered up all winter were now being exposed beneath shorts that made the imagination search for the soft secrets that lay hidden under clothes and between thighs of every hue. Breasts that once slept quietly beneath blouses and bras were now full and had the ability to hypnotize any man within a radius of a few blocks. But the only woman that Lennox Sutton wanted was ten blocks away. With a smile on his face, the taste of her Cinnamon Strawberry on his lips, he put one foot in front of the other and let the conveyor belt of summer beauties walk on by. He had something better waiting for him at home.

Destiny allowed herself the temporary pleasure of admiring her thick sexy frame in the bathroom mirror as she toweled off her body. The firmness of her 40D breasts felt good under her fingers as she massaged her nipples and gently squeezed them. She ran her fingers slowly down her stomach and through the thin layer of hair that ran from under her navel to the plump lips of her pussy. She ached to slip one finger into her rapidly expanding lips, but she had promised Lennox that she wasn't going to touch herself down there. That's my job he had said forcefully. It turned her on even more when he took control like that to claim his pussy.

She was an independent woman doing her thing in the world, but behind closed doors, she wanted to drop the façade she had erected for the world and just be a woman. His woman. There is nothing wrong with letting a man take over as long as he knows what he is doing. Lennox didn't need to be told what to do. He could find her sensitive spots in a blackout without any problems.

The mood was already set: curtains drawn, candles lit, and the lush voice of Luther Vandross filled her bedroom. She sat on the side of the bed swaying to Luther's voice while massaging her body with Victoria Secret's Vanilla Lace body butter. She was ready. She was a meal ready to be eaten and a drink ready to be swallowed. She was a woman ready to have her man taste the natural juices of her body that only thoughts of him could produce in abundance. She heard the door creak close downstairs. He was here and on his way up to their bedroom.

He found her facing him sprawled out on the bed as he entered the bedroom. Her arms were outstretched above her head, her brown hair caressed the softness of her face and lips, and her legs were up and spread open. This is my woman, was the first thought that raced through Lennox's mind and ignited the flames of passion and lust throughout his muscular body. He quickly undressed and let the muscular frame of his body and his scent fill the room with his presence. Destiny inhaled the scent of her man's masculinity and moaned with anticipation as tremors of desire caressed her body in every warm place where his tongue would soon seek the refuge that only her rainforest could provide.

Lennox rubbed his hands together to generate more heat so that when he touched Destiny's enflamed skin, there would be no doubt in her mind that her man had come to make her every wish come true. Her body ached in recognition of the pleasure that would soon be lavished upon it. His erection pointed the way to the bed and he followed without any hesitation.

The world outside didn't exist in their minds. They had created their own personal sanctuary which was governed by only one rule. Pleasure. The only form of communication would be spoken with moans, shudders, tremors, screams and the orgasmic release that she would be experiencing this afternoon. This afternoon was her special time, and when night arrived with its dark attitude, she would pleasure his body in the same way.

Lennox dropped to his knees, placed his palms on either side of her feet, and laid his head on the bed between her feet. The subtle fragrance of Vanilla Lace released from her skin filled the air, and he inhaled it through her cotton sheets. He felt his erection throb with desire as it grazed the carpet under his feet. It longed to be enclosed inside all four of her lips, but this afternoon wasn't about him. It was about the giving of pleasure to a woman who justly deserved having her body worshipped and ravished by her man. Slowly he slid his hands against the warmth of the sheets and placed both of them between her thighs. With the familiarity of a woman who knows what she wants, Destiny lifted her legs and swung them over his shoulders. Lennox grasped her thick thighs and let his fingers sink slowly into the soft warmth of her flesh.

Destiny sighed and knew that her man knew exactly what to do with her body. He had everything under control. All she had to do was let him be the man and let him do what came naturally. A warrior coming home to conquer and please his Queen. The heat of fiery passion radiating from between her thighs and her tender plump lips warmed Lennox's face with its heat like hot water cascading over one's body in the shower. He gulped deeply and licked his lips from thirst. The warmth emitting from her heated garden parched his throat, but it would soon be quenched when the first drops of her Cinnamon Strawberry touched his lips and tongue. He felt like a wino thirsting for that next sip, that next swallow that would make everything right with the world. He sucked the insides of her thighs like he was sucking on a mango extracting its sweet juices. He kissed them softly in preparation for the bountiful blessings that awaited him.

Every pore in Destiny's body screamed as if she was being tortured and tormented; the kind of torture that you pray never ends because it feels so damn good. She gripped the sheets tightly to steady herself, but it was already too late. She was swimming deep in a sea of passion and drowning under the weight of her desire for the heavenly release that her man's lips and tongue would soon fill her with. His huge hands had slipped under the roundness of her ass, and he pulled her onto his erect tongue as she released the sheets from her grasp to let herself float away into pleasure.

The day melted away into nothingness; stresses of work, life and finances didn't matter anymore as the first sweet drop of Destiny's Cinnamon Strawberry warmed his lips. It was the perfect aphrodisiac to end a long day. Some men like to unwind with beer or a shot of rum, but Lennox looked forward to drinking his woman's Cinnamon Strawberry after a long day. It was the preferred drink of the gods that could instantly replenish any man's strength and faith. He spread his thick lips wide open and smacked them together as if eating barbecue ribs at a cookout. He used his lips skillfully to squeeze both of Destiny's pulsating lips together between his to suck on them simultaneously. He enjoyed making his own pussy sandwich, and the moans that sang sweetly from Destiny's lips hardened his erection. A tremor trickled throughout Destiny's body as waves of pleasure surged over her, and she palmed his shaved head to pull him deeper into the center of the monsoon shower that she was about to unleash all over his face. He was due for a pussy bath and he relished the thought of being drenched in the warmth of her love.

A steady flow of Cinnamon Strawberry dripped from Destiny's pussy like a faucet that could not be turned off. Lennox spread his tongue across her fevered lips to plug the leak and flicked his tongue around her clit but it only made her wetter and hornier. Her soft whimpering cries of ecstasy sang his praise as his tongue met the fury of her beautiful release. She twisted and turned like a fish caught on a hook to escape the grip that his lips had placed on her enlarged clit and pulsating lips, but it was to no avail. His body was nimble and every turn that she made, he followed her and continued to suck and lick her dripping pussy lips and clit until Destiny thought that she might lose her mind. She was so overwhelmed with passion that her cries and screams soon turned into sobbing tears that shook her body—and still he would not stop.

Lennox had heard her cry this way before. It was a mixture of delicious pain and unbelievable ecstasy. He reveled in knowing that he could bring her to the point of experiencing such pleasure without actually having intercourse. When she reached this state of frenzied arousal there was no telling what she might do. It was as if she was having an out-of-body experience and being inhabited by someone else. She made him promise to never stop pleasuring her no matter how much she begged; no matter how much she claimed that she was about to die from an orgasm heart attack.

"It just feels soooo fucking good." she said with a smile and a shy look of embarrassment that Lennox would never forget the first time she reached this point of Nirvana. "It's an amazing instrument, this tongue of yours. Never stop using it on me."

When used correctly, a tongue can extract the same amount or more pleasure from a woman's body that an erect dick can; and if they both are working in concert, a woman's Holy Grail for sexual satisfaction will have been attained. Destiny wished she could bend her knees in prayer and give thanks by taking Lennox's throbbing manhood deep inside the warmth of her throat, but he was too busy lavishing licks of praise on her moist lips and she had no intention of disturbing him. He had entered pussy heaven and the master was hard at work to bring pleasure to his woman.

The full length of his tongue darted in and out of her so quickly that it took a moment for Destiny's body to communicate to her mind that she was about to go into orgasmic overflow. The honey sweetness of her Cinnamon Strawberry would be swallowed into the waiting reservoir of his mouth. A final slow seductive circular lick of his tongue around her throbbing lips, Destiny let go of her senses and relinquished all control. He was in control right now. His lips and tongue were all over her as she cried and pleaded for mercy from the swelling of pleasure that was exploding every second inside of her. Random images flashed through her mind of every time they made love and with every flick of his tongue, kiss of his lips against her lips; she fell deeper in love with him.

She lay on dry sheets even though a monsoon of Cinnamon Strawberry had surged through the tender wings of her pussy, and Lennox rested his head against the still pounding heartbeat pulsating between her legs. Not a single drop of her sweet nectar had been wasted or allowed to touch her sheets. The rhythmic beat of pleasure seduced Lennox into a peaceful sleep as he and Destiny closed their eyes knowing that any dreams they might have could not come near the passion they had just experienced. The night held promises of more pleasure to come, and Destiny fell asleep with images dancing in her mind of all the things that she would do to Lennox when they woke up with rested bodies.

01/13/09...4:17pm

# Sweet Fragrance of Passion

The scent of summer's heat covered his face like a pillow pressing down hard against his skin cutting off his oxygen. It was 3 a.m. in the morning. The sweltering summer heat clung to the sheets and his naked perspiring skin felt like Velcro against the white sheets. His eyes were wide open now, but the room was still dark leaving him unable to see anything inches from his face. His face and chest were damp with sweat. The musk of his own scent mixed with the heat made him feel like he was inhaling fire. The sound of someone crying had awakened him. At first, he thought it was a dream, but then the low moaning sounds continued to grow even more intense as if something imminent was about to happen. As his eyes adjusted to the dark room, and sleep left him to find elsewhere to rest, he began to realize that the sounds were coming from his girlfriend lying in bed next to him. She was masturbating in her sleep.

It wasn't the first time she had done this. He learned a painful lesson when he tried to wake her up the first time. She was so startled when he shook her that she had accidentally broken his nose. So now, he would either just listen or join her to participate in a sensual duet of passion.

He rolled over to give her more room on the bed just in case she lost control this time. After all, accident or no accident, bodily harm inflicted by your one hundred and twenty pound girlfriend doesn't go over well in the weight room. Her moaning had escalated and his eyes could now see the outline of her body slowly gyrating up and down next to him. The heat of her scented flower breathed hot from between her legs and it filled his nostrils as if he was inhaling his favorite perfume. He turned on his side to face her so he could listen to her pleasure her body, and inhale the sweet heat that was emanating from her pussy. It was like an air freshener being released to perfume the air with its sweet seductive scent. It made him want to get closer to taste what his nose was inhaling, but he would have to wait until she came before touching her. Every time her fingers probed her wetness, it sounded like rainfall and the room was being sprayed with the sweet fragrance of her pussy. They hadn't had sex in a few days because of conflicting work schedules and now both he and his erection were fully awake wanting to release all his pent-up energy between the soft folds of her pink fragrance of passion.

His hands slid down the full length of his erection and it felt like a piece of thick wood between his fingers. His balls were heavy with unreleased come and he squeezed them slightly to feel a jolt of pain. His pillow felt like fire against his face. The only thing that would cool him down was a cold shower or masturbating. The latter sounded better to him. She was tossing and turning as if possessed by some kind of spirit, but he didn't panic as he did the first time. He continued to stroke his pulsating manhood as the air around the bed became thicker with their combined sexual heat.

*He could always tell as he watched her when she was about to come.  Her moans would become longer like a singer holding a high note.  Her frenzy of passion would become more subdued as if she was in some sort of quiet pain, and then, it would build like a crescendo, like a rocket exploding into the sky and then it would be over.  She would sigh a few times then roll over onto her stomach and continue sleeping.  He would wait a few minutes before gently moving over her and parting her legs.  Her eyes would open and he could feel her smile even in the dark and they would make love until the darkness of the room would give way to early morning sunlight.*

He continued to masturbate, and when she came, the sweet fragrance of her passion flooded the room like sunshine bursting through the clouds after it rained.  It is always more intense then.

02/09/09…3:54pm

## Pussy Purrs Meows and Moans

When my pussy purrs, moans and meows it feels like a throbbing headache
Pulsating with an incessant ache that just won't stop hurting
My warmth just won't stop flowing until you take a swim and stroke your way into my depths
I want you to put a hurting on me that will make me scream your full name
Your name is long and so are you as you fill me with everything You
Here I am naked and in want spread open before your hungry eyes
Like a feast for the tongue to taste and lick every drop of my sweet delicious nectar
My ache is a pain so intense that the only way to quiet its purring
Is to feel the fire of your penetration feeding the flames of my moist lips
A hunger like mine that goes so deep cannot be instantly satisfied with a mere quickie
You have to dick me down with complete abandon and show me no mercy
Forget about making sweet love and unleash the full ferocity of your passion
Every stroke of your unsheathed manhood
Every lick of your erect tongue

Will slowly replenish my body and soothe this ache for
you that cannot stop throbbing
You have to take your time this pussy isn't going
anywhere now
You will have every chance to back up all your stories
I hope I cannot walk when you are done laying down the
pipe,
Your words and not mine
I hope I scream so much and lose my voice
Your words and not mine
I hope you penetrate me so deeply that you cannot find
your way out
Your words and not mine
I hope you are a man of your word and I want you to
hurt my pussy sweetly
With every lash of your tongue with every stroke of your
manhood
You peel away my resistance there wasn't much to begin
with
My pussy purrs meows and moans in anticipation of
getting the sweetest dick
Do not disappoint me when a woman is this hungry for
the passion she craves
A man has to deliver on his promise or his words will
forever be empty
Come and fill me with the girth of my curved master
It is time to make my pussy purr meow and moan like
never before.
10/09/08...9:15pm

# She Loves Him (Ode to Jill Scott)

A fever runs through her body and comes to rest at the center of its birth in the smoldering wet sun of fire that awaits his touch, his lips and his full and undivided penetration between the ebony of her legs. To touch her scorching black sun hurts. The only thing that will calm the fire of her sun is to be filled with his love until she overflows with liquid passion. It is the type of sweet pain that is addictive, and you feel compelled to make it hurt some more...just one more time. It never is just one more time. The fever of arousal becomes part of your breath; it beats to the rhythm of your heartbeat and whispers in your soul as you sleep. How did she get to this? A quivering, shivering pool of emotions, desires and secrets that you reveal without shame or embarrassment as your black sun explodes into the sky, illuminating the night with showers of your fevered fire. How did it come to this?

His voice is a sweet beautiful melody, like an old Motown tune, with every note working its bass deep into her soul as his fingers seduce her mind and body into a place of pure exultation. The distance between them bridged when she hears his voice on the line, and the night of her body is laid to rest as her sun rises to its apex of heat emission. There is no pretense of decorum or façade of not wanting her blazing fire to be stroked into a sensual beautiful explosion, which will rival the majesty of a full moon casting its light over the Earth. His voice, deep and rich undresses her and she stands naked waiting for his words to strike the flames that will set her skin, her mind...her soul on eternal fire. She is bathing in a sea of passion. She wishes not for air but for his breath to give her life, to give her back some of the dreams she has lost. She wants him to suspend reality and to take her back to a time before she knew the pain of heartbreak and the joy of innocent love was still something obtainable. She wants him to do the impossible. She wants him to give her back her innocence.

A hunger for everything he emanates from her core, invading all of her orifices, runs so deeply and sweetly, that it leaves her gasping for breath as her imagination brings him to life. He is inside of her, swelling; everywhere is available for his touch, his influence...his penetration. He moves in and out of her as deeply as her last thought, as fluidly as the depth of his penetration that settles somewhere between her hopes and dreams and he lives inside of her as she sleeps. How did she arrive at this place that to just close her eyes and feel his lips on hers makes her blush and there is no one around? How is it that love slips into you without your permission and stays without an invitation? Love, becomes that guest that you don't want to leave and open your heart to so that it can build a home and lay roots in your soul.

She loves him.

He is special.

Everything about him passionately moves and feeds her soul.

A rain cloud drizzles over her black sun of fire as the cold water falls from the round holes of the showerhead, and the heat radiating from her skin turns the coldness of the water into hot streams of relaxing pleasure. Love, when it is real, burns hotter than any emotion we can conjure; and when sustained by two people, it becomes its own source of energy that nothing on Earth can extinguish.

Hands are on her body, lips are kissing her shoulders, he enters her without consent because he knows that he can, and the sun between her legs releases rays of warm light that bath the walls in soft white paint of blissful pleasure. It feels too real to be her imagination. If it is a dream then she will keep her eyes closed until it all fades away and all that remains is the empty darkness to keep her company. Kisses move liquidly from her shoulders, they find the tender spot on her neck and linger there until she moans unrestrained. She shakes her head back and forth sending streams of water everywhere. His warm kisses lick her chocolate nipples; chocolate always melts when it is sucked with love. Her body yearns with desire as his kisses venture lower, licking the trail of warm water between her breasts, on her stomach; he sticks his tongue in her navel and sucks on it as if he is drinking a glass of cold water. The need to open her eyes to see if it really is him overpowers her, but she resists because she still remembers the last time when she opened her eyes, there was no one there. There are lips now on her throbbing sun, licking the hot rays of sunlight streaming warmly from her swollen lips; the roundness of a sweet mouth tries to swallow the ball of fire between her legs and she doesn't resist. It is his to have.

Her eyes open and her body remains on fire from her thoughts. He is still touching her, everywhere. He is here. He is home.

He loves her.

She is special.

Everything about her passionately moves and feeds his soul. Her sun of fire overflows with love every single time it feels the warmth of his tongue expressing his love. His fever of hardened intensity swims deeper in her warm ocean, always in search of hidden treasures.

She loves him.

He loves her.

They flow in and out of each other like sugar melting slowly in hot water.

3/27/09...1:10am

## <u>Sweet Whispers of Sensual Ecstasy</u>

When sleep comes to visit you and takes
you away in her arms
I want to be there again to fall asleep
inside of your moist warmth
When she seduces you with her sweet
whispers of pleasure
I want to hear the words she is saying so I
can whisper them back to you later
Every night before I go to sleep it is still
your name that I call
It is still you that I make sweet love to
every time I come so hard
With the intensity of the passion we once
shared and we took for granted
We thought it would last forever and in
your absence, loneliness lives a happy life
My senses crave the idea of you and the
way you would inspire me without even
knowing
I miss you in a way that exposes my
vulnerability without me even caring who
knows
The ache that I feel living in my mind,
body and soul goes so damn deep
That not even multiple orgasms of self
pleasure can give me what I need

Simultaneously, I am reduced to sobbing
tears and the sweet sensation of sexual
release
Throbbing through my entire body like
dueling seasons of spring and summer
If I close my eyes long enough I can
recreate moments of our life
I can still feel the passion of your kisses
taking my breathe away
The sensual way you bit my neck so
deeply that the pain felt so damn good
Like an extra source of sexual energy
raging through my body you set me on fire
I would beg you unashamed not to stop
and you would bite me even harder
Multiple orgasms rippled through my
body with an intense power
Only you can arouse my passion with such
a hardened intensity
My body is famished for your touch and
your sweet whispers of sensual ecstasy
My mind yearns to be seduced to again to
feel that intense rush
It is a hunger that has gone unfed in all
these years since you left
My desire for you is beyond irrational
because I set you free
Knowing that the passion we shared was
once in a lifetime

Many have tried to please me and they
have all been good women
But, there could only ever be one you.
12/09/08...7:14pm

# Delicious Home Cooked Meal

Walking down the dirt road on his way home for lunch, George Olivier took off his workman's hat and tied his work shirt to his waist. This is what he loved about being back home in St. Croix: there was a freedom of self that you didn't have when you lived on the mainland. You were always rushing to catch a train or bus, hurrying to eat lunch to get back to work and life just seemed to be a series of forgettable days. He and his wife, Athenia decided to get out before the long winters wore them down and they became Americanized without their permission. Two years later, they hadn't regretted their decision to come back home to build their house and start their own construction company with about twenty employees.

The tropical heat of the noonday sun beat down on George Olivier's shirtless back, neck, and bald head. He stopped in the middle of the road, lifted his head to the noonday sun and stretched his black arms up to the sky. His round stomach rumbled like a pickup truck bouncing in and out of the potholes on the dirt road to his house. He turned the corner and walked down the path to his house. Mr. Young, the neighbor from down the road, waved to George Olivier from under the shade of a mango tree as he tended to his goats and cows. Mr. Young wasn't a man of many words so he was always right at home with his animals who just wanted to be left alone to graze all day. Every day was a vacation for animals.

When Athenia cooked, the spicy sweet scent of her food filled the air and just a gulp of air tricked your mind into believing that you had actually tasted one of her dishes. George Olivier opened the black front gate to his house and the smell of fried fish, curry chicken, fried plantains and tomato stew seduced his taste buds, and he felt the stirrings of his manhood as he became aroused as he thought about eating and sexing his wife. He sat down on the porch to take off his work boots and to wash his hands and face by the pipe next to the cistern. His wife was a tolerant woman, but her pet peeve was dirty hands. *"A man who won't wash his hands to eat in my house is a man who won't get any sweet dessert later tonight."* The threat of her withholding the sweetness of her specially concocted dessert dripping with her honey comb nectar was always a reason to do as she asked. A man knows when to do what he is told by his wife.

A wave of aromatic delights rushed out at George Olivier when he opened the front door to his house. The only thing he could compare the anticipation of eating his wife's cooking to was each time she straddled his round belly, and he felt himself growing stiff like a coconut tree for her dessert. The thickness of his manhood would first savor the warmth emitting from her dessert before tasting it, and when it finally became excruciatingly painful to withhold the head of his throbbing manhood from dipping into the center of her delicious dessert, he would rub his pulsating head around the outskirts of her warm dessert lips. He couldn't taste it or allow himself to be fully covered in its succulence until Athenia spread open her thick creamy thighs and a few droplets of her dessert's honey flavor would fall onto his manhood, kissing it with its warm lips. She would then know that he was ready to receive the gift of her dessert and slowly lower her dripping blossoming flower onto the veined fatness of his erection. He would just lay there for the first few minutes as he reveled in the heat that enveloped his manhood. Her arousal would start flowing slowly like intermittent raindrops and with each slow deep probe of his curved manhood; the forecast would change from light showers until he was drowning in a monsoon downpour of her dessert honey sweetness. The moistness of her dessert would soak the sheets beneath them while he was still rigid inside of her just waiting for that right moment when he knew that a few quick deep hard pounding thrusts would make her speak in her native Creole tongue of Dominica. Creole is like Spanish—everything sounds dirty when you are in the midst of a sexual Nirvana. Just saying 'thank you' in guttural moans will sound dirty. *Mèsi! Mèsi! Mèsi!*

Athenia didn't hear her husband slip into the house because she was at the kitchen sink washing dishes and wining her waist to "Nani Wine" which was a sensual soca song by Crazy. Her waist was still limber even after ten years of marriage and two children. She could still mesmerize George into a slow pulsating erection that would ache until he found the comfort of her dessert to soothe his ache and rob him of his strength when he came. As she dipped up and down to the sweet sounds of soca music, her pink towel threatened to fall off her body leaving her fully exposed round bottom at the mercy of George's hands and thirsty manhood. Her honey colored braids swung back and forth in perfect rhythm with her back and round backside. His lunch was on the stove right next to her and was simmering on low. He reached for a fried plantain and it burnt his tongue as he swallowed its sweet flavor. The heat of the kitchen pulsated around him as he watched his wife wine her waist. The seductive smells of her cooking had aroused him and now his belly. George was in need for his wife's cooking and her sweet dessert treat.

His hand slipped under her towel and her body reacted to his touch as if it was patiently waiting for him to make his move and do his husbandly duties. His fingers slipped into the fleshy moistness of her dessert and she rotated her waist at an angle that allowed him to slip a finger into the heat of her tender pussy lips and moaned, "*ay yi yi* don't stop—don't stop...*ay yi yi* you make my pussy catch a fire." The honey of her sweetness glistened on his fingers like guava jelly on toast as he brought it to his lips and slid it slowly into his mouth.

"I see you hungry today," she sang out without turning around. "I go feed you what you need," she breathed hotly as her towel fell to the floor leaving her naked and her firm backside begged to be fucked. Her fingers found his belt and unzipped his pants, and it joined her towel on the floor. Her long fingers curled around his manhood and stroked it to a heightened state of arousal. The cream color of her skin was a beautiful contrast to his sun baked dark skin and his erection pulsed with soca energy between the fleshy confines of her bottom.

Athenia leaned back into her husband's body and felt his round potbelly rumble against her backside. His hands massaged her shoulders, worked their way down to her heavy breasts and pinched her two nipples until she moaned out loud with delight. Her body and mind were enflamed with passion and the soca music was still thumping with words of seduction. *Suck my pussy*, she thought to herself, but she didn't care what he did—just as long as he did it to her.

She loved to fuck in the middle of the afternoon while everyone else was busy working and not enjoying life. It made her feel as if, at least for an afternoon, her pussy took precedence over everything in the world. That even God had to stop what he was doing to watch her make love to her husband. She loved the attention that George lavished on her body as if it was the first time they had made love. He would devour her food and pussy with the same intense fervor every time. It turned her on immensely to know that she was so irresistible to her man and that her pussy still had the power to make him as hard as concrete.

His hands reached out around her waist and he dipped them into the warm soapy dishwater in front of her. He caressed her body with the soapy water until it was slippery and smelled of fresh sunshine. He slid his right hand between the two full ripe halves of her bottom and squeezed the fullness of her pussy into his hands as if he was testing the ripeness of fruits at the local market. Athenia shuddered to feel her husband take control and show her who was boss. She enjoyed talking shit sometimes, but when it was time for a man to be a man; she wanted him to take what was his without asking her permission. What good is a man if he cannot control his pussy and dick it down into complete submission? The sweet sounds of Lord Byron spilled out from the radio just as George spread Athenia's ass open to release some of her pent up afternoon heat, and his fat bud swiftly penetrated the fat lips of her moist dessert. Watching her ass spread open like that reminded George of eating a ripe papaya and sticking his face and mouth into its sweetness. Athenia stood upright and his fingers were locked into her braided hair as they both gyrated in a slow circular motion to the pulsating music of Lord Bryon. *"Sweet sweet sweet like a Julie mango...sweet sweet I want to know how it sweet so"* George sang out the lyrics as Athenia hummed in tune as his backup singer.

"You too sweet gal," he murmured as he stared down at her round ass shaking in between his hands like a volcano that was about to erupt. His stomach rumbled again from hunger against Athenia's back.

"My husband hungry?'

He answered her with three quick pelvic thrusts that lifted her ass into the air.

"Lemme feed you somefing good."

She reached into the frying pan and took out two warm pieces of plantain. She cooled it down by blowing heavily on it and then slid them between her lips. She then rubbed them on her nipples, and without taking a bite she fed him. After a few bites, he swallowed it quickly and his erection pulsed inside of her to let her know that he wanted more food. She fed him the eyes of the fried Snapper fish which he loved and stripped off a piece of tender meat. She placed it under his nose so he could inhale its fried taste and then slowly slid it between his lips until it disappeared. She kissed him and tasted her cooking on his lips.

"No woman can cook like my wife," George groaned in between swallows.

"And what else baby…tell me." Her inner muscles squeezed around his fat bud to elicit an answer.

"No woman pussy sweet like your pussy. You have the sweetest pussy in the world. It sweeter than a Julie mango," he babbled in his off key singing voice as he pulsed deeper into her dessert and Lord Bryon concurred with him in the background. Athenia's moist pussy lips smiled and she reached for another piece of plantain. The warmth of it felt good in her hands and she dipped it into the honey sauce of her dripping pussy and fed her lips. The taste of her own juices sent thrills of pleasure throughout her body. It delighted her that *everything* she made was so tasty. She dipped another piece of plantain inside her warm dessert, this time she let it linger there a little longer to soak in some extra juices and then fed it to her husband who greedily swallowed her delicious home cooked meal. She rewarded his stamina and will to resist flooding her tender pussy lips with a torrent of his baby making juices by feeding him chunks of curry chicken, tomato stew, more plantains, and fried fish. George's appetite for his wife's pussy and her food were being simultaneously fed. There was no way they could have enjoyed each other this way back in New York. He would have to take a train back home and there are always delays; he would have probably spent his lunch hour stuck underground instead of being inside his wife's sweet dessert. Dinner would be served in a few hours and George smiled as he wondered what Athenia had in store for him later that evening.

His lunch hour was almost over. They had eaten almost everything in the pots as they sexed, fucked and made love. Athenia turned around to face her husband. She loved looking into his eyes to see the ugly face he made when he came. It was a thing of beauty for her to watch the intensity of passion in his eyes, how his lips would quiver and the feeling that being inside of her pussy would have on her husband.

"*Vini*," she urged him. She wanted him to come inside of her. She loved to feel his sudden burst of cum flooding her walls with his liquid passion.

George gripped his wife's ample ass and dug his fingers into her tender skin. He lifted her off the floor with his throbbing black manhood still pulsating inside of her and she wrapped her legs around his waist and her arms around his neck. The music of the Mighty

Sparrow was now rocking on the radio and he was crooning about the pleasures of Salt fish which was a euphemism for pussy. Athenia and George sang together with Sparrow while moaning, groaning and heavily breathing his lyrics, *"Salt fish nothing in the world sweeter than salt fish."*

"Baby, wet my salt fish with your special sauce," she moaned in his ears.

In mid-stroke, George let loose a gush of hot sauce that sprayed and filled every crevice of his wife's sweet pussy hole. The blast of hot lava sauce rocked Athenia backwards and triggered her own orgasm that met his cum blast with its own flow of warm honey passion. She bit into her husband's shoulder as he continued to pound away at her tender pussy hole. His fingers sunk deeper into her ass and he somehow managed to slip his middle finger inside the tightness of her ass. "Ohhhhh God boy," she screamed as she came again and the cream from her dessert slid down his bud to form a pool at his feet. George came again and with one last deep thrust, he emptied himself into his wife's sweet *kokot*. Exhausted from the effort and sweat glistening from both their bodies; Athenia released her grip from around his back and neck and George eased her down back on the floor.

His manhood hung heavily between his legs still dripping from his wife's hot cum. "All this sex make me thirsty," Athenia said devilishly while looking at his glistening dick. His body couldn't take anymore but what man can say no to getting his dick sucked especially by the lips of his beautiful wife. She dropped

135

to her knees and took his slippery dick between the confines of her full lips and sucked him until his erection rose from the dead again. He would be late going back to work that day, but that's the benefit of being the boss of your own construction company. Whatever she had planned for dinner would be hard to top this delicious home cooked meal that he was still enjoying late into the afternoon.

2/15/09...8:02pm

# Dinner is Served

Everything looks wonderful on the table
Dinner this evening will be extra special
When the light from the candles dance across your face
You look so beautiful and innocent no one would guess
How passionate and ravenous you get when you are
hungry
Just a glass of wine is all it takes to get you wet and ready
Your eyes illuminate the passion you are feeling
Staring into them, you hold me deep in your gaze
My blood is burning hot and bursting sporadically into
flames
I cannot wait until dinner is served
I am hungry right now and need to eat
Your lips this evening will be the tantalizing appetizer
Your nipples will be the first course served for dinner
Followed by a delicious helping of your beautiful breasts
The tasty treat of your nectar will be the cherry dessert
Served deliciously on the tray of my lips
By your special request we will eat dinner naked
You look even more delicious than the food we will be
eating
A bottle of Merlot to start the evening
A drop spills from your lips and I lean over to kiss you
softly
My arousal stands firm and unafraid close to your
beautiful face
My eyes are closed and I wait for what surely will come

One more sip and you take me deeply between your
moist lips
Massaging me with your tongue until I am fully grown
In one gulp you swallow your wine and drink my fire
It is a delicious blend of sweet and flavored
There is plenty more if you would like another serving
But first let me replenish what you have so greedily
swallowed
Dinner is on the table and waiting to be eaten
After dinner you can indulge in quenching your thirst
again.
5/11/08…2:51am

# I Still Love My Husband...But

How did Lucille end up with a stranger's dick buried deep inside her sweetest treasure and feeling for the first time in her life that *a real man* was fucking her? Why was she screaming a man's name other than that of her husband, Howard, and enjoying it so much? Howard always said her pussy was her sweetest treasure whenever they were having sex, and he had once again released his sticky load just in time before his show "24" came back from a commercial break. He seemed to love Jack Bauer more than he loved making love to her.

He was the sweetest man, a good provider, an even better father to their two kids, but as a lover, he had always been clueless when it came to pleasuring her body after twenty years of marriage. Lucille had become adept at faking her orgasms through the years and giving the appearance that all the "excitement" had drained her completely after three minutes of *glorious sex*. She could teach a class on the art of faking an orgasm. It had become almost comical at how easily she could fool Howard. If he ever found out she had been faking, then the damage would be irreparable to their marriage. A man's weakness and strength is his ego. If you play to a man's ego, he usually will do your bidding. If you make him feel less than a man, then he will pout worse than any woman.

Like most men after sex, Howard would fall asleep almost immediately, leaving Lucille's body still hungry to be touched and to be fed with his manhood. He would be fast asleep for the rest of the evening, and she would be undisturbed by any further advances or pleadings for sex. Her appetite was insatiable and most nights she would have to masturbate in silence at least five times before the unfulfilled ache inside of her body would dissipate. She screamed her cries of lustful release into her pillow, or suffocated it between clenched teeth because she didn't want Howard to see her pleasuring her body in a way that he was never be able to pleasure her.

On the nights when the *five-fingered* plan was ineffective, Lucille would call in re-enforcements. *Silent Pleaser* was the name she had given to her dildo. He was buried in her feminine drawer, a place where she knew Howard would never go. He was deathly afraid of her "womanly things" as he called them. Lately though, not even the *Silent Pleaser* was able to fulfill all of Lucille's expectations.

She missed being touched, romanced, and made to feel special by her husband. Howard only cared about work, sports, and the kids. He was still attentive, but minus the romance and affection. She was only forty years old and all the magazines said that she was in her sexual prime, and her body on a nightly basis told her that they were correct.

*So what should a woman do with a raging libido that just isn't being satisfied?*

Should she continue to play the dutiful wife and mother and forget about her sexual needs? Should she talk to her husband about her frustrations and his inadequacies as a lover?  Men are like petulant little children when their prowess as lovers comes into question, as if there's some unwritten rule that wives should suffer in silence through years of crappy sex.

Howard was a good man but overly sensitive about the things that dealt with him personally.  He only did things when the calendar said it was time: Valentine's Day, Mother's Day and her birthday.  It felt to Lucille that it was more like an obligation rather than something that came from his heart.

It still played in her mind the last time she tried to bring up the subject about their lack of intimacy, and it hurt every time she thought about it.  It was the day of her birthday, a week ago on January 8th.  She had spent all day fixing a beautiful dinner for two consisting of oxtails, rice and beans, steamed vegetables, mashed potatoes, and baked macaroni.  Desert would be slices of ripe mango, strawberries, and grapes and to quench their thirst, a pitcher of freshly squeezed lemonade.  Dinner was delicious and Lucille looked equally delicious in her form fitting strapless black dress.

Howard complimented the dinner and he could barely keep his hands to himself as he imagined separating Lucille from her dress.  Her body was literally on fire everyday now.  She needed her husband to fuck her and to lick her clean as if his tongue was a towel.  Instead, as she filled her mouth with his erection while on her knees, he unexpectedly came in spurts all over her face and breasts.  He apologized profusely but made no attempt to please her orally. In twenty years of marriage, Lucille could count on one hand how many times Howard had eaten her pussy. She lay there in shock as he slept like a baby. It was at that moment that she decided she had enough of this treatment from her husband. She was at her sexual peak and she needed to be made love to and fucked. If Howard couldn't do it, then she would find someone to do it for her. It was by accident, or fate, that a phone call the next day changed her life.

They had been looking for a painter to paint the basement, so Lucille's sister recommended an ex-lover of hers for the job. Lucille had never met Dante before but had seen a few pictures of him, and heard legendary tales from Marlene about his *dick game*.

"This is one brother who knows how to use every inch of his tongue and dick to please a woman. It's too bad one woman isn't enough for him. Brothers like Dante can have any woman they want, and they definitely try to get into every draws that will allow them entry."

A glazed look of reminisce would come over Marlene's face every time she spoke of Dante. She was still in love with him, but he needed more than one pussy to keep him happy. Marlene would go into the intimate details of their lovemaking and Lucille's lack of sexual satisfaction at home made her envious of what Marlene and Dante shared. Her clit would throb uncontrollably and moisture would escape her, soaking her panties during Marlene's tales.

*No man could fuck like that.*

Only in the movies do these things ever happen. Now, here he stood in her front door; tall, dark, and hung like a horse. Gazing at him, Lucille felt her skin tingling under her bathrobe. She never wore panties and bras when at home. Howard was always mortified when anyone dropped by and the sheerness of her silky white bathrobe was almost as if she was naked and asking to be fucked.

"I hope I didn't wake you, but you did say the earlier the better."

"It's okay. I just need a cup of coffee and I will be nice and perky," Lucille smiled at him as she let him into the house and pointed him towards the basement.

She inspected him like a piece of meat as he walked by her and subtly inhaled the scent of his cologne, *Obsession*. Her knees buckled for a second. Any man wearing *Obsession* made her weak, and the stories that Marlene bragged about created an instant wetness between her thighs. If Dante could read her mind right now, he would turn around, drop his paint, and stroke her with his thick brush right there at her front door. He was built, not in the bodybuilder kind of way—where you knew these guys were on steroids and had two inch dicks that were so small that even when they got hard it was hard to see it. Today would be one of the hottest days of the summer in Tampa, and Dante had dressed accordingly. He wore baggy red basketball shorts and a white tank top. His head was bald; face freshly shaven, and a smile that sent shivers throughout Lucille's pussy.

It was like having Michael Jordan in her living room, and if she were lucky, her ass would be bouncing all over his black dick before the day was over. That thought made Lucille giggle out loud; but Dante was halfway down the steps, so he didn't hear the lust in her laughter.

"Do you need anything?"

"I'm good."

*Yes you are so good, and I want to feel that dick I've heard so much about.*

For a split second, Lucille wasn't sure if she had said that thought out loud or just another one of her erotic thoughts. A wave of embarrassment came over her because she was craving her sister's ex-lover, but her body was so famished that she didn't even care anymore.

*Why can't you feel what I need and fuck me just like Marlene? Please fuck me Dante!*

She stood there for a few more seconds contemplating whether or not to just drop to her knees and pull down his shorts to suck him off. Lucille felt herself teetering on the edge of just losing her senses to the heat that was stirring between her throbbing lips, begging to be fed. She turned around and headed back upstairs to the kitchen.

The smell of coffee filled the house and intoxicated Lucille even more. Everything turned her on. She needed to be fucked in the worst way. Her hands wandered aimlessly over her full nipples and squeezed her breasts with practiced ease. A soft moan escaped her lips as she lifted both nipples to her lips and sucked them ravenously. The warmth of her breasts cascaded through her fingertips and heated her entire body. Overcome by what she was feeling, she took off her nightgown and it fell in a heap around her feet. She stood buck-naked in her kitchen not caring if someone walked in to see her in a state of arousal. The weight of unreleased passion ached in her breasts but just touching them wasn't enough anymore. She squeezed her nipples so hard that pains of pleasure shot through her body with rapid certainty that more pleasure would soon follow.

Lost in the feelings of pleasuring her body, Lucille didn't hear or feel Dante walking up behind her, and he stood there quietly observing and wondered what to do next. He had no moral issues concerning fucking his ex-girlfriend's sister, but the last thing he wanted was for her husband to walk in and find the painter's black brush buried deep inside his wife's thirsty pussy. By the looks of how turned on she was, it didn't look like her husband was handling his business in the bedroom. Dante fashioned himself as a humanitarian so he decided to give to the needy and to fuck Lucille in her kitchen. By the looks of how turned on she was (she had peeled a banana and was stuffing it into her juices), a good deep soul stirring *dick down* was needed to calm her ass down. Dante was just the man for the job. The *Maintenance Man* had clocked in for work.

Lucille bent over and parted her swollen lips. Slowly she inserted the full ripe banana into her tender sweetness and she shuddered with pleasure as it completely disappeared inside of her. Droplets of her heated nectar juices fell to the floor when she removed the banana from deep inside of her. Still bent over, she brought it to her lips and it reminded her of a banana split dripping with caramel. The taste of her juices against her full lips made her open her mouth wider to curl her tongue around its width and ease it slowly down her thirsty throat. The fullness of it made her gag momentarily, but she loved the feeling of being filled to capacity. It reappeared from between her lips licked clean of the honey produced between her thighs. Still aching and feeling that tingling sensation in the depths of her pussy, Lucille slid the banana between her wet lips, which were already open for entry.

The entire scene before his unbelieving eyes gave Dante an erection that had no place to go but deep inside of Lucille's banana filled pussy. Without a second thought, he took off his clothes and walked towards her with an erection that swung heavily from left to right, and confident in the fact that she wouldn't reject his advances. Lucille opened her eyes as if sensing Dante's lustful heat and saw the shadow of a massive, erect dick approaching her without breaking stride. She closed her eyes, relaxed her pussy muscles with the banana still buried inside of her hungry pussy and braced for his entry.

Dante's first thrust into Lucille's tightness met with resistance not by Lucille, but by the banana still buried inside of her wetness. She groaned with pleasurable agony as it went deeper into her sweet hole, and Dante pulled it out, laid it on top of his erection and simultaneously they both penetrated Lucille moistness.

Her knees buckled. A shiver raced from her pussy up to her spine and she pushed back hard against her multiple penetrators. There was no way after being sexless for such a long time that she would let a little pain get in the way of double penetration.

"Damn baby this is the tightest pussy I've ever had," Dante moaned as Lucille's pussy strangled his erection and pulled it deeper into the center of her heat. Her muscles contracted and massaged his throbbing erection, and it was sheer determination by Dante not to bust and release his load inside of her. He tried imagining ugly women, fat women and two men doing it so he could be turned off, but Lucille wasn't to be denied.

She needed to know that she was still a sexy woman and that men found her attractive. She wasn't looking for love or someone who liked her. The only thing she was looking for was to be told that she was still a hot piece of ass. She knew it was shallow of her to feel this way but a woman's sexual identity, the need to feel desired by a man, does matter. When you have it, it's not something you think about. When it's absent from your life, it can begin to dominate every facet of who you are as a person. If she couldn't make a horny dog like Dante bust like a geyser then she might as well stitch her pussy up and send it out to pasture.

With every thrust of his dick going deeper and deeper into her hole, it felt as if Dante was building an inner pussy inside of her pussy. In their twenty years of marriage, Howard had never even come close to fucking her like this. *How could she go back to appetizer sex with*

*Howard after having her inner slut fucked like this by Dante?*
It would be a problem for another time, but for now, she
wanted to feel his massive dick release every drop of
cum inside of her. She braced herself against the kitchen
sink, each hand grabbing on to the hot and cold water
knobs, and thrust her ass into his six-pack stomach. The
force of her pushing back on his dick rocked Dante
backwards, but he held on and went right back to work,
digging a hole in her back. He was mesmerized by the
way Lucille's ass would ripple forward every time he
stroked her. It was like watching water rippling across
the ocean. And that's when it happened.

Lucille squeezed her pussy muscles so tight that it
felt like a strangle hold around Dante's dick. He
foolishly feared that his rapid in and out stroking motion
would cause his dick to be pulled from his body because
of the tight grip she had on him. So he stayed still and
allowed his throbbing dick to be slowly milked by her.
They were both unaware that the banana had dislodged
itself from Lucille's pussy and lay at her feet covered in
her warm juices. Inside of her, Dante's erection pulsated
like a volcano about to blow and his suppressed
whimpering turned her on even more. She had the
pussy power all along. It took a stranger to give her back
her confidence. With one final squeeze, Dante shot his
full load into Lucille's sweet spot and he felt her hold on
his dick loosen but not before she reached back to grab
his dick and inserted it back inside of her wetness. Her
ass bucked backwards as if urging him on to make her
come.

"Make my pussy scream," she groaned. "I need to come." The desire in Lucille's voice touched Dante and he kicked up his stroking into fourth gear. He had nothing left but what's the point of having sweet pussy if you can't give a woman what she wants.

He dug his fingers deep into her fleshy ass and Lucille screamed in sheer agony, and for a moment Dante thought he had seriously hurt her, but in between whimpered breathes she urged him to do his worst damage. Hearing those words stiffened Dante's semi-erect dick and every time he plunged his erection into her pussy; the sound of ass meeting dick resounded like thunder crackling through the sky. The force that he was pounding Lucille's ass lifted her off the floor, and he inserted his hands between her legs and grabbed on to the side of her hips, and continued to pummel her.

The sheer force of Dante's pounding stunned Lucille. No man had ever fucked her so hard and so deep. The screams she had been dying to release forever came out in groans, tears, moans, and the ecstasy of pure unbridled passion. She held on for dear life to both knobs of the sink, but either she was too strong or was given a shoddy installation job because both knobs sprung loose and water gushed everywhere. Water was everywhere and surged upward like a water fountain. Lucille was too far gone to care and she felt her own geyser building inside of her. She wanted it to break free like a dam about to bust wide open.

Dante summoned all his strength from hours of pumping iron at the gym and slammed his dick one last time into Lucille. Her body quivered; she couldn't make a sound as if she had forgotten how to speak and her entire body turned into jelly. Streams of hot cum poured out of her pussy and puddles of her released passion formed around her feet. Every time Lucille thought it was over and relaxed, her body would spasm uncontrollably and she would come again. Dante's flaccid dick slowly slipped out of her wetness as she released him from her grip. She was slightly embarrassed but then thought better of it. This is what she wanted and for once in her life, a man had given her what her body craved—to be fucked into submission.

Her kitchen was a mess and her body felt like a tractor had run over it, but she didn't care. Months after their encounter, Lucille would use it as a way to get off whenever she had sex with her husband. Howard couldn't understand the change in her intensity and the way she would scream when he fucked her. He wasn't doing anything differently, but his ego let him believe that she was enjoying his same old *dick game* which was passionless.

Dante had given Lucille what she needed and he went about his life in search of his next conquest. One thing that will always remain true is that there will always be women in need of good dick. Good dick is always in fashion. It never goes out of style. He was sure she would call again, and when she did, he would dick her down the way she should be getting *dicked down* at home by her husband.

7:20pm…5/4/08

# When No One is Looking

The man watches them kiss from afar but close enough to see her lover's hands grab her wrists and roughly push her against a tree. She looks at her lover as if to taunt him, and a look of bewilderment crosses his face as he realizes what she wants him to do to her in public. Her lover looks around, hesitant at first, but there is no one in that area of the park. It is secluded and away from the path of joggers and nature lovers. They don't see *him* standing in the shadows of the willow trees, and the color of his clothes is like camouflage blending into the trees. The sunlight blinds their vision when they look in his direction and do not see him. He knows how to stand perfectly still without doing anything.

Her lover leans into her body and she braces herself against the tree to shoulder the weight of his tall muscular frame against her tiny body. Her hands reach down and disappear momentarily into his pants and his shorts fall to the grass soon after. His buttocks are exposed and her lover reminds her of one of those football players from the NFL. He thinks to himself, *anyone with an ass like that should naturally be well-endowed.*

The only sounds to be heard in the park are the rustling of the trees, the distant sounds of traffic on the other side of the park, and the occasional chirping noises of birds. Her lover's hands appear strong as he reaches under her red uniform skirt and she closes her eyes as his hands explore her down there in her moist secret. She has done this before; she guides his hand to where her warmth lives waiting for his touch.

The wideness of her lover's back has her almost completely covered and he cannot see her face, but her hands are on his ass pulling him deeper into her body. Her skirt falls on top of his khaki school pants, and he can see flashes of the black panties that she is wearing as their bodies move in a slow, unhurried dance.

He drops to his knees, hooks his fingers in the waistband of her black sheer panties and takes them off and hands it to her. Her pubic area is unshaven and stands out like a pitcher's mound. He runs his fingers through the mass of black feathers which hides her secrets and blows the heat of his breath into its center. Her hair flutters like feathers on a bird and his tongue darts out to savor the secret passageway that has opened up for him. She inhales the moist scent of her panties and tosses them away behind her.

*She is beautiful* the man thinks to himself as he keeps his eyes on her while reaching into his pants to stroke the thickness of his rising arousal. There is aura of innocent sensuality that plays on her face that is slightly obscured by her flowing reddish brown hair. Her movements are fluid, sure, like someone who has done this many times before.

Her fingers play in her lover's dark curly hair as she holds his face steady so she can direct him what to do. She knows what she wants. She likes to be in control. Her body goes rigid, her head tilts to the side, and she releases his face from her grasp.

Her lover knows what will please her now and he continues to use his tongue to swim inside her wetness with deep tongue strokes that has her panting something that he cannot quite hear, but he knows she is enflamed.

She has the look of a young woman who is in the midst of discovering her sexual self and finding the rhythms of touches that will bring her to her greatest explosion.

The rustling of the willow trees catches her attention and in an instant, when the wind parts the falling limbs, she sees *him* with his pants around his ankles, his hands strangling his erection and looking at them, but staring right into her eyes as if it is the most natural thing in the world. A shiver runs through her body as another orgasm envelops her and he watches her come for the first time. Strangely, the moment emboldens her and she stares right back at him.

He doesn't move as if daring her to go further.

She slowly unbuttons her white blouse to expose the youthfulness of her perfect stomach. He removes his shirt also, several rays of golden sunlight illuminate his chiseled, dark physique, and she mentally runs her hands up and down his chest. He could literally scoop her up in his arms as if she was weightless and take her deep into the woods of the park to ravish her and have his way with her. Her body reacts to what she is seeing and she wants to run to this man and give herself to him. It is insane she knows but in the midst of passion, common sense is not a luxury that most of us are blessed with.

His dick is swollen in his hands and he wishes it were her lips suffocating his fat head instead. Her lips are soft and full like a ripe fruit that would be succulent from the first taste. *Take off your bra* he thinks to himself as his stares become more intense.

*Take off* your bra he seems to says as his stares became more intense and gives her goose bumps all over her body. She understands what his eyes desire and marvels at the thickness of his swollen manhood as his fingers glide over its darkness. She now thinks her lover isn't half the man  as the man lurking in the woods is as he brings her to another orgasm with his slippery snake-like tongue; searching for the center of her deepest ache. He is now just a puppet, a minor player, an extra between her and the stranger lurking in the willow trees.

The black straps of her bra fall softly against her arms and she holds it there for a moment. She wants to tease the man lurking in the woods to make him harder and feel the ache that she is feeling. His stare sends tremors of heat cascading through her body, and she does as his eyes ask her to do. Her bra falls to the ground leaving her breasts exposed to him.

He inhales sharply as his eyes feast for the first time in a long time on breasts that defy gravity and stands up without any assistance. Saliva wets his lips and drips unaware down his chin and unto his erection.

She wonders what he would taste like between her lips. She is known at her high school for being experienced, but she has never been with someone as old as him or as endowed. He reminds her of one of her brother's friends in college. The thought of making love to him intrigues her young mind and it makes her nipples hard to think of him sucking on them with his grown up lips and easing the thickness of his erection into her tight young pussy. *He would probably blow his load the minute he enters me,* she thinks to herself. She has a momentary flash of guilt as she looks down at the top of her lover's head going up and down like a seesaw, but it is just that, a momentary thought.

Her lover finally stands up pleasantly surprised that she has undressed for him. It is the first he has seen her breasts even though he has felt her up many times. His lips saturated with her moisture finds her erect nipples and she moans as he excitedly sucks on both of them while cupping her ass.

It isn't her lover's lips or hands that she feels covering her breasts or nipples—it is *his* lips feeding on her tender sweetness. She wants *him* to know that she just isn't some stupid school girl but a young woman who knows how to please a man.

She strokes her lover's erect penis while looking at the man in the woods. He wants it to be him she is stroking and not her lover. It takes all his will power not to step out of the shadows of the willow trees and go to her and fuck her in front of her lover. Her lover has no idea how to fuck her young pussy. He is just a boy playing grown up games and pretending to be a lover. Something tells him she would not run away and would happily oblige him the sweet fruits of her youthful garden. The power she commands is not yet fully harnessed. She deliberately steps in front of her lover to give him a full frontal view of her naked body. His erection throbs with increased intensity as she slowly traces her fingertips across her lips, then down to her neck and squeezes both of her nipples so hard that her lips part and delicious moans of sweet pleasure greets his ears. Her moans are for him and not her lover.

With an open palm, she slides her right hand down her flat stomach, spreads her fingers open and combs her fingers through her bushy brown pubic hair. Her fingers stop at the entrance of her sweetness and his breath catches in his throat like an uncompleted thought as she inserts two fingers deep inside her moisture. She brings one finger to her lips and licks it slowly with her gaze fixed on his erection and reaches back to feed her extracted honey to her lover's lips.

He is too young to appreciate the delicacy that she is feeding him and he licks her finger too fast. He doesn't savor its sweet taste. Sweet young nectar like hers is like wine; first you inhale its aroma, and then slowly taste it before letting it slide your throat.

She reaches back with her right hand and wraps her fingers around her lover's erection and squeezes it. She does it to let both of them know that she is in control. That this is her show. She bends slightly forward and spreads her legs as he guides his dick inside of her. Her long hair falls in front of her obscuring her face, but *he* can feel her eyes still on him.

His hands grab both sides of her waist and he enters her slowly. He has wanted to fuck her from the very first day they met, but she had always resisted having sex with him—until now. *There was no way he would be able to go more than twenty strokes without shooting his youthful inexperienced load into her tight pussy.*

With each stroke of his excited dick, her breasts sway forward as if reaching for the man in the willow trees. On stroke sixteen, maybe seventeen, she eases her lover's pulsating wet erection from her pussy and falls to her knees. She wants the man to know what he is missing hiding in the trees with his dick in his hands instead of having it buried inside the warmth of her passion.

Their bodies are turned to the side for *his* benefit. She easily takes the full length of his erection between her lips, closes her fingers around it and slowly feeds it to her throat. When she releases it from her lips, her tongue curls around it causing her lover to beg for mercy. He is almost at that point of no return.

There is more she wants him to see before making both men come. The adrenaline of stimulating two men at once has her feeling a rush of power that she has never felt before. When she looks back on this moment, she will realize it was on this day that her true sexual self was awakened. The man in the woods and her lover will be a memory she can smile at and recall the wildness of her youth.

*He* shakes his head and a wry smile dances across his lips and moves up to his face. Her lover is lying on the ground and she mounts him with her back towards him. He studies her back and mentally kisses every inch of her flesh. A gentle wind passes by and she shivers, or maybe it is his eyes on her that feels as if her body is on fire for his touch and his thick manhood.

She sits straight up straddling her lover and inserts his erection inside of her. Her body moves up and down as his dick probes her tightness. He cannot satisfy her because of his inexperience so she turns around to mentally fuck the man and imagine that it is *his* dick delving into the tightness of her young pussy.

He wants her to see the full length of his manhood so he momentarily releases it from his fingers and it stays buoyant and points straight at her as if to ask her a question.

The thought of jumping into his arms and him sinking his fingers into her firm, round ass while pounding her young pussy causes a sudden release of reserved moisture.

He sees the lust, the desire in her young eyes, and he yearns to be that young boy lying in the grass without a care in the world and enjoying nature's sweetest fruit. He had only come for a walk, to clear his mind before going back to work and that's when he saw them. Young love blossoming in the park in the middle of spring. He had only intended to watch for a few minutes before heading back to the office, but something about her; maybe it was the sensuality of her innocent beauty or the raw, untouched sexuality of a young girl who was not quite yet a woman that made him stay. Then she saw him in the trees, and he wanted to watch her come with the same uninterrupted passion that spring had shown when it flourished throughout the park. He had taken temporary leave of his senses and allowed his misplaced desires to overcome him. And now, all he wanted to do was come and forget everything else.

She spins around on her lover's erection and gives him a full frontal view of her breasts and thick brownish bush of pubic hair. Her hips gyrate slowly as she feels him swelling inside of her tightness. All he can do is lay there and let her have her way with him. He grabs hold of her waist in a futile attempt to slow down her hips, but her body and mind left him a long time ago in search of a bigger challenge. She leans back and reaches backwards with her hands to place them on his chest as he thrusts himself into her. His sudden thrust causes her body to rise like a wave and her breasts rise as they hope that they too will be pleasured. He cannot stop himself from coming.

She removes his erection from her swollen lips, slides her pussy up his chest until her clit comes to rest on his lips and he slowly swirls his tongue around it then sucks her so hard that she screams. She uses both hands to bring his dick to her lips, flicks her tongue around his engorged head a few times then sucks it down her throat. Her fingers manipulate his shaft and for once, she has lost control as her body betrays her hunger when she comes all over his face like sunlight spraying its warm rays throughout the trees, and she swallows him in return. Their bodies are simultaneously convulsing because his tongue is still buried inside her wetness and her lips are still wrapped around his dick as she waits for him to come again.

*He* watches all of this from under the willow trees and imagines that is her lips wrapped around his dick and drinking him. He wants her to see him come so he closes his eyes and mentally fucks her until he hears her scream. His breathing becomes shallow, his hand moves faster over the full length of his erection and he comes hard. Harder than he has come in a long time. His body jerks, momentarily knocking him backwards but he regains his balance and squeezes the last drop of his come onto the grass.

He stands there, unsure of what to do next. She is looking at him with the yearning desire he wishes he could get at home. Quietly, he recedes into the branches away from her stare to put his clothes back on.

They do the same thing and walk away hand in hand. He steps out of the trees and walks in the opposite direction. She turns around hoping that he is looking, but he continues to walk without looking back.

It is easier this way.

02/08/09…4:55am

# The Man Who Didn't Eat Pussy

At first, it didn't bother Rachael that Aaron didn't want to eat her pussy. He was a fantastic lover so she didn't push the issue even though they had been dating now for about six months. She was confident that after one lick of the sweetness between her tender lips, he would be hooked just like the others before him. Her previous lovers had always taken great pleasure in satisfying her orally, and a few of them had even claimed to having become addicted to its sweet, fruity taste. She knew that several of them might have to attend Cunnilingus Anonymous to get over their need to bury their faces between her legs every time they had sex or made love. It had gotten so bad sometimes that she swore that her pussy had developed an attitude about it only being licked and not filled. A pussy that is only being licked and not filled with the hardness of an erection can easily turn gay and forget that it's supposed to be a straight pussy, she laughingly told an ex-lover. She enjoyed oral sex immensely, but a woman needs the feel of a concrete dick pulsating inside of her every now and then. The last thing that she wanted was a confused pussy thinking that it desired another pussy instead of a throbbing dick.

"What do you mean you've never eaten pussy?"

Aaron and his best friend, Danny, were standing in front of the vending machine in the cafeteria unable to make up their minds which candy bar to buy. They were both good looking black men who worked out religiously and had the bodies to prove it. Two women from another firm walked by and gave them the eye. They looked at each other and kept on with their conversation. Their looks didn't merit their valuable time.

"*Damn man*, keep your voice down. I don't want the whole company to know my business."

"Okay, so you've *never* buried your tongue inside any of your girlfriend's pussy?"

"Never."

"And they let you get away with that shit?"

"I guess that after I dick them down they are just too tired to ask for anymore," Aaron laughed. He decided to have a Snickers. Danny was still undecided. He didn't have a particular candy bar he enjoyed, but enjoyed choosing from a variety. He applied this same sense of equal opportunity to his dating life. He was a rainbow lover. He enjoyed the beauty of all colors of women and as far as he was concerned, monogamy was a word that should be banned from the English language. Any honest man would tell you that if he felt he had a choice and could get away with it; he would make love to every beautiful woman on the face of the earth.

"Well, you don't know what you're missing. I'm addicted to the shit. It's like when I'm sucking and licking my woman down there, it's like she becomes possessed or something. I love a bald tasty pussy. I can get right to it, you know? I don't have to worry about hair or anything. All that hair sometimes is like wading through a fucking jungle and by the time my tongue gets there—it's too fucking tired to enjoy the damn thing. It's like when you have to put a condom on your dick and you know if you don't hurry up then the motherfucker is gonna get soft and you'll just be lying there with a limp dick in your hand and an angry horny woman who wants to beat you with your own dick."

Aaron couldn't help but laugh at some of the stuff that came from Danny's mouth. He had a unique way of putting things. Danny finally chose the Almond Joy and they ate as they walked over to the bathroom to take a leak.

"So doesn't your girl get mad that you're not eating her pussy?"

"She's never said anything about it, so I'm thinking that she doesn't like it. I don't want to ask her because if she does like it then she will want me to do it all the time. Then I will have to plead the fifth."

"The fifth what?"

"You know, abstaining."

They entered the bathroom, finished off their candy bars and stood side by side at the urinals.

"So why don't you like to eat pussy? What are you some sort of vegetarian or something? Or against your religion?"

"I eat meat, you asshole. I guess I just never got into it."

"It's not something you get into. You have a woman, she sucks your dick and you eat her pussy. There's nothing to really think about. You just fucking do it. Besides, eating pussy is like eating ice cream. Everybody loves it. It's like a fucking American tradition—apple pies and hot dogs and all that shit. It's like going to a barbecue and not eating a cheeseburger. Everyone will think you're crazy. Your girl must think you're a nut job not to be eating her pussy. No disrespect or anything, but I've seen your girl."

"Watch your mouth."

"Let's just say if your girl was a chocolate cake, I would be obese by now because I would be eating her everyday. I would be a diabetic by now after eating so much brown sugar."

"You're fucking sick, man."

Aaron thought about what Danny had just said, and Rachael was a beautiful woman. Her dark complexion set against her almond shaped eyes and round face gave her an exotic mysterious quality when you first laid eyes on her. She was naturally beautiful without the accentuation of makeup, but would occasionally wear some on special occasions. Danny and Aaron stood in silence at the urinal for a few seconds looking straight ahead at the white walls. Streams of yellow and white urine simultaneously flowed from their penises as if they were engaged in a synchronized swim event at the Olympics.

"I know it's stupid but I have nightmares about eating pussy. I have this reoccurring dream of putting my head down there, and Rachael is enjoying it so much that she pushes my head inside of her pussy and I can't get the fuck out. I'm already fucking scared of the dark because my mom used to lock us in the closet when we misbehaved. And besides, you're sticking your tongue into some dark hole and you don't even know what's on the other side. At least when a woman is giving you a blowjob—the dick is right there in her face. She doesn't have to guess what she's sucking because it's waving around without any intentions of going anywhere until it gets sucked.

"Dude, I don't know what kind of fucked up things that are going through your head, but trust me, eating pussy will clear it right up. You love when she sucks your dick, right?"

"Yeah, I love it. If I didn't know better I would think that she was a professional."

"Don't tell guys that you think your woman is a pro. They will want to try her out. Keep that shit to yourself."

Three shakes and a waggle later they had finished up at the urinal and washing their hands. Danny decided that it was his duty as Aaron's best friend for all of their twenty-eight years to try to make him understand how important licking and sucking your woman's pussy was to her mental well-being. He had heard of some woman in Alaska who refused to suck her husband's dick unless he started eating her pussy again. "It's only right," she had said. Eventually the man gave in and started performing oral sex on his wife again. When questioned about why he had given in, he simply said, "it felt like he was about to lose his mind if he didn't get his dick sucked right now."

The more Rachael thought about it the angrier she became. Why wasn't her man eating her pussy? All her girlfriends bragged to her about how much their men enjoyed eating their dessert after a full meal of pussy. She was sure that in a pussy-eating contest that her stuff would win first prize. It made no sense to her as to why Aaron hadn't tried to taste the sweetness buried between her moist lips. Maybe it was the whole Caribbean thing about not eating pussy. He was more Americanized than most guys she knew, but he still had that island blood in him.

*Maybe he didn't know how to eat pussy and was ashamed to tell her.*

This mess had to come to an end tonight when he came over. She loved sucking his dick: the way it felt growing in her mouth, on her lips, the strength that vibrated through it as she held it, but if he wasn't going to give her the same pleasure, then her lips were going on strike tonight. It had worked for that woman in Alaska and she was sure it would work for her. She would break him if it was the last thing she did, but she would much rather him do it willingly than be forced to do it. A pussy that is licked and sucked without coercion always goes down better and taste much sweeter.

"Where the hell are we going?" Aaron asked Danny as they took the elevator down into the lobby.

"Just to walk around the block for a few minutes to conduct an experiment. It's a beautiful summer day. You know the honeys are buzzing out there," Danny said to an exasperated Aaron as they exited the building and the noise of 42nd Street greeted them.

He had work to do but agreed to take a short walk. Ever since they were kids, Danny was always making him do things he normally would not do. It was always interesting being around Danny, but sometimes he would go too far.

If New York is the city that never sleeps, then 42nd Street is the part of it that has an incurable case of insomnia. It was always easy to pick out the tourists as they tried to walk in groups, wore color coordinated clothing, cameras strung around their necks begging to be robbed and constantly looking up in the sky as if they were waiting for Spiderman to swing from building to building. Aaron tried to avoid coming out during the day and would normally order in his lunch just to avoid the crowds that were never ending. It always struck him just how naïve tourists from all around the world were, and any thief worth his profession could easily swindle them without much effort.

"So tell me what are we doing here again?" Aaron asked Danny as they waited at the light.

"We're going to conduct an experiment to prove a point to you. It won't take that long before you have your answer and join the millions of thirsty pussy lickers all around the world."

"Is that what this is about? Eating pussy?"

The light turned green and they walked up to Seventh Avenue towards AMC Movie Theater. A crowd had gathered to watch the new Will Smith movie, "*Seven Pounds*."

"Excuse me ladies," Danny walked right up in the middle of the crowd to disrupt their ongoing conversations. "I don't mean to disturb you, but my friend and I are working on a sex survey and we need your opinion." Aaron shook his head in disbelief and embarrassment at the spectacle that Danny was making. "Can you help us?" Most of the ladies shook their heads in agreement, but the loudest one in the bunch let Danny know that no freaky deaky sex would be happening on her watch. Aaron could almost read Danny's mind, as he looked up and down at the overweight, bookish woman but just smiled at her to soften her up to get her on his side. She melted when Danny looked at her with his piercing gray eyes and touched her shoulder.

"Okay ladies, here's the deal," a crowd had gathered by now to hear what Danny had to say. "My best friend has been dating this young woman for about six months, but for some reason, he doesn't feel the need to satisfy her by going downtown," he was trying not to say the words.

"What do you mean downtown?" A female tourist asked. She could have been the poster child for tourism with her "I Love New York" hat, shirt, and buttons. "Is downtown more interesting than where we are?" She asked innocently. Someone in the crowd whispered to her what downtown meant and her mouth flew open in shock.  A ripple of conversation surged through the crowd at Danny's admission about Aaron's sex life.

The crowd had grown in size as men and women from all walks-of-life stopped to listen to what was going on.

"So why doesn't Aaron want to taste the cookie?" Someone in the crowd shouted.  All eyes turned to Aaron for his response.

Aaron stood there in disbelief vowing to strangle Danny when they got back to the office.  His personal life was now fodder for the streets of New York and it would just be his luck if a News 7 truck drove by and put him on the damn news.  His mother would have a frigging heart attack to hear her son talking about eating pussy and acting as if he didn't have any damn sense..

"Well...it's not that I don't want to eat--*the cookie*," Aaron's face showed his embarrassment as he said the word.  *This could only be happening in New York or San Francisco* he thought to himself.

"I'm sure you enjoy your woman pleasuring you, but you won't do the same for her.  You're a selfish ass brotha!"  Another woman in the crowd shouted.  The other women nodded their heads and shouted their approval.  "I'm sick of brothers like you who always want these lips," she pointed to the fullness of her lips and blew a kiss into the air, "To deep throat them but they barely want to lick you for a minute.  What's up with that?"

"Listen," Danny implored the women before everything got out of hand, "Aaron is good brotha.  He just doesn't know how good the cookie taste when it crumbles in your mouth, drink it with milk and seeing how much your woman is enjoying you eating her cookie is sheer bliss. Tasting your woman is like eating that perfect piece of cake, like eating a ripe mango and the juices are dripping down your chin, or walking into your house and the smell of dinner gets you hungry. All you want to do is just eat and eat until you are full." Danny had a far away look in his eyes as he spoke, but the sound of clapping and laughter brought him back to the moment.

All the women clapped and laughed at Danny's words wishing they had a man at home who appreciated eating the cookie like Danny. Some of them had smiles on their faces as they were remembering the last time they experienced the pleasure of a long tongue plunging deep into the abyss of their moist pussy. Aaron looked around at their faces and thought that it wouldn't surprise him if a few of them were turned on just thinking about it.

"Tell the women what you don't like about eating the cookie," Danny turned to Aaron with a smile on his face. He was enjoying watching his boy squirm under the hot glare of a bunch of female eyes. If Aaron said the wrong thing they might just turn on him and rip him to shreds.

"Stop calling it the cookie" a tall light-skinned woman shouted over the crowd of noise. "Maybe the boy doesn't like cookies. Call it what it is—eating pussy!" The crowd roared with approval. A few of the women broke into a spontaneous cheer of "Pussy! Pussy! Pussy!"

One young woman who had been quiet through all the hoopla stepped forward into the circle that had surrounded Danny and Aaron. She was a pretty sister with short red dreads, round face and lips that made Aaron think of her on her knees pleasuring him. It was such a natural thought to him that it never registered as anything other than a man being a man in his mind. It was like going shopping and just browsing through all the clothes, but only buying one thing.

The young woman reached out to him confidently and put her right hand on his shoulders. "I saw that look on your face when you looked at my lips. You were imagining me sucking your dick, weren't you?"

Her boldness caught Aaron by surprise and the look on his face told the crowd that she was right. A few women barked at him as the young lady continued.

"Close your eyes," she commanded him. He did as she asked and Danny did the same. "Imagine me coming home from work, maybe running a bath for you, then laying you down and letting my lips enjoy every thick delicious inch of your manhood. Would you like that?"

Aaron lost in the moment forgot where he was and answered "yes," weakly. A noticeable bulge had grown in both his and Danny's pants, and the women in attendance giggled at their obvious arousal.

"Imagine these full lips making love, caressing…swallowing you. Damn! I bet that shit feels good."

Her voice had dropped and become even more sensual. Some of the women in the crowd tried to hide the fact that the young lady was turning them on also. Danny and Aaron tried discreetly to hide their erections but it was already too late. When an erection has risen, it is like a balloon, the only place it has to go is up. With her hand still on his shoulder, she leaned in close to him and whispered in his ears. The scent of her perfume exacerbated an already volatile situation as he tried to keep some façade of control.

Her words hit him hard, "Don't you think your woman deserves the same pleasure that she gives you? Go home and eat your woman's pussy as if you haven't eaten in days. Suck it, lick it, eat it, and swallow her like a man who is in love with his woman and that woman will do anything for you."

When Aaron opened his eyes, she was already sashaying through the crowd of women and disappeared around the corner. The other women who had gathered began to disperse and return to what they were doing.

"What did she tell you?" Danny asked as they walked back to work.

"Basically pleasure goes both ways. Do me a favor?"

"Anything man."

"Tell Mr. Jones that I got sick over lunch and I'm taking the rest of the afternoon off. Okay?"

Danny nodded in approval and slapped Aaron across the back. "Go ahead, boy! Go eat that pussy!" They both laughed as Aaron hailed a cab to Rachael's apartment in the city—luckily one stopped for him within a few minutes. Twenty minutes, he was standing at Rachael's door with flowers in hand and lips that were ready to taste his woman's sweet pussy.

The knocking at her door woke Rachael from a sound sleep. It was her day off and she couldn't imagine who could be banging her door in the middle of the afternoon. She had taken a long bath, and the warmth of the sun streaming through her open bedroom windows had sent her into a restful sleep. The sight of Aaron through the peephole made her remember why she needed that bath to relax, and she could feel the tension returning to her body. She was about to give him a piece of her mind. Rachael flung the door open naked and before she could light into him; Aaron handed her a dozen red roses and carried her to the bedroom. She was too shocked to protest and looked at him as if he had lost his mind when he deposited her on the bed.

Aaron hurriedly took off his clothes and rested the weight of his full body on top of Rachael. "I'm sorry it's taken me so long to do this," he said as his hot kisses found the softness of her lips, her neck and worked his way down. She wasn't sure what he was talking about *yet* as her body responded to his touch. The strength of his hands massaged her nipples and his lips closed gently around them. Her body arched upwards to greet his lips and his hands wandered to her ass. His touch

173

was surer than it ever been before and she was swept away as he lowered his body down to her navel. His tongue filled the hollow dimple of her navel while his hands held her around her waist to keep her firmly in place. Rachael wasn't sure what had come over Aaron. Or whoever this man was who kept going lower and lower to touch her in places that had been a secret to him until now.

Aaron closed his eyes, rid his mind of images of women having babies, rid his mind of their periods, and inhaled the scent of Rachael's heated pussy. He had never eaten pussy in his life and relied on his instincts to take over. *"It's like kissing,"* the young woman had whispered. *"Kiss her down there as if you are taking her in your arms to kiss her."* He licked his lips and gently kissed her directly on her engorged vagina lips. Aaron's tongue instinctively slid between the small opening of her throbbing lips and tasted the sweet nectar of his woman's pussy for the first time. She waited breathlessly for him to continue. She wanted more but waited for him to proceed on his own. She needed to know that he enjoyed licking her without her prodding him to do so. What is the point of asking your man to eat your pussy if he doesn't want to? It's like asking him if he loves you. If he loves you—he will tell you.

The taste of her juices on his lips, his tongue…on his face was something new to Aaron. He was only accustomed to seeing her juices dripping from his dick and marveling at how she would lick it off with the full length of her tongue wrapped around his girth. The thought of it made him shudder, and he wanted to bring that same pleasure to her. The taste of her wasn't what he expected. Instead, the flavor of her warm juices reminded him of honey, and he was pleasantly surprised to find that he enjoyed it. He slid his tongue deeper into the center of her moistness and swirled it inside of her as if he was licking an ice cream cone.

Rachael couldn't believe how good his tongue felt inside of her. He was thirsty and sucking everything in sight. Her moans of pleasure kissed his ears letting him know just how much she was enjoying the pleasure he was bringing to her body. Her pussy was swollen with sweet nectar, and every time he flicked his tongue on her clit, she would come in spurts which he swallowed hungrily. Aaron smiled to himself and was almost angry that he had waited this long to please his woman. He promised himself that he wouldn't take her pleasure for granted anymore and would do whatever it took to keep her satisfied.

Rachael lost count of how many times her body exploded with the release of her orgasms. She lay there exhausted, unable to come again. As Aaron came up for air, she licked his lips to taste herself. Their lips met in a passionate embrace as he slid effortlessly inside the cocoon of her tight pussy.

"Thank you baby," Rachael gasped as the full length of his manhood touched every nerve in her body.

Aaron withdrew himself from her and slid back in again. He enjoyed watching the expression on her face every time he entered her. "Don't thank me baby. I'm your man and giving you pleasure gives me pleasure."

They spent the rest of the afternoon in bed, in the shower exploring the secrets of their bodies that would slowly unfold with each touch, each kiss, bringing them closer together.

01/21/09…3:48pm

# Beautiful Release of Pleasure

Just the thought of licking you deep in your moanful
center
Sets my tongue instantly on fire
I can already hear you moaning, softly purring
And it is only my breath that is setting your skin on fire
Imagine the walls you will soon be climbing
When the full force of my love fills you up
You will know you are loved there will be no room for
doubt
Every word you moan from your whispering lips is like
Greek to me
After you come you will be fluent in every language
Your nectar always tastes like the finest wine I have ever
swallowed
Your body is trembling and ready for that beautiful
sweet release
You are eager to wet my palette and feed me what I
crave… what I need
Not yet…it has been a long day and I want to savor your
taste before it all disappears
Every drop is as precious as gold and the way you moan
makes my tongue harder
I want to go deeper to find the eye of your pleasure and
be swept away in your storm
Unleash the torrent of your hurricane swell and let the
current take me under

Toss me to and fro my love and have no mercy on me for
that is what I want
You don't have to do anything my love except lay there
and look beautiful
Your nectar is like fresh spring water bubbling from the
earth
Your moist swollen lips affect me in the same way
As watching a beautiful sunrise rising to greet the world
How blessed these eyes are to witness one of God's most
sensual creations
Let me show you how thankful I am my love use my
tongue for anything you want
No task is too menial ask it of me and I will grant your
every fervent desire
For your beautiful release of sweet pleasure I will
patiently wait
The longer you take to drown my tongue in your sweet
nectar is the more pleasure I am able to give you
Do not be afraid of overwhelming me all at once
Whatever you have been saving for me
Release it until your whispering lips are quiet once again
I will lie silently at the mouth that feeds my thirst
Just waiting for another burst of your beautiful release of
pleasure.
3/10/09…2:42pm

# Room 104

They always got the same room every time they stayed at the Clarion for a few hours. She loved having the big Jacuzzi in the middle of the room to take baths, scrub him down, and make love. Their time together was precious. Stealing moments was what she called it. The drive from Virginia Beach to Maryland always seemed to take forever even though it was only a four-hour drive up to College Park. Knowing that she would see him that day always made her body ache with anticipation of having him swollen inside of all her orifices. Her body needed to be nourished by his sweet island dick. Her mind needed caressing by his poetic words and the hint of his island accent still dancing in every word. She checked her rear-view mirror to make sure there were no cops around and stepped on the gas. Her lover was waiting.

Anyone driving by on the highway that might happen to glance over at her smiling broadly would think that she was a few moans short of an orgasm, but she didn't care. If they knew the sweet dick down that she would soon be getting—they would be smiling too and maybe hoping to get in on the action. It had only been three weeks since their last rendezvous, but when your mind, body, and soul craves to be near the one you love—even a few hours can feel like an eternity.

At first, she tried valiantly to hide the feelings she felt washing over her every time they were together; and it became even stronger when she had to leave him and know that his nights were being spent in the bed of another. Absence doesn't make the heart grow fonder. It only makes it yearn for what it cannot have everyday. She tried to keep it casual and light, but she wasn't the kind of woman who could make love to a man with every fiber of her being and then pretend that it was only sex. Sex is something you have with a stranger you've just met in a bar or with some fool who claims to be a great lover and he comes in one minute. He then stupidly asks you "if it was good for you too?" When she took a man in her arms, in her bed, into her confidence; and inside the pleasure of pussy, it was an invitation for him to share a part of her that was reserved for only him and no one else. She would willingly give all of herself to him. All he had to do was ask and she would be his forever.

There was no time for these kinds of thoughts, she thought to herself, as she pulled into the parking lot of the Clarion. He hadn't arrived as of yet so that allowed her enough time to freshen up and get ready for him. The clerk at the front desk recognized her and offered a smile as he handed to her the keys to room 104. She wondered if his smile was the normal customer service smile or maybe he knew that she would soon be making love and about to feel things that she had never felt before in her life. She smiled back at him and the clerk thought to himself that he had never seen a woman so happy before. He wished more of his customers had her smile instead of the guilty expressions they wore on their faces when they came to check in or snuck out in the middle of the night.

She received a text from him letting her know that he would be there in fifteen minutes. She shook her head in amazement as she opened the door to the room. Just seeing his name on her cell phone was enough to get her excited. She felt embarrassed that it took so little to make her smile, but she lived with the alternative—finding it dissatisfying. This felt much better. He brought something into her life that she had only dreamed about and never thought possible—until he came along. Men had touched her body before. They had even given her pleasure, but making love to him, being with him, was a surreal experience that she still found indescribable. Every time they were together, inside of each other's body, kissing so deeply—it felt as if her skin was on fire. It intensified her feelings of passion and she felt as if she was caught up in a beautiful love song. She was the singer and she was writing and singing all the lyrics just the way her heart wanted to sing them. There was nothing sad about this love song. It was a song filled with unrequited passion about her heart finally being touched and allowed to bloom into its full beauty. If she had more time before he arrived, she would have sat down and cried tears of joy. She didn't want him to see her crying because he would worry, which was actually kind of cute, but it would take away from their afternoon together. There would be time for tears later on when he left her and went back home.

The warm water washed over her naked body beating down on her tired muscles in much the same way he would soon do to her pussy. She laughed out loud at her naughty thought and felt herself blushing. She was a grown woman with kids and blushing at having a naughty thought, but she knew that it was a thought not based solely on desire or the yearnings aching in her pussy hole. It went deeper than that for her. She felt complete as if all the bad things that had transpired in her life happened so she could fully appreciate the bond they were sharing. In so many ways, he had saved her life. His presence and his words had found her at a time in her life when she wasn't sure if her life made any difference to anyone. Something happened when he found her... or she found him. The gray began slowly to lift, and the smile that once laid dormant inside of her found its way to the surface again. He would humbly brush off her words of gratitude for saving her life as merely being kind, but she knew...she knew that maybe if he hadn't arrived then everything after would not have happened. She was happy now that she hadn't succumbed to the dark feelings that had overwhelmed her spirit before him.

The knock on the door announced his arrival. Her heart thumped and she had to remind herself not to run to the door and throw her arms around him, but that's exactly what she wanted to do every time they were together. She stepped behind the door and opened it to let him in. She was shy about her body and didn't want someone wandering by to see her in a towel. It was only for him to see and to do with as he wished.

"Hi honey," she embraced him as the door closed behind him.

"Hey. I see you're ready for me," he smiled mischievously because he knew she would blush when he said so, and she did. Her face turned bright pussy pink and she tried to look away, but he held her face in his hands and kissed her. One kiss from him. One touch from him and her body and mind responded as if they were being touched for the very first time. In many ways, she felt like a virgin experiencing the joys of love and sex for the very first time. It's amazing what a man's touch can do to a woman's body when she craves him from the depths of her soul.

In his arms, she felt protected as if there was nothing that he could not do once he set his mind to it. Her body felt perfect against his. It was always so warm and the mixture of his cologne and scented deodorant made her high. It was the natural high of a woman who was in love and soon to be ravished by her lover.

His kisses felt like candy coated raindrops falling sweetly on her lips. She had an image of running in the rain naked but of course, she never would. "Kiss me like that again," she said as her towel fell to the floor while his lips ignited her skin and her nipples grew fatter as they rubbed against the hairs on his chest. She was alive and reveling in her feminine beauty. His hands felt like magnets connecting her body to his. She helped him out of his clothes because even having the thinnest layer of clothing between them was too much distance from his body. She craved skin on skin. She wanted the illusion of being in love even if the real thing wasn't possible. Although she knew it was too deep of an emotional state for him, her heart, mind, and body craved it—reality be damned.

He never had to ask. She was always ready to please him in whatever capacity he demanded. The only way she knew how to love was with her very soul. She dropped to her knees, laid him on his back and took his erect manhood between her quivering lips. Her senses became flooded with the heat of his thickness thumping against her lips, and he forced his dick down her throat by grabbing hold of her damp brown hair. When he did this, it made her feel special that he instinctively knew what turned her on without her having to draw him a road map to her erogenous zones. He followed the trail of heat vibrating from her body and tasted the heated desire on her skin to have him inside of her. He was a generous lover in the truest sense; he always made sure that she was completely satisfied. His ultimate pleasure was derived from knowing that all her cravings had been fed. Making love to him wasn't just simply about penetration or hearing her moans of passion. He had made love and fucked scores of women but there weren't many who he could recall fucking and making to love to simultaneously. With her, the lines were blurred because passion cannot differentiate what the body and mind are feeling at the apex of its release. You allow yourself the possibility that things exist that transcend our physical understanding and experience passion so soul searing that it leaves your mind in awe. It's a beautiful thing to feel. Most people never get to experience true bliss. They read about in books and see it in movies but always as an observer and never a participant. She was the star of her own production and every line and scene was scripted to perfection.

Her moist hands closed around his fat black dick and stroked it back and forth as it slid smoothly between her hungry lips. She wanted to drink all of his babies, feel them sliding down her throat and filling her stomach. They would never have any babies because her tubes had been tied a few years ago. Every once in a while, she would give in to the fantasy of what their child might look like if they had one. It would have been a beautiful baby.

"Lay down baby. I want to taste you," she said without looking him in the eye. Her eyes cast downwards on the matted hairs of his chest. She found it difficult to tell him things of a sexual nature while holding his gaze. It was a form of her submission to him and performing her womanly duties as a lover. Maybe she was pretending to be the submissive one because life and love had taught her that men, even the strong ones needed their fragile baby egos stroked once in a while to keep them performing at their highest level. It was something she didn't quite always understand but she knew that it was a necessary function of keeping her man happy. It was just as important as sex because it made a man feel virile and necessary. The small things in a relationship can keep it in motion without it ever needing mention, but take it away and the importance of it becomes glaring once it is gone.

Her eyes never left his naked body as he lay down and waited for her to please him. His dick lounged semi-erect between his thighs. Even when he wasn't fully erect, he could put her past lovers to shame with the length and girth of his manhood. Comparing them to him was like asking an amateur to do battle with a master or pitting a child against a man. The outcome was already pre-determined.

His dick waved in front of her like a beacon of light docking a ship into port. A physical pain filled the ache in her pussy as if someone was stabbing her, but she refused her carnal instinct to mount his dick and use it like a trampoline to levitate her into the air with each deep thrust. Her tongue encircled his big toe and she sucked on it hard as if it was a three-inch dick deserving of her best tongue job. He squealed like a pig squirming in sty. With each suck, his moans intensified and it made her pussy drip liquid fire to know that she was turning him on so much.

"Come here," he called to her with hands outstretched to her as she kneeled on the floor. "I need to fuck you now." Hearing the gravity of his desire made her clitoris jump for joy. When a man expresses his need for you and not merely a want, you can expect to be thoroughly fucked by every inch of his dick.

"You don't have to tell me twice," she said smiling as she crawled up between his legs and his erection slapped the right side of her face. She straddled his upper body with her knees and she bent down to kiss him again. His touch ignited bombs inside of her as he caressed her back, her ass, and wrapped both hands around her neck to kiss her deeper. She loved when he took control of her in the bedroom. *That's what a man is supposed to do*, she thought to herself—*handles his business before somebody else does it for him*.

Her pussy dripped onto his erection with the promise of squeezing every ounce of come from his dick. "I'm here honey. Do what you want with your pussy."

He kissed her again, this time so deep that it felt like his tongue was caught in her air passage, and he entered her heated cunt without pretense of foreplay. His penetration was swift, like an unsuspecting slap to the face that leaves you stunned because you never saw it coming. She screamed with her every thrust of his manhood opening her pussy wider and deeper. Her pussy was like a one-way street trying to accommodate two lanes of traffic. It felt as if he was trying to burrow a hole into her stomach through her pussy cavity. He was trying to steal her breath, make her lose her voice as her moans and screams ricocheted back and forth on the walls and settled in the empty Jacuzzi waiting its turn to get in on the action.

"Damn baby…that's how a man is supposed to fuck…just like that."

"You like it? Tell me how you much you like it," sweat poured down his baldhead and onto his face. She had an insane thought of trying to fit his big baldhead into her pussy, but in the throes of passion, people begin to fantasize about some crazy shit that isn't humanly possible.

"I love how you fuck your pussy baby. You are the best lover I've ever had." Hearing those words made his dick harder and she felt it growing another inch inside of her. If she died right now, she would die a happy woman on a fat dick that was stroking her into multiple mind numbing orgasms.

His hands slid down her sweaty back, cupped her ass and spread both cheeks wider. He was preparing her body for the penetration of his fat head into the tightness of her anus. The full length of his manhood slipped out of her pussy and teased her soaking lips as she moaned for him to enter her again. He granted her request as he entered and exited her slowly. He was in complete control as he played her body like it was his own personal instrument. Every stroke, extracted a sweet note of sensual passion from her quivering lips, and her pussy dripped with applause.

She was his.

He was hers.

In this moment, no one else mattered and she hugged her chest as she felt the throbbing head of his dick say hello to her tight anus. Her tight hole never frowned, told him to go away, or kept its hole closed for his entry. It smiled for him and he kissed it with the slit of his eye on his dick. Deep breathes...one more deep breath and he was inside of her again—where he should always be. He slid into her tiny space easily because the

188

warm juices of her pussy coated his entire dick and her asshole swallowed his many curved inches until it was choking on dick meat. Her body shuddered and the sweetness of temporary pain washed over her as she stretched open to take all of him inside of her. His hands were now around her waist, digging into her flesh, controlling the depth of his penetration. He knew that he couldn't go crazy and pummel her back there without a care in the world. He was gentle when it was necessary and rough when it was needed. The perfect lover.

"Fuck my ass deeper, baby."

"You sure you can handle all of this dick?" he asked her cockily.

"Yes baby, give it to me. I've been craving this dick stretching my ass open all day," she almost begged. "Don't deny me baby—please."

The sound of her voice, almost begging, so girlish and innocent tapped into the dominant side of him that few had ever been exposed to. His hands tightened around her waist, he lifted her into the air and slid almost completely out of her ass, but she tightened her muscles and held him there, choking his thick head until he returned into her dark sanctuary.

"Come in my ass baby. Water my hole with your sperm."

"I...I can't stop it," he murmured as his eyes closed, his dick twitched violently and he got ready to flood her anal canal with two weeks worth of fermented sperm.

"Feed your ass baby. Give me every drop of that sweet shit," she urged him. She wanted to milk him dry so when he went home all he could do was go to sleep like a baby who had just been breastfed. No one else would be getting her dick tonight after she was finished with him. She loved spoiling him and giving him everything he wanted. There was so much more that she wanted to do for him. To show him that not only did her body scream for pleasure when he touched her, but also her heart. When he was inside of her, growing thicker and thicker with each spurt; she felt a stronger connection to him than she had ever felt for another man. Her thoughts overwhelmed her as he sprayed her quivering insides with rapid bursts of warm come. Her ass was on come overload as he let loose with a sustained torrent that spread quickly through her anal cavity and left her dripping like a faucet that couldn't turn off. He always seemed as if he was in pain after he came, but it wasn't pain that he was in; he was engulfed in a moment of sheer bliss that was unsustainable, but in that moment of orgasmic release, it felt like it could go on forever.

"Stay inside," she whispered to him as she laid down on his sweaty chest and he stroked her beautiful brown hair. The heated scent of their sex filled the air and his erection decreased slowly from strength to being flaccid. She loved when his thick head would finally slip out of her ass and her tiny hole would release him. A plopping sound would resonate through her body giving her the shivers all over again.

They laid in silence letting the moment they just shared speak for itself. His heart was still pounding against her chest as if he had just finished running a marathon, and at any moment, he might be in need of open-heart surgery.

"That was intense," he breathed heavily into the air between closed eyes.

"Yes, baby. You are such a wonderful lover. How do you do all these wonderful things to my body over and over again?" It was a rhetorical question. She knew that she would never get an answer.;

He learned a long time ago when women asked you these kinds of questions, it was never really just one question. It would be followed-up by a sustained cross examination which would slowly evolve over days, weeks and months. He learned a lot by being quiet, watching women lay the foundation for their eventual goal. They would make great hunters in the jungle, he often thought, because they would be patient and be able to wait out their prey. She didn't strike him as the preying type, but it's the mark of a true hunter; when you don't see them coming and the shocked expression plastered all over your face as you are devoured.

His stomach rumbled beneath her like a New York train in need of maintenance. "You hungry baby?" He nodded yes. "You need your strength for round two unless you can't handle this pussy again."

He smiled in bemusement at the absurdity of her statement. His smile made her smile as she got off the bed and went to the bathroom. Splotches of red filled her face, as she was still enflamed by the fervor of their passion. It felt like his dick was still lodged inside of her body and her steps were weighed down by the sensation of having his manhood still buried inside of her. The water ran in the sink for a few minutes until it got warm and she splashed some on her face. Her hands trembled slightly as she did this, but it was probably the remnants of a secret orgasm shuddering to life. She took a warm rag and walked back to him.

"Turn over honey let me wipe you down." Lovingly she took his now dead penis into her hands and wiped it down with the warm rag and soap. After two more trips to the bathroom sink, she took him in her mouth again, and she felt life slowly returning to his manhood. She was sucking him back to life. She wondered to herself as his thick head invaded her throat if his girlfriend at home tended to his needs with same level of passion as she did. Creative men like him become easily bored. Their minds are always in constant motion so they never maintain focus on one thing at a time. Passion sustains them and keeps them from visiting the darkness too often. She wanted to be the light that illuminated all his dreams even if she could not be with him everyday. *If I had you everyday*, she thought to herself as she turned on the hot water in the Jacuzzi, *you would be treated like the King you are*. She kneeled by the Jacuzzi as it filled up with water and bubbles from her favorite bubble bath, Sensual Amber. Her fingers tested the water to make sure it wasn't too hot for him and when she was satisfied that the temperature was just right, she removed her hand and licked her fingers to taste the warm fragrance.

"What do you want to eat, honey?" She wanted him to say that he wanted some sweet pussy dessert on his tongue. If she had a minor complaint about their lovemaking, it was that his talented tongue didn't go swimming often enough between the warmth of her pussy lips. He made up for it in many other ways, but she knew better than to ask. He did everything in his own time and when the mood suited him, he would take swift, deep tongue plunges into her sweetest ache.

"I'm okay, not really hungry. Just give me two of those bananas you have and I will be as good as new."

"Are you sure that's all you want to eat?" she asked again.

"Yes, that's all," he looked at her unblinking as he said it. Her eyes fell downwards as she turned around to get the bananas for him.

He watched her as she entered the steaming water and slowly slid into the deep Jacuzzi until her entire body was covered in bubbles.

"It's good baby. Come on in, let me wash you up."

He took the last bite of the banana and gingerly tested the water before getting in. He stood straight up and the bubbles came up past his knees. She had placed a bottle of cold Dasani water on the side for him because she knew that he got thirsty when they stayed in too long. She slid over to him, covered in bubbles, and blew some at him. He swatted them away from his face and looked down at her with a half smile on his face. She blushed as she rose to her knees and rested her head against his wet stomach. He waited, expecting her to fill her lips once again with his erect manhood. He loved making love to her and fucking her almost as much as he enjoyed having her sweet lips sucking him dry. It was a tossup as to which hole he enjoyed most; she didn't make it easy on him because every time they were together; it just got better and better. At some point, sex and its passion levels off, but that day for them was faraway in the future.

His back stiffened when he felt her soapy hand slide between his legs and gently but firmly caress his balls in her hands. She played with them as though she were playing dice; about to toss two 6's. His hips gyrated on command when the warmth of her mouth engulfed his hardness and he steadily dropped to his knees. She reluctantly released the happy prisoner from one of its three favorite homes and they were shoulder deep in bubble suds. The hot water felt good against her skin. It felt like his hands touching her all over all at once. Her body trembled at the thought of having him touch her everyday. It was a thought that she didn't dwell upon but when it snuck out from her secret thoughts and into the light; it would weigh upon her so heavily that only the presence of him and making love to him could soothe her mind.

"Stretch your feet out, honey. Let me wash them for you." He rested comfortably with his head tilted back and did as she asked. For the next few minutes, she washed and scrubbed his feet with the tenderness of a woman taking care of her man. "You could have this everyday, honey." He didn't respond and kept his eyes closed.

The jets of hot water streams swirling around and beneath her had created some sort of suction vortex making it feel as if the water had turned into pussy sucking lips. His erection bobbed back and forth above the surface of the bubbles in the water like a buoy in the middle of the ocean. It was calling her home to ride his dick on the high seas, and the lapping waves of water pushed her towards him and into his arms. He reached for her neck as his dick bobbed around in circles looking for a way to enter her pussy. Unable to wait any longer to feel him inside of his pussy, she reached behind her back and rubbed his manhood all over her smiling lips.

"Do you know what you do to me?" She asked him not really expecting a response.

"Tell me baby. Tell me what I do to you." He scooped up a handful of water, raised it above her head and as she looked up, he let it fall on her face and down her chest. She felt baptized, as if she was given a new life.

"You make me feel so beautiful," she gasped as the thickness of his engorged head spread her lips open and she descended onto his erect manhood making sure to say hello again to every inch with sweet whispers of deep appreciation from her thirsty pussy.

"You are beautiful."

"Say it again."

Actions, when shown at the right time, can go deeper than a thousand beautiful words strung together. Every thrust off his dick inside of her tightness said much more than anything he could ever say. The depth of his penetrations signified the level of affection he had for her. If he could go any deeper, he would drill a hole in her uterus and into her stomach where he planted gallons of his liquid passion. A village of unborn babies would live within the walls of her stomach.

Water splashed all around them and spilled onto the white tiles. He brought her closer to his body, held onto her waist as if it was a life preserver, and fucked her like a man possessed. Tears of joy rolled down her face and sunk into the water below.

"You fuck me so good baby," she moaned as if in disbelief of his prowess and stamina. "No man has ever fucked me this good and made love to my body like this before baby," she moaned deeply as her body shook simultaneously from her tears and the sweet dick down he was ministering to her body. "How do you do it…how? How do you know exactly what my body needs every time?"

"You deserve it, baby. You know how to fuck and suck this dick."

"Yes honey. This pussy is all yours…do whatever you want to it," she sobbed as tears flowed freely down her face. She felt embarrassed at her show of emotion, but he took pride in bringing her to tears when they made love. It let him know that he was touching a part of her soul that was in need of his touch, his words and the cravings of love that she desired to feel. He kissed her face. Her salty tears fell against his lips. He showed her no mercy and continued to fuck her until he felt the warm release of her passion come down on his manhood drenching it in her warm lava cream.

"Baaaaaaaaaaaaby," she moaned. "I can't stop coming. Shit!"

He went as deep inside of her as her body would allow his penetration and remained still as her heated arousal continued to shower his throbbing thickness with its warm praises of love. The warmth of her love came down thick on his manhood like a cum waterfall. It triggered his own passions, and before long; he was thrashing about like an out of control mechanical bull, but she held on for the ride as he came inside of her again. *Another baby for me*, she thought. His thrashings subsided and he lay still as he collected his thoughts and slowly went soft inside of her. Her body rested against his chest as their cum and the hot water swirled around them in unison.

"Here baby." She knew he was thirsty without having to ask him. He drank the entire bottle of Dasani in a few deep gulps.

"It's too hot for me now," he said as he stood up in the Jacuzzi.

"Stay here baby; let me get your towel."

She got out of the Jacuzzi to quickly dry off, and then he stepped out to be dried off by her.

He looked at her in silence as she dried his feet, legs, balls and dick before turning her attention to his upper body. No words needed. The words were in the way she touched him as she dried his body. He reached for her, held her close, and allowed the warmth of her body to merge with his.

"One more time before you leave?" she looked up at him with a quiet plea in her eyes. He nodded yes. He wanted to make love to her as much as she wanted him. They had two hours before he had to leave so they laid down in bed, naked under the covers. Their bodies wrapped tightly together. She listened to the sound of his heart beating against her face. It was a sound she would not mind waking up to everyday and having him naked in bed next to her. He was still here in bed with her but the thought of leaving him, and him leaving her, crept slowly into her mind. Tears stained her face again as she buried her face in his hairy chest. He was fast asleep and she closed her eyes to join him in his dreams.

3/21/09…12:42pm

# Crack Dick

Every few minutes J would peek out the window of her 3rd floor apartment window in the projects to see if Mitchell was walking up the block. The usual gang of suspects from the projects was hanging on the corner smoking weed and blasting rap music below her apartment window, which was close to the street. A haze of smoke drifted lazily through her bedroom window; J expertly inhaled, and then swallowed it as if she was swallowing Mitchell's *babies*. J thought she recognized one of the street pharmacists on the corner as her ex-boyfriend Spliff, but it turned out not to be him. He was a crazy-ass ex-boyfriend who still thought that the pussy was his and claimed to have *mad* love for her even though he was fucking everything in sight.

They didn't have sex anymore but he still looked out for her, and everyone knew not to mess with her or else they would have to answer to Spliff. He was never able to tame her pussy the way that Mitchell did. Licking all those blunt papers to smoke his weed had gotten him the name Spliff. His tongue had become quite good at licking the papers and licking her pussy, but his *dick game* wasn't anything to brag about. It was lame but she never threw it back in his face that he couldn't fuck her the way that she needed. You just never know how a man might react if you tell him that his dick game is soft. He might take it well or he might kill your ass. The King Projects was still abuzz with activity as if it was the middle of the day. J checked her voice message again to make sure her cell phone was working, but the motherfucker *still* hadn't called as yet.

He never called.

She always waited.

He was always sorry and promised to do better. She always forgave him as soon as he pried her legs open to fill her pussy up with his crack dick. She would forget all her bitching and moaning, and get high on his ten-inch crack dick pipe. Her pussy would smoke it to the very last inch until she lay quivering in bed in need of another fix. J had never been addicted to anything in her life before Mitchell. All she did now was constantly daydream about him and having sex with his dick.

She didn't think about him—just his dick. She sometimes wondered if she loved his dick more than she loved him. Sahara, her best friend, joked that the next time he fell asleep; she should make a cast of his dick. That way, she would always have his dick without needing him. J was strung-out and needed a doggy style hit—a few back shots of him riding her ass would do the trick. She shook her head at how pathetic and needy she was for this man. The first time they fucked, she came so many times that she lost count and had to call in sick from work because she was so exhausted. He bent her body into so many positions that she felt like a used pretzel after he was through with her. Sweat dripped down their bodies and they lay in a pool of sweat and cum. Half an hour later, they were back at it again and it was the beginning of J's dependency on Mitchell's crack dick.

Like a pusher, he knew just how to keep her hooked. Some weeks he would come by everyday for seven days straight to feed her pussy, and life would be blissful. Her body would be accustomed to having him inside of her, but then, he would just disappear for about a month without even calling. He would claim to be working odd hours on special projects (she still wasn't quite sure what he did for a living), and she would offer to come to his place but he always found a reason to decline the invitation. At first, his mysterious nature sparked her interest, but after a few months of his cloak and dagger act;, she felt stupid for allowing herself not to see the truth. After a month, he would show up and soothe her anger by slowly fucking her into a coma until she forgot everything and forgave him again.

It was a pathetic cycle of dependency, which held her pussy in its grip of dick addiction. The power of the dick can leave even the strongest minded woman quivering in a pool of her own cum and waiting for her next orgasmic release. Every time she tried to get off the crack dick and go about her life; something would happen to start her reminiscing again the way his dick spoke to her body. She would masturbate until she had Carpal Tunnel in her fingers and still her pussy would be on fire. She would curse her stupidity as she dialed his number, but was unable to help herself. She needed a fix. He had her strung out worse than a wino who loved his liquor.

Two hours earlier, Mitchell had called talking that sweet shit that always got J's panties wet, her clit throbbing, and her pussy smiling like a stupid schoolgirl in love. She was far from a schoolgirl, but still held on to the belief that she would fall in love and be loved by a man deserving of her mind and heart, and not just her pussy. They all seemed to fall in love with her pussy but never with her. Her heart had been broken many times before by silver-tongued men who promised to love her until the day she died, but they always left after the pussy became too familiar. She was always replaced with someone new, but definitely not better. New doesn't mean better, but men just seem incapable of being satisfied with one pussy, no matter how sweet it is to them.

J was pushing thirty, and she was tired. Like most women, J was still hopeful that there was still one good guy left out there to love her. Men knew that this belief kept most women going long after they should have given up on their sorry trifling asses and it was that simple belief of finding a good man in a city of players that kept the pussy flowing for every man who knew how to work a woman's mind. They fed them the drink of hope with sexy smiles, empty promises and sex that felt like love—but in the end just turned out to be sex. A momentary distraction from reality.

"Just make sure your sweet ass is naked," Mitchell told her. "We fucking like rabbits as soon as I get there. I got a dick headache and your pussy is the aspirin."

The stupid chauvinistic stuff that came out Mitchell's mouth always made J laugh out loud at his arrogance, but it also made her cringe at how she was wrapped around his finger like a piece of string. All she wanted was for a man to see past the sweetness of her pussy, and see how beautiful her heart was also. There should be a timer on your pussy. It would stay locked until there was reasonable assurances that a man was genuine with his affections, and only then would it open to release the honey to the bee buzzing above it. The problem is when most men smiled at a woman, all four of her lips usually got wet, and the combination to the pussy could easily be read in her eyes. It's not a conscious unlocking, but soft drizzles of arousal start to flow and he knows that the combination is just a kiss away waiting to be tasted on your lips.

"You always chat that bullshit when you need this pussy, but you never be answering your damn phone when I call." J's voice was angry now. Drinking almost an entire bottle of Alize and smoking two joints always made her more emotional. "Why you treat me this way all the time like I'm some kinda fucking *jump off* or some whore bitch? I know I'm not your woman, but I ain't no *jump off* either. You better start treating me right or someone else is gonna get this sweet pussy you say you love so damn much."

Drink in one hand and cell phone in the other, J walked around her apartment in black thongs and high heels and continued to rage to Mitchell about how he treated her with disrespect. She was near tears but got it together before the waterworks started to fall.

This drama with J had been going on for a year now, so Mitchell knew the deal. He would let her vent, and then soothe her with the words that always got him through the door and into her panties. Ultimately, that was all he cared about. She was great in bed and gave great head. He would miss her pussy should he lose it, but there was always more pussy to be found in a place like New York. Some other man could have the rest of this drama, woman bullshit she was trying to lay on him. All he wanted was to bust a big nut, have his dick sucked, and then fall asleep. You would think that after a year, she would know this by now; some women need a building to fall on them to get the picture that they are nothing more than a piece of pussy to a man. Funny thing is, even after they know that a man is just sticking around for the pussy—they will try to change his mind. If it starts off as a pussy thing—it will end up the same way. A man can't lose even when he fucks up. Pathetic.

"I'm sorry baby," he said for the thousandth time. "There's no excuse for my behavior especially since you're always so good to me. I miss you baby and I need to see you."

His voice had dropped to barely a whisper to emote sincerity and longing. J would fall for his bullshit every time. Mitchell knew how his words and dick affected J. He knew she was crying silently at his sincerity, and he promised to make it up to her as soon as he got there. Two hours later, he walked through the projects empty handed and headed to her apartment. From the corner of his eyes, he saw her looking out the window already naked, and she was probably having a pussy stroke at being kept waiting again. He would soon make her forget her anger and replace it with moans of intense passion. Mitchell knew the one thing that he needed to know, J had low-esteem, and he used it every time to get what he needed from her. It was like a pimp taking money from a hooker, every time it just got sweeter.

Slumming down to the projects about twice a month to fuck J had been a new experience for Mitchell. In this instance, the stereotype of what he imagined was all too real: the stench of weed permeated the air, music of the most profane kind filtered through the radios and rapped to precision by the young black men loitering in front of J's building. With his IPod blasting the sweet sounds of Dave Matthews in his ears, he would hurriedly walk by them and exhale a sigh of relief once he was in her building. He never took the elevator because it was too slow and there was always a surprise of some disgusting kind waiting for his eyes and nose. The staircase wasn't that much better. There were a few times he would have to navigate around a passed-out, drunken person, a drug deal going down, and even a couple in the throes of passion. He might as well have been invisible because they never paid attention to him. He was safe. They knew he was either slumming to get some project pussy or looking to score some weed.

Either way, he didn't care what they were doing so they let him go about his business in the projects.

A few minutes had passed and still she hadn't opened the door. *Every time I have to go through this shit with this girl*, Mitchell thought to himself. *Why the fuck do I keep coming back?* It was the best damn sex and blowjobs he had ever had in his thirty-five years, and he wasn't about to give it up that easily no matter how much a pain-in-the-ass seeing her could be at times.

He lived out in Long Island with his wife and three kids who were away visiting relatives in Connecticut. He loved his wife but in ten years of marriage, she had never once made him feel the way that J did when they had sex. The sex was good between them, but there was a comfort level that felt rehearsed and lacking spontaneity after a lifetime of marriage. It's true what they say about a man wanting a *lady in the street and a whore in the bed*. The whore in his wife didn't exist. She wouldn't allow herself to just cut loose. On the few occasions when she would give him a blowjob, it often felt like a stranger was touching his dick and was inspecting it like a doctor and not a woman who relished sucking dick. She would make faces and look for a spot that was least offensive to her delicate sensibilities. She wouldn't really suck it like a dick is supposed to be deep-throated. It was more like a tasting test. The whole thing was quite frustrating to Mitchell, and he would get more satisfaction masturbating before taking a shower.

He loved his wife, but sometimes he didn't know if he was in love with her anymore. With J, the sex was

206

the kind of sex you saw in porno movies. She would let him fuck her anywhere, at any angle; she moaned and screamed from the minute he entered her, and it made him feel virile. His wife behaved as if his dick was an intruder into her pussy and mouth, but J welcomed it in all of her sweet holes. In some ways, he knew that he was addicted to her pussy, but would never admit or show it. He had to keep the upper hand in order to keep their relationship in balance.

"It took your black ass long enough to get here," J said to him when she finally opened the door.

She had been standing there the whole time and wanted to make him suffer, but she was the one dying inside to feel him close to her again. She could see his juicy lips through the peephole of the door and was unconsciously rubbing her clit. Not wanting him to change his mind and leave, she finally opened the door and pretended to be upset, but she was happy that he came to see her again. Mitchell would smile at her and hug her, but it always felt distant to J as if it wasn't a genuine hug of affection. More like something that felt necessary to get her into bed. It was only during sex would he allow himself to open up to her when she spread her legs—then he would become vulnerable and treat her with compassion.

She was far from a beautiful woman. However, she was sexy with her size two waist and small round *Love and Basketball* ass; but once men gazed up from her ass to her face; the look on their faces usually was a telling sign for J. There wasn't anything discernibly *fugly* about her except that the lower right side of her face was slightly burned. An ex-lover in a weed-induced haze had poured hot water on her face forever scarring her dark skin. She wasn't able to afford plastic surgery, so the alternative was make up and long weaves to hide her scar. In the year that she had dated Mitchell, he never asked about it and she didn't volunteer any information. She sometimes wondered if it didn't matter to him that she was scarred or maybe that he just didn't give a shit, and all she was to him was a warm, tight pussy.

In the dark of her bedroom, Mitchell would shut his eyes and the only thing he could feel was the ecstasy rummaging around in his balls and aching in his dick. He might as well be blind because he kept his eyes shut the whole time and saw her with his hands, mouth, fingers and tongue. They were his eyes as he fucked and made love to her.

Dressed in a flimsy black thong and high heels, Mitchell imagined J as a streetwalker, and the erection in his pants shifted at the scent of pussy in his vicinity. Her apartment was dark and lit only by the light from the streetlights streaming through the windows. It was more than enough to give him a full view of her body. What she lacked in beauty was aptly made up with a body that screamed sexuality. Her breasts were a nice handful with dark nipples that always seemed erect; a line of soft baby hair ran down the middle of her flat stomach and led directly to her clean-shaven peach, which was always wet and ready for penetration.

"You see something you like, fucker?" J said with a smirk in her face. She was already wet from being angry, the liquor and the weed. Her pussy was horny and didn't care if Mitchell was an asshole. He was an asshole with a crack dick.

"Bet you won't be talking that shit in a minute when I'm fucking the shit out of my pussy."

"Stop running your damn mouth and do it. If I wanted to watch a fucking talk show I would turn on Oprah. This ain't your pussy by the way— motherfucker."

J turned around to give him a look at the ass he'd been neglecting and started walking back to the bedroom. He grabbed her at the elbow and she spun into his body. Before she could protest, the heat of his tongue had snaked into her mouth and she swallowed her words. His erection pressed against the outsides of her pussy and made her clit throb with excitement. She turned to the side to avoid his penetration. She knew this would only make his dick harder when she resisted him. The fact that he was two hours late was slowly fading into her memory because she didn't need to be angry right now. She needed to be pleasured. It never took much for J to forget how angry she was at Mitchell for often treating her like an after thought. She thought the least he could do was bring some flowers or candy to make up for his bad behavior, but now, candy and flowers were the last things on her mind. The only thought raging in her pussy was the need to be dicked down for hours, or until she couldn't take anymore.

209

Mitchell never left her unsatisfied, which in her book was a big plus. It was only after he left that she felt like a whore for letting him treat her like a *jump off*. For now, she just wanted his *cock-of-pleasure* to be buried like a bone inside her hungry pussy.

Mitchell never wasted any time when he came over. He was on the clock. Conversation was limited to the pleasantries and he would toss in a few soft compliments to feed her ego, but he never asked about her day, how her job was going, or just basic stuff that a man who cares about you would ask. Other than that, it was straight to the bedroom, or not unlike this very moment, up against the wall. J was a tiny woman; Mitchell could stand to lose a few pounds from his two hundred and seventy five pound, six foot frame, but J liked her men big like Mitchell.

She enjoyed the feeling of being lost in a man and overwhelmed by his physical presence and sexual prowess. The high heels had slipped off her feet and her underwear lay at her feet in a bunch. She had assumed the position for penetration: hands laid flat on the wall, head tilted forward, and ass cocked slightly in the air to receive Mitchell's erect manhood; but the fucker always teased her by letting the head of his dick tease her enlarged pussy lips. That shit drove her crazy because it built up her frustration to a crescendo until he plunged his dick deep into her waiting wetness.

"Don't tease me like that baby," her voice was low and aching with passionate lust to feel him inside of her.

She was *feening* for his crack dick. Mitchell knew his dick was like crack to J because she repeatedly told him how addicted she was to it, and in the next breath, would tell him how much she hated him and wished that a building fell down on his black ass. J had good dick before, but the way Mitchell fucked her was the way a man should fuck a woman. He fucked her body, mind, and soul, and he wouldn't stop even after she came—he would continue fucking her. She would lie in bed after they had finished fucking, her body physically unable to take anymore dick, but she still craved to feel it inside of her. She needed dick rehab in the worst way to wean her pussy off it, but she was too weak to even contemplate being without him. Right after he was finished spraying all of his cum inside of her pussy walls, sleep would take him away to *Snore Land*. While he slept, J would turn him over on his side and suck his flaccid penis. She felt pathetic for wanting him so desperately, but grateful to be the one on the receiving end of his dick.

After a brief half hour nap to recuperate, Mitchell would spread her ass open from the back and squeezed it so hard that J cried out in pleasurable pain. She loved when he did that before submerging his dick inside of her pussy. So forceful was his penetration that she almost literally climbed the walls like Spiderwoman until they rolled off the bed onto the carpeted floor. Mitchell wrapped his hands around J's tiny spider waist, and with his dick still inside her pulsating wet pleasure; he lifted her off the floor with her back against his and her ass bouncing off his chest. J somehow spun herself around and jumped into his arms, landing directly on his erection. The force of her landing on his erection caused her to shudder and scream out like a cat being beaten by its master. Mitchell grabbed J's ass like store bought melons, and fondled them knowingly while he continued to pile drive his dick inside of her crack dick addicted pussy.

"Fuck me baby," she whimpered as she bounced up and down on his cock like a trampoline. "You fuck me like a dream!"

"Tell me it's mine! Tell me you love me," he ordered her as J's pussy juice dripped down his shaft. He savagely fucked her and J bit down into his shoulders to stop from screaming. She didn't want her neighbors to hear her coming with a force that would leave her weak and professing love for a man she didn't even know. She knew his dick, but she didn't know him.

"I love you baby," she said in answer to his question. *"You know this pussy is yours. It's yours anytime you want it, daddy."*

The muscles of her pussy gripped Mitchell's shaft and milked it until he erupted like a volcano inside of her. J had already come multiple times, and feeling Mitchell's geyser of hot cum exploding inside of her brought her to another one. They both laid down on the bed; Mitchell on his back still trying to catch his breath and J in a fetal position with her weave sweated out, and her pussy throbbing like a migraine headache.

"You want some water, baby?"

He nodded yes.  A stupid smile of self-satisfaction was etched on his face.  J glanced at Mitchell's dick still semi-erect, and kissed it as she left the room.  It didn't take much to put him to sleep after sex.  *What is about men that one minute after sex, they suddenly lose interest in a woman?*  It's as if all their strength is in their penis, and once it's emptied of all its cum—they're useless for everything else.  It doesn't take much too just hold your woman in your arms and let her know that you appreciate her as you fall asleep.  *Selfish bastards, the whole lot of them,* J thought to herself as she bent over in the refrigerator butt-naked.  The cold air felt good against her still hot skin.  If she didn't know any better, it felt as if Mitchell's dick was still inside of her, and was being used as a third leg to prop her up.  J cracked open a bottle of Corona, tilted her head backwards, and drank half the bottle in three swallows.  Mitchell's snoring had left the room and followed her into the kitchen.  It sounded as if someone was choking him as he struggled for air.  She finished off the rest of the Corona and walked slowly back to her room with a bottle of water.

J wondered what it would feel like to put a pillow over Mitchell's face and suffocate him in his sleep.  The thought made her smile as she watched him from the doorway of her bedroom.  She was sure no one knew where he was, and he probably had never mentioned her name to any of his friends.  She was a ghost in his life.  The sudden realization saddened J and she knew once again that it was time to get this monkey off her back.  She didn't know where this man lived, his real name, or

213

anything that could prove he existed in the world. Every time she would ask him anything personal, he would automatically change the subject and try to get in her panties. He had a one-track mind. There were worse men in the world than him, but he did nothing to dispel the notion that he possessed only one single, redeeming quality. She loved him and there was no use in fighting the truth—her heart and body were addicted to him and his crack dick.

"Here baby," she whispered and opened the bottle of water for him. He took a long drink without even opening his eyes, and handed her back the bottle expecting her to be there waiting to receive it.

In an hour, he would be going back to his family and this excursion to the projects will be the furthest thing from his mind. The beauty of being in J's company was that it allowed him not to think, allowed his predatory instincts to take over. In his mind, it was purely sex. J had done the unthinkable by falling for a man she could never have; he didn't want her in that way. How could she love a man so deeply that she would do anything for him? J was certain that beyond the sex Mitchell didn't care for her in the slightest. A few times, she had threatened to stop seeing him, but he remained unfazed. Mitchell told her that he would understand if she couldn't see him anymore. Afraid of losing him, J always quickly relented. She was hooked, and the only way that this sick dependency would end is if he ended it. She crawled into bed next to his naked body and limp penis, and lifted his arms to put around her. Maybe in time, when he realized that she was a good woman and that she truly loved him, Mitchell would come to his senses and appreciate her. Hope was all J had left as she fell asleep in his arms dreaming dreams that would never come true.

9-17-06...1:14am

# The Sexy Marriage

"You look beautiful this morning, Ms. Robinson," Malik said to his wife of five years as he stepped out of the shower leaving a trail of water dripping behind him and quickly disappearing into the green bathroom rug. His manhood was already rising as he eyed her large honey colored nipples and slid his tongue over his lips in anticipation of sucking on both of them like a hungry baby in need of its daily feeding.

Dominique hated when Malik stepped out of the shower without toweling off, but that was one of the small things she learned to let go of during their marriage. In a marriage, you pick and choose your battles and the ones worth battling—win them. Don't sweat the small stuff because they only cause a distraction. Besides, no woman in her right mind would complain about seeing a specimen like her husband stepping out of the shower looking like a wet, black god coming to claim his queen with a dick so thick that her mouth ached for days after sucking it. It was the kind of sweet aching that she enjoyed feeling and Dominique loved giving her husband pleasure just as much as he enjoyed pleasuring his wife.

Dominique inspected her husband's wet, naked body as he approached her with his dick swinging between his legs as if he were Tarzan and a cheesy grin plastered on his dark cleanly shaven face. That look was his mating call alerting her that he was hungry, and his "lion" needed to be fed the plump lips between her now thickened thighs.

She didn't feel beautiful anymore. She felt fat and insecure about her weight gain. She knew it was ridiculous, but the rapid increase in weight around her ass, legs, feet, face and belly had come as a shock to her.

"Baby, you're not fat", Malik always insisted as he would kiss her cheeks and lips, rub her round belly and her massage her swollen feet. "You're eight months pregnant with our first child. How would you look being skinny and eight months pregnant?" He always knew what to say to make her laugh.

The image staring back at her in the bathroom mirror was that of a fat woman. Gone was her thick shapely size ten curves, replaced by a belly the size of four basketballs, her breasts were now a 40DD and her nostrils looked like an open highway for trucks to roll on through. Malik either was a bold face liar, blind or just loved her regardless of what she looked like. Whatever it was, she was thankful that his desire for her had not waned during the pregnancy. In fact, it seemed that he wanted her more than ever. If it were possible to get pregnant while you were pregnant, he would have impregnated her with an entire village by now. "There just seems to be an extra fire that's been lit in your pussy since we've become pregnant," he would say. He always said we when referring to her pregnancy.

Steam rose from the shower as Malik ran his wife's bath for her. He made sure that it was exactly the right temperature because he didn't want it to be so hot

217

that she couldn't soak comfortably. During the last eight months, he tried to anticipate every conceivable thing that could go wrong and fix it before it happened. His job as her husband was to make sure that he gave her what she needed to be happy and comfortable. The bathroom had an aroma of Rainwater, which was Dominique's favorite bubble bath scent. Later, when she slipped into her bath, Malik would turn off the lights and light a few of her mango scented candles. It always relaxed her and she would often fall asleep and awaken to Malik gently stroking her cheeks and kissing her forehead. Sometimes she would pretend to still be sleeping just so he would continue kissing her like that.

The sight of Malik's throbbing manhood briefly angered Dominique because it was his dick's fault that she looked like a fat cow. It had fed her all of its cum until she was now literally bursting out of her panties. Despite her feelings about her weight gain, Dominique was excited about becoming a mother for the first time, and Malik would make a great father. All the kids in her family loved coming over because Uncle Malik was so much fun and so cool. Even after ten years of being together, he still managed to take her breath away. He was the kind of man where even on his worst day, his kindness and compassion could outshine everybody else's.

"I was raised by good women," he always said. He was a man's man with the sensitivity of a woman.

It didn't hurt that he was very easy on the eyes and blessed with a dick and stamina that would put any man to shame. He stood six feet tall, a dark skinned complexion that enticed you to touch him to feel its smoothness. He had dreadlocks that were shoulder length and immaculately maintained and teeth that shone when he smiled; a smile that could make even a blind woman wet with desire. Sometimes she thought that he was too good to be true, but over the last ten years he had proven himself a man of his word possessing a character of men from a different generation. He was the kind of man that women prayed for but never got. Dominique knew how lucky she was to have Malik as a husband—especially after everything she put him through.

"Feed the lion," he breathed into her right ear as the heat of his naked body enveloped her nakedness from the back. His body, still wet from his shower pressed hard into Dominique's back, and she felt his manhood growing stiff between the slit of her plump ass cheeks. He wrapped his arms around her protruding belly and laced his fingers together to hold her closer into his body. The thumping of his heartbeat vibrated against her back and Dominique closed her eyes to feel the love Malik felt for her and their unborn child. They shared a connection that didn't need to be expressed in words or any discernable action. It was palpable in the silence of their thoughts when they read the paper together, when they held hands together, when they watched their favorite movie, "Love Jones," when he reached for her naked body under the covers to pull her into the center of his warmth and when she could feel his eyes caressing her body at anytime during the day. She knew that she was loved. At times, reflecting on his love for her gave her goose bumps and would often bring her to tears. He would never wipe her tears away when she cried, but would kiss her cheeks as her tears stained his lips. He would kiss her and the saltiness of her own tears would make her even hungrier for this man—her husband.

The temperature of his skin rose with each kiss that he planted on her shoulders and back, setting her body on fire—he was the match. His body felt like a warm blanket draping over her and it made her swoon as if she was suffering from heatstroke. Dominique grabbed the edges of the bathroom sink as Malik used his tongue to make circles under her shoulder blades. It was one of her weak spots and he lightly bit into her fleshy skin to arouse her even further. A sweet moan of desire trembled from between Dominique's lips as her body anticipated his next move. He would usually kneel down and lick the fullness of her ass, but this time, he changed up his tempo and spread her ass open. The lion was **very** hungry and couldn't wait any longer to be encased inside the heat of her pregnant pussy.

"I can't wait any longer, baby. Feed the lion some sweet pork before he dies from starvation," he growled in between kisses on her back and neck.

A smile crossed Dominique's face and Malik gazed at her in the mirror. Her beauty was undeniable to him. Her brown eyes were always smiling and her pregnancy made her eyes even warmer. He knew the weight gain had been hard on her, and he had done everything to reassure her that he still found her beautiful and sexy—which was the absolute truth. Her light complexion had grown increasingly darker as the months went on and everything just got bigger and wider. At 6'0, 200 lbs, Malik was a big man so he didn't have any problem handling his wife in the bedroom. The pregnancy had added on an extra 50 lbs to her 5'9, 145 lbs figure. There was something extra sexy and wonderful about pregnant pussy that made Malik hunger for his wife. Maybe it was just his freaky imagination, but it just felt as if the fire between her lips was always set on high. She was hot before the pregnancy, but being inside of her now felt like a sauna.

Dominique eased away from the bathroom sink and backed Malik up against the green wall that they painted together when they bought the house. He unlocked his fingers and was now gently rubbing her belly. The touch of his hands slowly caressing her roundness stimulated her body and she felt her wetness begin to pour. His hands wandered all over her body; massaging the thickness of her thighs as his erection grinded slowly behind her, kisses of heat surged through her body when his lips closed around her ears and he bit her gently. Her body vibrated against his as she went weak, but she knew that she would not fall. Her man had her wrapped strongly in his arms.

"Do that again baby," a voice that didn't sound like hers said hoarsely.

"Like this?" he asked innocently as the tip of his tongue probed her inner ear. "Yesssss"…like that baby," she could barely get the words out of her mouth before she felt the familiar engorged head of his manhood probing her outer lips. Her body was on *go* and there were no roadblocks up ahead to deter his penetration. Pregnancy had made Dominique hornier than normal— which wasn't saying much. She always wanted sex and Malik was always ready to deliver like the maintenance man. He was gentler now since the pregnancy even though the doctor had assured him that he couldn't hurt the baby. He remained unconvinced. "This dick has far reaching powers. The doctor doesn't know how long I am. Fuck around and I might be tapping the baby on its head." His silly and doting nature made the pregnancy easier on Dominique. Her mood swings had made her quite demanding and, at times, she would break down in tears apologizing for her unseemly behavior. "Don't worry baby. Nothing you say can get rid of me," and then he would hold her and kiss her belly.

Malik mumbled something unintelligible sounding like a man inebriated on passion as the smooth thickness of his erection filled the tight pink walls of Dominique's pregnant pussy. She loved the feel of him sliding in and out of her and his dick seemed to have a mind of its own—as if it could instantly sense the right rhythm to stroke her to elicit her passionate moans. His fingers manipulated her erect nipples and gently massaged her aching breasts as they fell into his waiting hands without any resistance.

She reached over her head with both hands and worked her fingers into the thickness of his dreadlocks to massage his scalp. He loved it when she played with his hair. It was an extension of his dick, and the more she pulled and massaged it, the harder he would get until he would explode inside of her with a passion that left him drained and panting like a dog thirsty for water. She kept her eyes closed because the image of her big belly wasn't the mental picture she wanted during sex. She imagined herself fifty pounds lighter with smaller thighs and breasts. Her man was turned on by it all so it couldn't be all that bad.

Malik struggled to keep his composure as he lengthened his strokes to keep himself from coming. Dominique's hands reached under the weight of his hair to massage his neck. It was her way of letting him know that it was all right to come. He had been an attentive husband and deserved this quickie. Today was Sunday and they had the rest of the day for her to get hers. Malik braced himself against the wall, tilted his head backwards and allowed himself the pleasure of feeling his passion for his wife leave his body and enter hers with repeated explosions of his warm fluids. He stayed still inside of her wetness as their fluids mixed and his erection gradually lost its strength to fall limply from inside of her.

Dominique turned around and both his hands met her protruding belly as they gently massaged her belly. His breathing was still heavy as if he had just run a marathon. She reached between his legs and closed her hand around his sticky manhood. Her fingers closed tighter around it and he closed his eyes as she stroked him back to life.

"The lion is still hungry?"

"Always hungry for you baby," he said as he bent down to kiss her lips.

She released his growing manhood from her hand and wrapped her hands around his neck. They kissed with a passion that went beyond their ten years of being together. It was as if they had just met for the first time and were discovering the slippery wetness of their tongues and mouths coming together to feed the hungry desires of a new couple. His kisses always made Dominique certain that Malik's love for her was forever. The way she kissed him often made Malik feel as if he were watching All My Children or General Hospital. It was the intensity of those kisses that made him sure that he had chosen the right woman to marry, share a life with and to have his children.

The tub was now filled with water and the aroma of her Rainwater bubble bath intoxicated the air. Malik loved how she smelled after a bath and how she would meticulously rub her body down with those delicious lotions from either Bath and Body or Victoria's Secret. They smelled so good on her that he sometimes thought about rubbing himself down with it. A few of the women at the office had commented on how secure he must be in his masculinity to go around smelling so sweet. As long as his wife didn't have a problem with it, Malik could care less what anybody else thought about his masculinity.

Dominique put one foot into the tub while Malik held her hand and she slowly descended into its warmth until her entire body was submerged. The top of her belly stuck out above the water level and she cupped two full hands of bubbles to cover it.

"Just relax baby," Malik said to Dominique as she stared up at him and his dick swung back and forth like a pendulum. "I will get you a glass of orange juice and some fruits."

With her eyes closed, she nodded in his direction. He lit her favorite mango candles and hit the play button on the CD player. Stevie Wonder's "Isn't She Lovely" started to play. It was their wedding song and he had tried to sing it to her as they danced, but finally relented and let Stevie do his thing. He gently closed the door behind him and walked downstairs to get her some OJ and a bowl of fruit .

Earlier that morning, they had braved the cold winter temperatures outside to attend the Catholic Church where they had been married five years ago. Father John's sermon was lively and his words seemed to speak to Dominique and Malik about communication and their reasons for getting married. He also warned the congregation of *haters*, and hearing him use that word made the congregation laugh out loud. "There will be people who want to see you failing," he warned them, "by whispering in your ears untruths because they want what you have. The devil is trying to steal your happiness. Don't let him! Hold on to it as if it was your last breath. Can I get an Amen?" Everyone in the church sang out amen in unison and burst into the next song, "Amazing Grace."

Malik and Dominique tried to sneak out just as the service was over, but Father John had the eyesight of a hawk and called out to them as Malik helped Dominique down the church steps. Malik quickly scanned the stairs looking for any slippery spots but did not find any. Father John hurriedly brushed by a few parishioners and promised to speak to them later. A few of the older ladies cut their eyes at him and muttered under their breaths, but they would wait for him as long as it took for him to notice them again.

"Here's my favorite couple trying to sneak away before I caught up with them," he said jokingly but they knew he was serious. Everything Father John said had an intended message. He embraced Dominique and shook Malik's hands. "It looks like you're about to give birth at any minute," without asking for permission, he patted her belly under her winter coat. Dominique cringed but didn't say anything. Even strangers had taken to touching her belly without her permission.

"It's good to see you Father. I'm just trying to get my wife home before the storm hits this morning."

Father John looked off into the sky and saw the increasing dark clouds were coming closer. He seemed to want to say something but decided better of it. Dominique discreetly tugged Malik's hand signaling they should make their getaway now.

"We will see you next week Father John," Dominique said as they started to walk down the steps.

"Be sure to let me know when your blessing is born so I can drop by the hospital to say a prayer," he said to their backs as they walked away. Father John was a wonderful man, but he could talk the ears off Don King if you allowed him. He had been very helpful when they were going through a rough patch in their marriage and they would always be grateful to him for his insights. The sky opened up and shed its tears right after Dominique buckled herself into the front passenger seat.

Malik heard Dominique humming to the baby as he walked back upstairs with her orange juice and an assortment of sliced fruits. He stopped outside the bathroom door for a few minutes and listened as she spoke to their unborn child.

"You are a child born into love and mommy and daddy love you so, *so much*," Dominique whispered softly as she rubbed her belly. "God brought you as a special gift to us. Your brothers and sisters would be so happy to have met you."

At the mention of the children they had lost, tears rolled down Malik's cheeks freely as he remembered the loss of their previous three children. Dominique had been unable to carry their previous three children to term. The loss of each child brought a deeper sense of loss for both of them—especially Dominique. She had taken each loss personally as if God was punishing her for her past transgressions. Fearing that she would be unable to give Malik the children he so desperately wanted, she tried to push him away, but Malik knew her heart and waited until the real Dominique came back.

She belittled his manhood by telling him that his sperm was weak and that's why all their children died. She openly flirted with men while he was with his friends and family; one of those flirtations turned into a brief affair and still, Malik stood by his wife's side. His friends and family urged him to leave her. No man should endure the mental abuse that he suffered, but Malik would patiently tell all of them that he knew his wife and this woman doing all these hateful things was not his wife. His wife was somewhere, locked inside all of this imposter's self-hate and he knew that she was fighting and trying to find her way back to him. Although, there were times when Malik had his doubts, he kept them to himself. He was a prideful man and anger and embarrassment swelled inside of him, but somehow he knew, that Dominique would find her way back to their love—he just had to hold on.

"Why are you still here? Why haven't you left as yet?" Dominique had shouted at him after coming home late again and smelling of alcohol and cheap cologne. "What kind of man stays with a woman who doesn't have any respect for him and treats him like a little boy?" She practically spat the words to him.

"The kind of man who knows the kind of woman you are and I know this isn't you, baby. *This isn't us.* I still love you and I know you still love me," Malik said to Dominique with tears brimming in his eyes.

"Love? Love didn't save our children. God didn't love us enough to save our babies!"

"There is no limit to God's love for us and there is no limit for my love for you. We will have more children I promise you that, but right here, right now, we have to save us."

Malik approached his wife and continued to tell her how much he loved her and that nothing she did would drive him away. He rested his palm on her abdomen and again promised that they would have a baby. Dominique tried to pull away, to hide from the pain, but Malik wrapped her tightly in his arms as she broke down in tears. She cried for the three children they lost, she cried for herself and she cried for all the pain she had caused her husband. The next day they went to Father John to seek counseling and in the last year, they had become faithful Christians with a better understanding of themselves and the true meaning of what it means to be married.

"Who is that man crying by the door?" Dominique asked out loud as she continued to rub her belly. "That's your daddy little one," and a sudden kick from the baby sent gentle waves through the water. "Come here baby. Come give mommy and your baby some sugar."

Malik rested the orange juice and fruits on the wooden hamper and walked over to his wife. He knelt down on the floor, dipped his hand into the soapy water and placed it on his wife's round belly. Her large, erect nipples bobbed up and down above the water like a buoy in the middle of the ocean. The connection between Malik and Dominique was stronger than anything they

229

had ever felt in their life as the heartbeat of their unborn child pulsated between them. Soft tears rolled down Dominique's face because it was in that moment she finally realized all that she could have lost had it not been for her husband's belief in their love. Malik leaned over into the tub and kissed the tears streaming down his wife's beautiful face and he entered the large, circular tub. He helped his wife to her feet with her body covered in bubbles and he eased his long frame into the warm water.

"Come here."

Dominique lowered her body onto Malik as his strong hands guided her slowly onto his throbbing manhood and his fingers dug deep into her fleshy ass. A look of sweet pleasure flashed across her face and her lips trembled slightly when the thickness of his dick stretched her pussy open. He remained still, leaned back and watched his wife take all of him inside of her. Her body was barely moving, but inside, her muscles gripped his shaft and slowly massaged him into a frenzied arousal.

"You know just how I like it," Malik breathed heavily as he leaned forward carefully so as not to hurt his wife's belly. He leaned over to plant several kisses on it as she continued to ride him without a destination in mind. Their future was an adventure as long as they were together.

"Mmmmmm, you feel so damn good baby," her voice trembled as their lips met and the fire of their passion connected them once again.

Malik continued kissing his wife hungrily while using his fingers to gently squeeze her erect nipples. Her moans echoed with every squeeze and every time he pierced the heat of her pussy deeper, her body shuddered in anticipation of more inches of him. It felt like they were in the deep ocean, surrounded by water and the only thing that mattered was the love they felt for each other and their unborn child. Thoughts of how close she had come to losing her family surged through Dominique as Malik's wet tongue filled her mouth and his hands made love to her body bringing her to an orgasmic climax. Her fingers caressed his face and, as his eyes fluttered open, he released the heat of his passion into the tight walls of his wife's pussy.

"Stay inside of me," she whispered into his ear. "Don't ever leave me...*please*."

"I won't baby. You know I won't."

Dominique rested her head on Malik's wet shoulders and mouthed the words *thank you* as another orgasm rippled through her body. She had many things to be thankful for and she promised herself never to take her husband for granted ever again.

4-23-09...9:02pm

# The Sweet Dick Down

All day long Nina's clit had been throbbing and banging her like a drum major, knowing that in one hour it would be getting the sweet dick down from Jeremiah Heat. Her office was set at a cool temperature, but on days like this when she knew she would be getting the sweet dick down, everything she touched felt like it was on fire. She wanted to rip her blouse off and stick her throbbing nipples in a bucket of ice to cool them down, but her ache was so deep and intense that it would probably melt ice cubes. She needed the services of Jeremiah Heat to release all this excess energy being stored inside of her body.

If there wasn't a huge see-through window in her office, she would have already closed her office door, shut the blinds and stripped naked. She had done it before, late one evening when she was sure that everyone had gone home and masturbated herself into an orgasmic frenzy. The thought of maybe one of the cleaning women catching her gyrating naked on the carpet excited her even more and it made her come hard and loud. She came so hard that she squirted like a geyser in Central Park all over the carpet.

Nina also knew that the men in the office loved to walk by so they could sneak a peak at her. They were all so obvious in their pathetic attempts to be discreet but she didn't mind as long as they stayed in their lane, they could look but not touch. Nina never mixed business with pleasure.  At 6'0, 170 lbs, Nina Rogers was an intimidating woman to most people.  Her height and beauty intimidated most men and women.  She wore her hair in dreads, which were shoulder-length and colored with a touch of auburn.  She carried an air of arrogance that she fully cultivated and embraced.  Her brown eyes and round face were filled with the fire of a woman who knew her place—which was anywhere she wanted it to be.  Nina Rogers had more balls than most men did, but every woman craves to be a woman and wants to feel sensual and beautiful in the arms of a man.  Jeremiah Heat satisfied that desire within her.  He saw through all her bullshit facades and saw the woman inside.  He knew how to take control without her giving it to him.  He knew how to be a man.

It was quiet outside of her office because everyone had abandoned ship at 5 p.m. to haul ass for their trains. She relished being alone at this time of day.  It was hard work being the Vice President of the New York office of a successful magazine, Today's Woman.  Everyday was a stressful day.  Nina wondered sometimes why she did it, but she loved her job and wouldn't trade it for any other job in the world.  She got to hobnob with celebrities and politicians and made a ridiculous amount of money in the process.  The solitude of this time of day gave her time to think and plan for the next day's activities.  She had to be on her game everyday or someone else would take her place.  When you are black woman in charge, you have to work twice as hard to prove yourself everyday to your white bosses; and when you are a black woman you have to not only justify why you have this position, but prove that being a woman isn't a handicap-- it's an asset. It's no wonder that she needed a dick down pronto.

Her plump ass felt embedded in her chair so she got up to stretch her long legs. Her muscles were still sore and felt bruised from their last encounter just a week ago, but it was a sweet pain that made her body hungry for more. Beneath her gray business skirt suit, she was braless and her 38D breasts ached to be sucked and bitten until the pleasure was too much to bear. She also wasn't wearing any panties. She enjoyed knowing that when she spoke to her employees in the office that she was practically naked and within inches of them. The thought excited her and would often make her moist and make her warm nectar run down the inside of her thighs. The joys of going braless and without panties were an extra stimulation to help her get through these hectic days. Besides, the extra second or two it would take Jeremiah to remove her bra and panties were two more seconds that she would be without him inside of her. She couldn't wait that long.

She was listening in to her last conference call for the day with the California office which was three hours behind New York time. Talks about budgets, marketing strategies for the new fall campaign for the magazine couldn't hold her attention. She needed an extreme dick down to clear the cobwebs in her brain. The only thing on her mind was thoughts of having Jeremiah Heat deep inside of her and hurting her pussy until she screamed for mercy. The only mercy she craved was to be savaged and ravaged by his dick. He knew how to hurt her unlike any man she had ever been with before. She knew he would show her no mercy. It was part of their agreement in their contract. Her clit throbbed again in recognition of her thoughts. She soothed its anxieties through her cotton skirt, and if she wasn't on a conference call, she would have made herself come. There was nothing quiet about Nina Rogers when she had an orgasm. The thought of seeing the faces of the executives in the California office when they heard her screaming almost made Nina laugh out loud.

She kicked off her prized black pumps from Neiman Marcus and placed her feet on her desk. It felt good to be barefoot, and she sighed softly as her feet sunk into the plushness of the carpet. Her hands were free as she listened to the droning female voice of the VP of the California office fill up the remaining time with talking points. Finally, it was over and Nina hung up without even saying goodbye to anyone. The car service would be here in ten minutes to drive her to her apartment on Park Avenue and 86th street. She needed to freshen up before she left. A woman always has to have on her best face because you never know who you might meet in New York on any given night. New York is a stage and every night you have to give your best performance or there won't be an encore.

Jeremiah Heat was pissed. He was so upset that he almost ran into the car in front of him, but managed to swerve away just in time. He gunned his black Jeep

Cherokee onto the Bronx Expressway into Manhattan to meet Nina, but he wasn't too happy about it. It was his night off and told the agency not to page him under any circumstances, but they had called anyway because Miss Nina Rogers had demanded to see him or else she would take her business elsewhere. In any business, the customer is always right and usually gets their way. In his business giving the sweet dick down made his clients even more demanding and agitated when they couldn't get what they wanted. A horny woman was worse than a woman scorned in his line of work. Jeremiah had to make another bogus excuse about his brother being in trouble to his fiancée and left before she could really tear him a new asshole. There would be hell to pay when he came back home later that evening. He had to save at least one nut for her to swallow when he came back to quiet her down. Being blessed with a twelve inch dick came with its privileges. It was his *get out of free jail card*, and he used it like a Black American Express Card—he never left home without it. It was ready to be activated at all times.

Nina Rogers was his best client and she knew it. Lately, she had become more demanding and bossy. She would call him at random hours during the day at the agency, and now, was even sending him texts. She had even begun sending him flowers and other gifts at the office. He wasn't quite sure how she got his cell phone number because all transactions were done through *Well Hung* agency and clients were not allowed to have their Dicker's phone numbers for reasons of avoiding situations of sexual harassment. Jeremiah had been with *Well Hung* for five years and had been seeing Nina for over a year now, and engaged to his fiancée for the last three months.

He noticed that's when everything changed with Nina, when he accidentally mentioned his fiancée's name in passing and finally confessed to her the true nature of their relationship. She was quiet at first but then seemed genuinely happy for him. He should have known better because women in her position are used to being in control and don't like being second to anyone. He hated women like Nina Rogers who acted as if they ruled the world because they made more money, had their own office and could basically have any man they wanted. She had chosen him out of every man from the agency. She paid very well and that's another reason why he tolerated her, and she knew it. Money will make even the most independent person think twice about compromising their moral integrity.

Their initial meeting had been for drinks over a year ago at a local bar in the city during lunchtime. She ordered an Apple Martini and he ordered Cranberry juice. Jeremiah Heat never drank on the job. It was the first rule of being a maintenance man. Any inebriation could impair your performance, be it mental or physical, and that was bad for business. He had browsed her file earlier, which came with photographs and a background check before meeting her. The agency always e-mailed a potential client's complete records as an initial introduction. She seemed to be the typical busy business woman who just didn't have time to date or meet men. That's where his services came in for the many busy and wealthy working women of New York. His clientele was like a beautiful rainbow of women from all shades of African-American, Caucasian, Spanish, Asian, and European women. Jeremiah's dick did not discriminate when the call came to perform an immediate dick down. He prided himself on always being able to deliver. He was the Mailman; through any weather or situations, his package was always confirmed and ready to perform. He was their stress releaser so they could walk into a board meeting the next day completely relaxed and ready to do battle with corporate America.

As pissed as he was at Nina for pulling this shit on him; the sex was addictive because she was insatiable in her need to be pleased and to please him. Since he had mentioned his fiancée to Nina, she would ride and swallow him every time they were together until she was so sure that he had nothing left to give. Her motives were transparent to him, but he was too weak to stop her. Sex with Nina satisfied Jeremiah's deepest cravings, but he was smart enough to know that it was just a business arrangement and she enjoyed playing games with him. Just as much as she desired him, Jeremiah knew that she could easily discard him like a used condom and move on to the next man.

All of her friends warned Sedra that Jeremiah was the living incarnation of the Devil, but her girlfriends tended to exaggerate. They were all just jealous of this fine black man who had chosen her when he could have had any woman he wanted. Sedra loved her some Jeremiah Heat. He was the man she had been saving her virginity for all these years. At twenty-nine years, she was six years younger than Jeremiah, but he never treated her as if she was naïve and that made Sedra love him even more. They had been dating for almost a year now after meeting in the elevator of the Grand Hyatt on 42$^{nd}$ street. She was there for a conference with her church, and he was meeting an associate named Nina Rogers for dinner to discuss a new business venture. Sedra was instantly attracted to Jeremiah and that familiar dull ache of desire and lust sprung forth hard from between her thighs.

Her desires for sex would often consume her mind and body, and Sedra would pray fervently for deliverance from her sinful thoughts of fornication. Every week she would have to say at least one hundred Hail Mary's after confessing her sins at church. The thoughts she was having about Jeremiah would need an infinite amount of prayers before God could forgive her. Sedra could barely look at him as the elevator went up. The scent of his Eternity cologne made her flush. She was embarrassed about how she was feeling, but couldn't help wanting this beautiful man. He stood 6'9, dark complexion, broad football shoulders, shaved head, no tattoos or earrings, and lips that made her want to suck him like a baby sucking on a pacifier. He wore a tailored black suit that made him look as if he had just stepped off the covers of Ebony Man. Sedra felt the desire to step right into his arms and let him ravish her, but her religious beliefs had guided her life until now so she resisted all temptation. Later that evening, she ran into him again in the lobby and a conversation ensued. They had dinner that night and she informed him that she planned to stay a virgin until marriage. That confession didn't make him yell for the check, and a year later, they were still together.

There were many nights when Sedra wanted to give in to her desires to have Jeremiah fill her up with the same fervor that she felt for Jesus Christ. She loved two men, her Lord and savior Jesus Christ and Jeremiah Heat. God lived deep inside of her heart and soon she would have Jeremiah's thick heat deep inside of her hungry flesh. Her body and spirit would finally be fulfilled and she could scream for both the men she loved. The thought of that would make Sedra smile because the day was coming soon when Jeremiah would make love to her on their wedding night and every night after that.

After Jeremiah left to go meet his brother in the Bronx, Sedra tidied up all their clothes and sheets that they had thrown to the floor as they wrestled and she pretended to resist his advances. She loved how his dark naked body would cover her light skin and make her feel weak and protected at the same time. Sedra rationalized that being a virgin meant not being penetrated vaginally so she and Jeremiah engaged in oral sex on a regular basis. At first, the thought of having a man's penis inside of her mouth repulsed her, but after the first few minutes of feeling Jeremiah growing and pulsating inside of her mouth and between her lips, Sedra enjoyed the feel of his dick rubbing back and forth against her lips.

It excited her and made her feel powerful at the thought of this huge man moaning like a baby as she stroked him with hands and teased him with her lips and tongue. She was unprepared the first time when she felt his dick stiffen like a piece of brick inside of her mouth, and he held her head tightly between his hands until every inch of his erection slipped deep down inside of her throat. She had no choice but to swallow him as he came for over two minutes and fed her throat with his warm passion juice. Sedra thought he was having a seizure or maybe she was doing something wrong, but the look on his face told her that her man loved every second of the pleasure he had just experienced.

From that day on, Sedra relished sucking and swallowing her man's thickness. It was the least she could do for him to alleviate his sexual frustrations. He had been so patient and understanding about her wanting to stay a virgin until they got married. He never asked for sex and respected her wishes completely. Every time she performed oral sex on him, the urge to forget about being a virgin intensified as her legs would quiver without stopping, her pussy lips would ache so much that it hurt when Jeremiah would lovingly stroke his tongue over them. She would then sit on Jeremiah's face and he would suck on her lips hungrily as if drinking the sweet juices from a coconut. She loved how his lips felt on her bald pussy and couldn't wait until their wedding night to feel him inside of her.

Sedra was by all definitions a fox, a hottie...even for a church girl. She had a killer body that was hidden beneath conservative clothes. Her breasts were 38C with nipples that wouldn't quit. Her 5'7 frame was equipped with an ass that bounced like a yo-yo on a string and would definitely be bouncing high and hard when it finally got a sweet dick down from Jeremiah. When Sedra looked at any man with her grey eyes and pouty lips, even a man of God would think twice about giving his life to the church. It's hard to think about Jesus Christ when a woman who was molded by his hands is staring at you, and the only vision you see is her naked body calling to you to feed it dick. God made her in his image so he of all people had to understand how difficult such intense beauty can be to resist for any mortal man. Any man who desires God more than he craves the supple flesh of a woman is definitely a man of God who has a higher calling than any earthly pleasures. God bless that man!

It was always good to come home to her 18th floor apartment after a long day at the office. Nina closed the door behind her, but it remained ajar. Her pussycat ran to her and purred and rubbed up against Nina's bare legs. She popped in a Jill Scott CD and quickly discarded pieces of clothing as she walked to her bedroom. By the time she entered her bedroom, she was naked and ready for a shower. Bonkers purred again, this time more insistent.

"Mommy's baby is hungry?"

She bent down to stroke her Persian cat and her fingers got lost in its thick white fur. Bonkers purred as if she was starved for attention. Both of them had something in common. They were hungry to be fed. Both pussys would be fed, one with food, and the other with dick. Nina walked to the shower in her bedroom and turned on the water with Bonkers right at her heels. The hot water needed a few minutes to heat up so she walked back to the kitchen to feed a hungry Bonkers. Jill Scott sang to her as she walked by.

"My love is deeper, tighter…sweeter, higher didn't you notice…"

Only Jill can make pussy sound so innocent and naughty at the same time. Nina had tickets to see her next week at the Convention Center in Washington, DC. She would be there on business for the magazine.

She still had some time before Jeremiah got here. She knew he would be hitting traffic right about now, so she poured herself a glass of white wine and stepped onto her porch. Spring was her favorite time of the year. It wasn't too hot or too cold; a harmonious balance of nature. The cool air kissed her naked body then whispered kisses on her nipples and her shaven pussy. She closed her eyes and took a sip of wine and allowed the moment to take her away. Five minutes later, she entered her steaming shower and felt a little woozy from the half glass of wine. She wasn't a drinker and always had a hard time recollecting things the next day.

Jeremiah pulled in across the street from Nina's building and sat in his Jeep for a few minutes to cool down. His entire evening had been *fucked-up*. He had to leave his fiancée naked in bed. Nina was a bitch out of control. He had gotten stuck in traffic, and to make matters worse—an asshole cop had given him a ticket for speeding. It took thirty minutes before he was able to drive away. His mood was foul and he wanted to hurt someone to release all the tension he was feeling. He gathered his thoughts, stepped out of his Jeep, and took a black duffel bag from his truck. He was so focused on what he was planning as he crossed the street that he didn't notice it was starting to rain, and the car that pulled in two spaces behind him.

The security guard was nowhere in sight so he went straight to the elevator without signing in. As he got closer to the 18th floor, Jeremiah reached into his duffel bag to get his equipment ready. He didn't want any surprises tonight. He knew exactly where Nina kept her spare key. It was under a loose tile under her doormat. As Jeremiah approached the front door, he could see it was ajar; it wasn't the first time that Nina had forgotten to lock the door. She was careless that way. He had warned her that one day she would regret leaving it open. Tonight would be that night for Nina Rogers.

Jeremiah stepped inside and softly closed the door behind him. He heard the lock snap shut. She would have nowhere to go. The stupid cat with its bionic ears heard him come in, but didn't purr to alert Nina that he was here. She had just been fed and was laid out on the couch like a guest. Before he could take another step, the CD stopped and all was quiet. He heard her singing in the shower and knew he was safe. Quickly he put on a pair of black gloves and placed a stocking cap over his head to cover his face. He was dressed all in black and blended in nicely in the darkness of her apartment. She had exquisite taste. A few expensive art pieces hung on the walls and she had every piece of new electronic gadgets scattered all around her apartment. Finally, the next CD came on and instantly added energy to the quiet of the apartment. It was the frenetic rap patois of Busta Rhymes rapping, "Put Your Hands Where My Eyes Can See" it made Jeremiah want to break out in a dance. He resisted the urge and instead walked over to the stereo and put the song on repeat. It would be the perfect cover for what he had planned.

He stepped into her bedroom as her singing became clearer. She was rapping to Busta. No one would peg her for liking rap music. She just didn't fit the profile. Goes to show you that you should never judge a book by its cover. Her cleaning lady had been by that day. The bed was made up, all her clothes were put away, and the rugs were freshly vacuumed. *How lazy must you be to have a once a week maid for an apartment* Jeremiah thought to himself as he stepped into her huge walk in closet and waited for her to come in. He set his duffel bag down at his feet, got what he needed from it, and bobbed his head to the music that filtered into the bedroom.

Nina loved taking long hot showers, and loved how the hot jets of spray relaxed her body. The air in the bathroom was thick with fog as she stepped out of the

245

shower.  She had to use a towel to wipe off the mirror to see her reflection.  She was always struck by the sensuality of her naked body as she caressed her breasts and squeezed her nipples.  It was ironic that people paid so much money to buy beautiful works of art, but the most beautiful creation was a woman's naked body and it was always covered-up with clothes.

Jeremiah should be here soon she thought to herself as she lathered up her body with Victoria's Secret Cucumber Melon.  It was her favorite fragrance and she wanted to smell nice for him.  Nina slipped into a pair of sheer lacey see-through panties that hugged her ass tightly.  It made her feel sexy and flirty.  She then slipped on a see-through red nighty that felt wonderful against her warm skin.  She was ready. *Where the hell was Jeremiah*?  He knew how she got when she needed a sweet dick down.

Nina's mind was only focused on getting fucked by Jeremiah so she didn't realize that her CD was on repeat as she lit a few candles in the living room and walked into her bedroom to light two more.  She walked a few feet by her closet and before she realized what was happening; she felt the presence of something quickly approaching her and she was propelled into the wall ahead.  She braced for the crash by extending her arms forward.  There wasn't any time to think, scream, or even turn around before she was completely overpowered.  She was a tall woman but this man was bigger and heavier than she was and would have no problem hurting her.  She felt a sharp object in her back and her blood ran cold as if death was waiting for her. It felt like a knife so she dared not scream unless she wanted to end up in a pool of her own warm blood.

He pushed her up against the wall roughly and pressed his body into her. Nina felt the thick strength of his erection pounding between the crack of her ass through her nightgown. She didn't want to think of what would happen next. He wrapped his left hand around her throat and squeezed it just a little to let her know that he had to power to end her life. Nina gasped for air when he released her and allowed her to breathe again. It was a knife that he had jammed into her ribs because he quickly removed it, and she felt the cold steel slowly grazing up her thighs. Nina felt her heartbeat racing and pounding against her chest like fists against a door. What was he going to do to her? He hadn't said a word as yet, but his intent was clear. She had to find a way out of this but how? He was so much bigger than her that there was no way she could overpower him. There didn't seem to be anyway out of this. The thought of being raped frightened Nina, but she wouldn't allow herself to succumb to the fear...not yet.

The knife slid smoothly between Nina's skin and the waistband of her panties, and sliced through it cleanly. He roughly parted her thighs with his legs from behind and her panties fell to the floor; and were quickly followed by her red nightgown that he savagely ripped from her body. Nina stood there naked and in fear for her life and knew that if she screamed that she would be dead in seconds. The damn security guard was useless.

How else did a stranger slip into the building and her apartment? The music was playing so loud that no one would probably hear her blood curdling screams as her throat was slashed and she was left for dead. Who would take care of Bonkers? It was a stupid thought to have but she loved her kitty.

He released his grasp from her throat but still had the side of the knife pressed into her back. In one swift motion, he roughly brought her two hands behind her back and clasped handcuffs on them. He then placed a blindfold around her eyes. She was helpless and completely at his mercy. As an added reminder for her to keep quiet, he placed the knife on the right side of her neck. "You're all mine," he seemed to be saying to her. Nina could hear him slipping his gloves off, and the touch of his hands against her naked skin sent chills throughout Nina's naked body. His touch was gentle as if coaxing her to relax, but fear gripped her and she was unable to breathe.

He was a stranger who intended to rape her. His hands smoothly glided over the firmness of her ass, and he caressed it as if it were some priceless piece of art worthy of being admired. Then he slowly ran his fingers between the cheeks of her ass and Nina moaned reluctantly. It was one of her many weak spots. She wasn't sure if her moans were out loud or in her mind. He continued up the curve of her back, then down both of her arms and gently massaged her breasts. Nina was helpless to struggle so she just stood there and waited until it was over. She prayed silently for a miracle as he squeezed her nipples hard, right in the middle of one of her prayers. The pain was so intense that she screamed, but her scream just blended into the background of the music. The thumping beat of the music and her heart reverberated loudly in Nina's ears. She couldn't think straight and she felt as if her body was no longer her own.

For a brief second, she thought he had left the apartment and that she was finally safe. She turned around still blindfolded, hands handcuffed behind her back and took one-step forward. She ran directly into him. He was still there observing her as if she was his prey. She stepped back and felt the coldness of the wall against her back. She felt him approaching her and she had nowhere to turn. The full weight of his body pressed against hers and this time he was naked. He had been undressing quietly while observing her. The thickness of his erection pressed hard into her and slipped down to the soft folds of her pussy. Without thinking, she screamed as loud as she could and her screams were quickly followed by two hard slaps to both sides of her face. The shock of being hit caught her by surprise, and he placed his hands over her mouth before securing it with tape.

The helplessness of the situation hit Nina and she almost broke down crying, but she didn't want to give the bastard the satisfaction even though she was scared to death. He might not only rape her but kill her. The thought of her mortality made Nina think about her family members that she hardly spoke to, friends whom she never called back, and her employees who respected her but didn't like her. She wished she had more time to make amends.

He was toying with her. Breathing in her face, flicking her erect nipples with his fingers and his growing erection threatened to enter her, but every time he pulled back just to let her know that he could have her whenever he wanted. She could almost feel the smirk oozing from his face. He bent down closer to her and his hot breath ignited her neck. He held her in place by putting his hands on her waist as he sucked her nipples. It was raw animal lust and *her body*, not Nina, responded to how he was making her body feel.

*This is crazy* she thought to herself. *This man is about to rape and I can't stop my pussy from throbbing.*

Nina didn't know what scared her more, being raped or the fact that she was turned on by this perversion. She rationalized that it was her body doing the reacting and not her mind.

*But didn't her mind control her body?*

His hands slipped around behind her ass and he squeezed it as if he owned it, as if she had given him permission. Maybe her moans were the permission he needed to feel entitled to touch her in such a familiar way. Nina gasped when she felt his fingers slip inside of her wet pussy. His body pressed against her and impaled her against the wall. His fingers slipped in and out of her, and he massaged her throbbing pussy lips. Her breathing became shallow and she clamped down on her lips to stop from screaming with pleasure. She didn't want to give him the satisfaction. The handcuffs were cutting into her skin, but the pleasure that was vibrating throughout her body was even more intense, so she ignored the pain. Nina wanted him to release the pressure that was building inside of her pussy walls. Her initial fear had now turned to excitement then back to fear again. She was all fucked up.

Her clit was fully exposed and she knew from experience that the only way for it to retract into the folds of her pussy was for her to have an orgasm. Slowly he used the tip of his finger to massage her clit in a circular motion, and then counter clockwise. Nina was fighting a losing battle. She knew it and he knew it. Her lips parted open to release the many moans that had stayed quiet until now. She purred and meowed like Bonkers until her body shook and her knees knocked together like two pieces of wood being hit together. It was hard to breathe with her mouth taped up, but the tape had come slightly loose around the corners of her mouth to allow her some air. She inhaled the cool air and exhaled more moans.

He bent down in front of her on his knees, and his lips quickly found her exposed clitoris. At first, he sucked on it slowly as if building a rhythm, and when he found it, he sucked it so hard that Nina's moans turned into tears. Her body was numb with pleasure. She was embarrassed, humiliated, and angry for feeling this way; but God help her—she was loving it. With one last deep suck, she came hard in spurts and his mouth was ready for her onslaught of warm nectar. He swallowed every drop and waited for more. Satisfied there was no more for now, he stood up and forced Nina to her knees. She was still shaking from coming so hard so she felt disoriented and unsure of what he would do to her next. It didn't take her long to find out what he wanted from her.

He removed the tape from her mouth and she felt the heat of his manhood close to her face. She would have to suck his dick. He grabbed her by her dreads and started to rub his erection all over her face then he slapped her across her face with his thickness. It felt heavy like a real slap as it assaulted her cheeks. Nina's mouth reluctantly opened and twelve inches of black meat filled her mouth and throat. He grabbed her fiercely by both sides of her head and continued to force himself down her throat. Nina gagged and gasped for air, but he showed no mercy. She couldn't see what she was sucking, her hands were still handcuffed behind her back, and for a brief insane moment she had the stupid idea of biting it off, but she quickly discarded that thought. He would surely kill her. Relentlessly, he force-fed his erection to her until she felt his body tense up, and she knew he was about to come in her mouth. Nina braced herself and fought the urge to vomit at this humiliation, but her anger wasn't as strong as before. He came forcefully without making a sound and stayed inside of her mouth until she swallowed every drop he had given her. There seemed to be no end to his cruelty. He helped her back to her feet, wrapped his hands around her waist and threw her on the bed.

Nina laid there in a fetal position listening to him use the bathroom as if he was a guest in her home and not a rapist. Between all the sweating and the lotion on her body, her skin was slippery and she managed to slip out of the handcuffs. But before she could escape, he flushed the toilet and came back into the bedroom. She was lying down on her back. She tried to remain calm because if she panicked now and tried to escape she wouldn't have any leverage. He would surely overpower her. She needed the element of surprise on her side. The room was completely dark now and she heard him shuffling towards her. Removing the blindfold would have indicated to him that something was amiss if he touched her face. Her instincts were now so in tuned with her surroundings that she could hear his penis swinging between his legs and slapping his inner thighs as he approached her. He had grown confident and turned off the music. Nina wondered if he had killed Bonkers because she didn't come running when Nina screamed. She almost wished that she had gotten a dog but she hated dogs and the way they smelled after they got wet.

The weight of his body weighed the bed down as he sat next to her and ran his damp fingers over her pussy. He had washed his hands and smelled of her Dove soap. Casually, as if he was squeezing fruit to test its ripeness, he enclosed her breasts in his hands and squeezed them harder than before. Nina gritted her teeth in defiance of the pleasure she felt shooting through her body. She swallowed hard and killed the moans of pleasure before it escaped her lips. She didn't want this fucking bastard to know that if he squeezed both her nipples at the same time—she would come again. He seemed to know her pleasure points and squeezed both of her nipples and her body came again, but her mind refused to give in to the pleasure. There was no way that she would have give him that satisfaction

He got off the bed and walked away. Nina could feel him standing at the other end of the bed as if plotting his next move. She sensed a little indecisiveness in his walk, but then he quickly made up his mind. He roughly spread her legs with his hands, and she momentarily resisted, but she relented quickly when the cold steel of the knife touched her inner thighs. The full weight of his body descended upon her, and his erection was beating fervently like a heartbeat against her skin right below her navel.

It was happening.

Nina was about to be raped.

His lips were on her neck. She could feel his hot breath assaulting her under his stocking cap. The material scratched her face as she tried to turn away from his advances. He pried her legs open again with the implicit intention of penetrating her against her will. A rage of defiance boiled over in Nina that this wasn't going to happen. If he was going to rape her, then she would fight him with every fiber in her being. Summoning strength from places unknown, Nina managed to wriggle her hands free from behind her back. She felt emboldened because she heard the knife drop to the floor. The playing field was more even but still in his favor.

The thick head of his dick was inches away from penetrating her tight pussy. She knew he was large and it would hurt if he was allowed to enter her. She had to act now! With the element of surprise on her side, Nina delivered a kick to his groin that momentarily stunned her assailant, but he didn't get off of her and regained his balance almost immediately. She tried to bite anywhere that she could; his chest, arms, face—anywhere, but he deftly sidestepped her gnashing teeth. He used his body as a weapon and continued to pin her down against the bed. Her blindfold was still on, but was slowly coming loose as she battled him. She used both her hands to punch him repeatedly on his chest, and then assaulted his face with numerous slaps that were so hard that under normal circumstance would stun any normal person.

They were now both operating under the rush of adrenaline and excitement. He seemed to get stronger with every slap and punch that bounced off his body. He was relentless and smothered her like a blanket. Nina felt her resolve weakening, but the thought of a stranger penetrating her made her fight on. He pinned her arms forcefully behind her head and wrapped his hands around her throat to silence her screams. Her breath was caught in her throat and it felt as if she was going to pass out. The blindfold had come loose over her right eye, but it was so dark that his body looked like a dark shadow gyrating over her. He wasn't going to let her go. She would have to fight her way out of this or just let him have his way. Nina Rogers wasn't used to giving in to any man, and she damn sure wasn't about to let a man rape her in her own bed.

Sweat poured profusely from his face and through the stocking cap he was wearing to hide his face. Drops of it splattered on Nina's face and lips. She spat it back in his face, and he became so enraged that he let go of her hands for a split second to slap her again. That's what she wanted. The rest of the blindfold fell off and got lost on the bed. Nina's fists slammed into his throat and her assailant screamed in pain. He rolled off her clutching his throat as he tried to catch his breath, and Nina bolted for the door. In her haste, she didn't hear Bonkers purring, and tripped over her and went flying to the floor. She lay on the carpet for a split second as she tried to regain her composure, but that was all the time he needed.

He was on her again. She had angered him even more and would pay the price. He viciously slapped her again and she cried out like a child being reprimanded. He pinned her to the carpet with both her hands stretched out over her head. Her legs were pried open and his throbbing thickness entered her swiftly and deeply. She was instantly filled with him and he pumped his manhood furiously into her tightness. Her screams and cries went unheard and with every withdrawal of his erection, he entered her deeper.

Conflicting feelings raged through Nina's body and she was unable to control how she felt. Her body responded and she began gyrating her hips to accept his deep thrusts. She didn't want to enjoy it but God help her-it felt too good to resist, and the familiarity of having a big dick inside of her turned her on. She didn't want to resist anymore. He let her hands go as if reading her mind. He took hold of her legs and tossed them over his shoulders. He pulled her deeper into his erection, and his dick felt like heaven inside of her pussy.

She wanted more. With every thrust, he pummeled and assaulted her pussy and Nina moaned in complete submission. She couldn't help herself. Her body was in control and it wanted this sweet dick down. With a final thrust, he exploded like a rocket inside of her and Nina's clit throbbed with excitement. He continued stroking her slowly until her legs began to quiver and her body was overheating and ready to explode. She came hard and furious without any apologies. She wasn't sure if she had been fucked, raped, or dicked down; but her body told her it was satisfied. He collapsed besides her as if he had forgotten that he was the bad guy...the rapist. Nina lay next to him unable to move and weak from the force of her orgasm. A few seconds passed by without anyone saying a word until he pulled off his mask and looked at her.

It was Jeremiah.

He bent over and kissed her lips tenderly and she kissed him back with the passion of a woman who loved her man. She slapped him playfully on his bald head.

"You almost kicked me in the balls and busted my fucking throat—that wasn't the plan," he said to her as he looked down on her lying on the carpet. He still couldn't believe that he had gone along with this rape fantasy of hers. What if she had changed her mind and called the cops? That's why Jeremiah had insisted that before he did anything, she record on camera that this was a fantasy and not a real act. Experience had taught him that a woman scorned is capable of anything. He wasn't about to go to jail for some crazy ass woman.

"You're lucky I missed it by inches," Nina laughed devilishly. She was aiming for his groin and was still pissed that she had missed it. She wanted to hurt him as he had hurt her by getting engaged to that church girl, Sedra Simon. "Those handcuffs were too tight. You need to get a better pair next time, okay baby?"

Jeremiah nodded yes, but in his mind there would be no next time. Even a blind man could see that Nina was trouble. And yet, here he was. He had to be either stupid or retarded—or both. *Can pussy be so good that you would be willing to risk everything to get inside its warmth?* It was a rhetorical question, and he knew the answer because he was laying on the floor with this crazy-ass bitch that had set up this entire rape fantasy. They lay on the carpet exhausted because of all the energy they expended and were lost in their own thoughts. If they could read the other's mind, they would both back up cautiously and walk away.

An hour after Jeremiah left her apartment, Sedra's phone rang. It was a blocked ID that she didn't recognize, but she picked it up anyway. On the other end was the pleasant voice of a woman and Sedra relaxed, until she brought up Jeremiah.

"Do you know where your man is going right now?" The female voice asked her sweetly.

Sedra was about to hang up, but paused when the voice mentioned Jeremiah's brother.

"I bet you that lying bastard told you he was going to see his brother. That's the lie I told him to tell you."

"Who is this? What the hell do you want?"

Sedra was scared of where this would lead. Her worst nightmare was coming true that her girlfriends had been right about Jeremiah, that he was a male whore and just playing with her love for him.

"If you really want to know what your man is into then come to this address and be here in half an hour."

The voice on the phone had given Sedra specific instructions and told her where to find the key under the rug at the front door. Sedra's head was spinning with questions, but she had to know the truth. Was Jeremiah really a male escort as the voice had told her? Was he really about to enact a rape fantasy? Sedra's stomach lurched and she rushed to the bathroom to vomit before leaving her apartment.

Something must have happened because Jeremiah was still in his Jeep when she pulled up and parked two spaces behind him. She had a clear view of him as he crossed the street. He didn't look like the gentle man that she loved and had promised her love, heart, and virginity to. This had to be a mistake, but it was happening right in front of her as the voice had told her.

Twenty minutes after Jeremiah entered the building; Sedra followed him and went up to the 18th floor without any problems. The key was right where the voice said it would be and Sedra entered the apartment. Thankfully, the cat was stretched out like a princess on the couch and fast asleep. The last thing she wanted was to be attacked by a cat and scratched to death. Sedra listened intently and heard the sounds of a struggle. She followed the sounds of a feverish struggle and watched unseen by Jeremiah.

Nina saw her watching in the hallway and smiled to herself. It was show time. Jeremiah and his church girl would know the wrath of Nina Rogers. There was no way she would allow this Bible thumping, supposed virgin to steal away the best man she ever had in her life. Even though Jeremiah didn't know it—she was in love with him. He wasn't intuitive enough to know that her independent façade melted away whenever he came around. This was the only way to get rid of Bible girl.

Sedra watched in disgust for a few minutes as her beloved Jeremiah, wearing a ski mask and gloves, proceeded to assault the woman who had called her earlier. His vicious slaps and repeated assaults on her body stunned Sedra that a man as gentle as Jeremiah could be so cruel to a woman. She knew it was just a game, but it seemed so real that it was hard to distinguish fact from fiction. The brutality of Jeremiah's actions was too much for her to bear watching so Sedra slipped out undetected by Jeremiah. She sat in her car and cried for a few minutes. She was humiliated and embarrassed for believing all his lies.

Everything he said was a lie. The man had a crooked tongue, incapable of telling the truth. Sedra was hurting. Her heart was broken and she wanted Jeremiah to feel the same depth of pain that he had caused her. Without contemplating the consequences of her actions, she picked up her cell phone and dialed *Well Hung*. She told the operator that she needed a man ASAP at her apartment within the hour. Money was no object. The gift she was going to give Jeremiah, she would now give to another man. He didn't deserve her. Even a stranger deserved her more than this lying con artist she had fell in love with. The operator promised to have a man at her apartment in thirty minutes.

One thing about *Well Hung*—they could deliver faster than any fast food in the five boroughs of New York. You could get a dick faster than you could get a large pepperoni pizza with cheese.

Nina stood over Jeremiah as he lay out on the carpet, and for a brief moment she wanted to tell him that Sedra had seen everything and now knew what kind of man she was engaged to, but decided she wanted Sedra to break the news to him. It would hurt him more. He would be angry with her for a while, but he would come back. They always came back like the dogs they were. She loved him, but she knew that he was still a dog. Half the battle is knowing what you are up against and not fooling your heart to believe otherwise.

261

Jeremiah stared up at Nina and she looked like a tall tree blowing in the wind. Her legs were spread wide open and gave him a clear view into her shaved pussy. His dick moved a few inches, but it was time to go. He dressed quickly and made his excuses. Nina seemed understanding for once about him having to leave to go back home to his fiancée.

Jeremiah should have known it was too good to be true.

As promised, *Well Hung* had a man at Sedra's apartment in less than thirty minutes. The policy at *Well Hung* was the same as Domino's Pizza; if what you ordered isn't there in the allocated time then it's free. There is almost nothing better for a horny woman than a free sweet dick down with no strings attached. The strings attached are always invisible and can only be seen after it's too late to return the pleasure.

The male escort sent over by *Well Hung* was Johnson Fire. He was second in popularity to Jeremiah. The Dicker who had the most calls for the month would get an extra two thousand dollars. Jeremiah Heat won every month. Johnson hated Jeremiah more than anyone he had ever known in his life. He wanted to get back at that cocky son of a bitch in the worst way, but up until now, he had not been able to even the score. Johnson Fire was a pretty boy with wavy hair, light skin, and green eyes. He had the same build as Jeremiah, but didn't pull the same kind of action. Johnson wondered if Jeremiah's dick was bigger than his, but there was no way to prove it. Everyone assumed that dark-skinned black males could throw down better in the bedroom than the light skinned brothers, but Johnson Fire backed down to no man. He could sling dick with the best of them, or so he thought. Men always overestimated their sexual prowess and never kept it within the limits of mediocrity. Johnson Fire was no exception.

He rang the doorbell and in mid buzz, the door swung open. Johnson smiled his best smile and introduced himself. His erection instantly stiffened when he saw Sedra. She was a beautiful woman. She could have any man she wanted and tonight he was thankful that he was that man. Her face looked familiar, but he couldn't quite place it. She must be a model or something and maybe he had seen her face in a magazine. His mind drifted back to her as she wordlessly let him inside, and he followed her to the bedroom. Johnson's eyes cast downwards and he shook his head in disbelief at his luck tonight. Sedra had opened the door in a black thong and short pink t-shirt that only came down to her mid-section. Her ass bounced rhythmically as Johnson followed her into her and Jeremiah's bedroom.

There was nothing romantic about this so there was no music playing or candles lit. She wanted Johnson to take action without her telling him what to do and he did just that.

Johnson approached Sedra from behind and pressed his firm body into hers. Her ass felt delicious against his erection. He slipped his hands into the waistband of her thong and glided it down her legs until she stepped out of them. He massaged her breasts through her t-shirt, but she still didn't respond. He wasn't deterred by her being inhibited. Quickly he slipped out of his clothes and slipped off her t-shirt. Johnson felt like a kid in a candy store on Christmas Day and everything was free. She was the most beautiful woman he had ever laid eyes on, and in a few minutes, she would be riding his dick. *I love my job* Johnson thought to himself as he guided Sedra onto the bed.

She wanted this to be over quickly. She wanted him to take her virginity and be gone before Jeremiah got here, but he was taking too long. For the first time in her life, Sedra took control of the bedroom. Johnson was laid out on the bed and she mounted him, but not before slipping a condom on him. She was heartbroken but not stupid. His dick was long but thin. *Jeremiah could easily break his dick in a dick fight* Sedra thought to herself, but quickly pushed him out of her mind. She hated him for what he had done to her. She guided Johnson's dick to her pussy and rubbed it on her lips a few times.

This is not how she imagined it would be for her first time. This is not how she planned to lose her virginity. She had planned to lose it to the music of Marvin Gaye and imagined her and Jeremiah coming together as Marvin sang, "I Want You." Sedra pushed that thought of her mind and Johnson's erection slipped inside of her. She held her breath for the pain she had read about but there was no pain. She rationalized that since his dick was pencil thin then he couldn't fill her up and hurt her like Jeremiah. Without any concern for her pleasure, Johnson started pounding himself into Sedra's indifferent pussy.

When she looked at him with the saddest eyes he had ever seen on a woman, did Johnson finally realize where he knew her. A few months ago, he had run into her and Jeremiah on the F train. He introduced her as his fiancée, Sedra Simon. Johnson's pulse quickened at his realization that finally he would get even with Jeremiah. The knowledge that he was fucking Jeremiah's woman excited him and he fucked her even harder. It made it doubly sweet for him because he had overheard their conversation on the train about her being a virgin until their wedding night. Sweet virgin pussy. It had been years since Johnson had gotten him some virgin pussy. In New York, it was like being on the endangered species list. You didn't run across too many virgins anymore. They were all probably hiding out at church or something with a crucifix around their necks. It didn't take long for Johnson to come. If his cousin hadn't been the owner of *Well Hung*, he would have been fired a long time ago for unsatisfactory work performance. Sedra had expected to bleed but there hadn't been too much blood. She climbed off Johnson's penis and reached for some tissue on her night stand. She wrapped it around Johnson's limp penis and pulled the condom off to discard it into the toilet bowl.

The person staring back at her in bathroom mirror was a stranger. This wasn't her. She dropped to her knees and started to cry, but didn't ask for forgiveness as yet. There was one more thing she had to do.

At the door, she thanked Johnson for coming over quickly and was about to close the door behind him when he knocked on it.

"One more thing. Tell Jeremiah that Johnson Fire said hello and that your pussy was the best pussy I've ever had in my life."

Sedra slammed the door angrily as Johnson walked away with a smug look on his face. She had used him. He had used her. Everyone was using everyone without any regard for each other's feelings. Her head was spinning, but there was still one more thing left to do. She took a quick shower to wash the scent of Johnson from her body, and by the time she stepped back into her bedroom, Jeremiah had come home.

"Hi baby. Sorry it took so long, but you know how my brother can be."

"I know baby. I missed you," just saying the words made Sedra sick to her stomach.

Jeremiah smacked her ass playfully and kissed her lips. Sedra returned his kiss without any emotion. Her mind and body were numb. Images of Jeremiah and Nina were still playing in her head, and added to that was the fact that she had just lost her virginity to a man she didn't even know. Everything in her world was unraveling. Just two hours ago, Sedra thought that she had the perfect life and the perfect man. It had all been a lie.

Jeremiah was used to playing it cool. He was an expert at the art of deception, and he thought that everything was under control as he left her to get a drink of water.  When he came back, she had turned the lights down, candles were lit and she was naked. The only thing she was wearing was a smile.

"What's got into you girl?  You know how I get when I see you like this.  I can't resist wanting to make love to you."

"So why resist?"  Sedra said seductively as she approached him.

Jeremiah was momentarily shocked by Sedra's boldness.  Normally she was the one, who had to fight him off, and now, she was the predator and he was the prey.  She approached him with hate in her eyes which he mistook for passion.  If he had looked closer, he would have seen the anger and hate smoldering in her eyes.  She undressed him like a woman possessed then pushed him towards the bed.

"Take it easy baby.  You want our first time to be memorable.  This dick ain't going anywhere.  It's all for you."

Hearing those words made Sedra sad and angry at the same time.  How can a man say he loves you and cause you so much pain?  Was he the Devil coming in the guise of man and trying to corrupt her faith?  All these questions raged in Sedra's head as Jeremiah laid her down and started kissing all over her body.  His kisses were filled with an extra dose of fire tonight because he was about to get some virgin pussy.  Jeremiah didn't question Sedra's motives for changing her mind.  He didn't wonder how this would affect her faith.  If he really did love her, then these questions would be

267

paramount in his mind instead of having sex with her. He cared more about sex than her heart. He just assumed she was horny and tired of not getting the dick that laid next to her every night. She was about to get her first taste.

His tongue felt good inside of her. *He definitely knows how to eat pussy* Sedra thought to herself as she closed her eyes and plotted her next moves. If he only knew that he was tasting another man's dick inside of her mixed with her nectar—he would have a coronary. She wanted to be on top so she could see his lying face when he heard the news. She wanted to see the pain in his face. She wanted to see his heart break in his eyes the same way he had broken hers earlier.

Sedra used to love the feel of being on top of Jeremiah and feeling the power of his body between her thighs. It felt like a powerful engine just idling and ready to take off at any minute.

"Are you ready baby?"

Sedra nodded yes in answer to his question.

His hands palmed her ass and caressed it to relax her. He slowly spread her ass cheeks and the thickness of his head stretched her lips open. Sedra shuddered as his first penetration forced itself into her. She didn't expect him to be this big as he filled her tightness and plunged deeper into her wetness.

"Aw shit baby…damn…damn…fuck baby this is what I've been feening for. Sweet tight ass pussy."

"You love it baby…you love this tight-ass pussy."

"Yes…yessssss…you're gonna make me come quick."

"Not yet baby. Let me feel my man's dick inside his pussy."

Jeremiah slowed down his rhythm as he closed his eyes and felt the sweet tightness of Sedra's muscles strangling his erection. He was in pussy heaven. Images of Nina flashed through his mind, and now he had Sedra riding his dick—he was the ultimate player pimp. A smile danced around his closed eyes and Sedra looked at him with hate in her eyes. It finally hit her what she was losing, and she had gained nothing at all except for a broken heart and her lost virginity. She felt as if she had let herself down and also God. She was ashamed of her actions, but unable to stop herself from doing things she knew were wrong. *God is a loving God* she thought to herself and tears flowed freely down her face. Jeremiah again assumed that her tears were tears of joy and that the dick was just so damn good that she was crying for more.

It was time.

Sedra leaned in close to his left ear, strands of her hair waved in his face and her nipples pressed into his chest. The sweat of their bodies merged as he grunted with every deep sweet stroke. It felt so good to have him inside of her. His dick felt as good as it looked, but he wasn't the man he claimed to be. Her body wanted more as she continued to ride him harder and her unreleased passion neared an explosion.

269

"You love me baby?" she asked him in her sweetest innocent voice. Behind her sweetness was the sadness of a woman whose heart had just been broken. Everything she believed in was a lie. All her hopes for the future were dead.

'Yes baby…I love you."

Jeremiah was barely able to talk and fuck at the same time. Her pussy felt better than Nina's. *Tighter…sweeter…deeper*, and Sedra loved him. It suddenly made him sad about all his deceptions. It was in that moment that Jeremiah had an epiphany that he would confess everything to Sedra and hopefully she loved him enough to forgive him for all his cheating ways. Maybe he should have stopped her right there in the moment and bared his soul. Maybe things would have turned out differently that night.

"If you love me so much baby why did you hurt me? Why were you fucking other women! Why were you fucking Nina?" The bitterness and disillusionment flowed from Sedra's lips like the pain flowing from her heart.

Jeremiah's eyes shot wide open when he heard Nina's name. How did Sedra know about Nina? Their bodies continued to operate on auto pilot as Sedra grinded her pussy onto his shaft. She needed to come to release all this pain she was feeling.

"Who told you about Nina? It's all a lie baby." He was trying to buy some time to come up with a plausible lie.

"She called me and told me. I saw you raping her! I was in the fucking apartment, Jeremiah. I saw your sick ass game! What kind of sick perverted man are you?"

That fucking bitch had fucked me for the last time Jeremiah thought to himself. There was no way she was getting away with this. She would pay dearly for this betrayal.

Their bodies were tense, the air filled with anger and intense passion. Sedra wanted to get off but Jeremiah's strong hands were wrapped around her waist and kept her in place. She was about to explode but not before giving him the shock of his life.

"I'm not a virgin anymore," she whispered in his ears. Saying those words didn't feel as empowering as she thought it would feel. It made her feel cheap and unworthy of her faith. Faith is needed when you are at your darkest hour, and at her darkest hour; she had allowed herself to succumb to anger, jealousy, and revenge. She had failed to adhere to all the principals of faith.

Jeremiah was about to come and words couldn't find their way to his lips. He grunted loudly as if unsure of what she was telling him as her muscles contracted around his erection and massaged him into an orgasm. He came with a fury and an anger as Sedra continued to taunt him. He moaned as she whispered in his ears and said the words that would make any man want to kill his woman.

"Your boy, Johnson Fire was over here about half an hour ago. When you were eating my pussy—you

271

were licking his cum inside of me. He fucked me so good without any condom," Sedra lied. "He fucked me better than your sorry black ass!" She taunted him in his ears. His body spasmed as he came and heard the news of her betrayal with Johnson. "He took my virginity that was meant for you. He fucked your pussy," the moment as the last words left her lips, Sedra came and it felt like everything left her body. She felt empty and lost. She felt like a sinner and she felt saved at the same time. In that moment she started to pray silently for God to take away her pain. She prayed for forgiveness, for understanding of her human frailties.

Jeremiah's body relaxed after coming but his anger had just started to boil over. He was still inside of Sedra and her eyes were closed. He knew she was praying. His mind snapped, and in that moment, he lost control. He reached for her neck with both his hands and clamped them tightly around her throat. Her eyes opened, surprised at what was happening. She struggled at first to remove his hands from around her throat as her body jerked back and forth like a ragged doll caught in the crossfire of an angry storm.

His hands were strong and quickly cut off her air passage.

He wanted to stop but he couldn't.

He wanted to tell her that he loved her but couldn't.

Sedra looked at the man she loved and stopped struggling. The life she wanted to live flashed before her eyes. The faces of friends and her family smiled at her.

She accepted that death had called her name and the Devil was in her bed. She said one last prayer before closing her eyes and hoped that there was a place for her in Heaven. Maybe there, she would find her happiness.

Jeremiah took his hands away from her neck and she slumped forward onto his chest. She couldn't be dead. He hadn't intended to kill her. He only wanted to scare her, but now she was dead. He got off the bed and paced around for a few minutes unsure of what to do next. Every time her words came to mind about Nina and Johnson, his rage bubbled over again. They both would pay for crossing him. Nobody fucks with Jeremiah Heat and got away with it.

Calmly, he called *Well Hung* and asked for Johnson. He was out on another job. The operator at *Well Hung* had the hots for Jeremiah so it wasn't too hard to get the address which was only twenty blocks away. Jeremiah quickly dressed and took one last look at Sedra's naked dead body. He wouldn't allow himself to feel any remorse. In ten minutes, he was parked a block away from where Johnson was meeting his customer. Patiently he waited in the shadows of a building next to Johnson's car. Johnson would soon know that anyone who fucks with Jeremiah doesn't fuck with anyone anymore. *Enjoy your last piece of pussy, motherfucker.*

Johnson exited the building smiling like a man who had just hit the pussy lottery. Two beautiful women in one night and he even got to fuck over Jeremiah Heat. He laughed out loud to himself as he opened his car door.

273

"Laugh now, die later motherfucker," an angry voice growled in his ears. The stench of death filled Johnson's mind as he tried to stay calm.

"Listen man, I have a few hundred dollars on me. You can have that to get your drink on and fuck some hoes. If that's not enough we can go to the ATM down the block—Okay?"

"Not okay," the voice growled again. You're gonna die tonight like the bitch you are. Turn around!"

Johnson turned around to face his death. He wasn't a brave man and had already pissed on himself. His assailant's face was uncovered and the barrel of a Magnum sunk in between the space of Johnson's two eyes.

It was Jeremiah Heat.

Both men looked at each other and knew the other's truth. Johnson knew that Jeremiah knew he had fucked his woman and that he was about to take his last breath. Jeremiah knew that he would be two for two tonight in killing people who had betrayed him. He pulled the trigger and Johnson Fire was no more. He died on the street like the dog he was. One more loose end to clean up Jeremiah thought to himself as he drove away.

Nina fell asleep completely satisfied after having Jeremiah fuck her and her fucking him over with Sedra. Not bad for a night's work was her final thought as she fell asleep. She didn't hear her front door open and she didn't hear Bonkers meowing a warning that death was coming to claim her last breath.

Jeremiah stood in the shadows of the bedroom he had just been in less than an hour ago. He watched her sleeping peacefully. *That's a peaceful way to die* he thought to himself but he wanted her to suffer. He reached into his duffel bag and got his handcuffs and the knife. Nina was a sound sleeper so it was too late by the time she realized that she was being handcuffed again. She struggled to sit up in the bed, but strong hands pushed her back.

It was Jeremiah.

His face looked like death. In that moment, Nina Rogers realized that she had pushed him too far. You can only push a man as far as he is willing to go until he snaps and loses all perspective. Jeremiah Heat had lost all perspective.

"This ain't no game this time bitch. You've fucked with me for the last time. You had no right to tell Sedra about us. What the fuck did you think would happen?"

This time the handcuffs wouldn't slip off. He had tightened them. "I'm sorry baby. I was jealous of her. I love you, but you couldn't see that. I had to show you that I was the woman for you."

"*Love me?*" Jeremiah paced back and forth with the knife glinting in his hands. "You don't fucking love me! You wanted to control me! You wanted something you couldn't fucking have!"

He approached the bed and sat down next to Nina. She screamed knowing that there was no use in trying to reason with him. He was beyond reason. Death shone in his eyes.

"You can scream all you want," he looked at her as their eyes met. We will both be dead before anyone gets here.

Before Nina could say or scream another word, the knife sliced through the air and the last thing Nina would see was how it glinted in the light as it plunged into her throat. She died instantly. The coroner would tell the daily newspapers that the cut was so clean that it appeared to be the work of a professional killer.

Jeremiah slumped over in the bed with the knife still in his hands and reached for the Magnum in his jacket. His killing spree was almost over. He didn't regret killing Johnson or Nina…*but Sedra*. She didn't deserve to die. She didn't deserve a man like him. She had paid the ultimate price with her life. Grief overwhelmed Jeremiah as the knife dropped to the floor and he placed the gun in his mouth.

The police found his body slumped right next to Nina. It would be weeks before they were able to tie in the murders of Johnson and Sedra to Nina and Jeremiah. The case became known as *"The Well Hung Massacre"* and it wasn't surprising that the escort business in New York, and all around the country, took a hit for the next few months. Everyone was scared that some crazy ass escort would slash their throats or put a bullet in their fucking head. But after a few months, things got back to normal and it was as if *The Well Hung Massacre* had never happened.

10/06/08…12:42pm

# My Sweet Addiction

Shallow gasp of breaths announces your arousal
The temperature in the room is almost unbearable
Your body writhes in the agony of pleasure as if giving
birth to the sun
Drops of warm honey nectar dew flow steadily from
your throbbing pussy
It is an amazing sight to bear witness to passion giving
birth
I am in awe that one person can give another such
intense pleasure
Fever of desire breathes hot from your skin
Your breasts sigh upwards as if praying to God for
salvation
You are consumed by a passion that has no name
The only name you moan is mine over and over again
until you come
It is a feeling that will haunt you because it is not easily
recaptured
Something so deeply arousing that it shakes the fountain
of your soul
You can live your whole life and never again know such
intense passion
Everything you are feeling right now is fully exposed to
me
I know how to touch your body to elicit your moans and
groans of pleasure

I tenderly stroke your cheek and the heat emanating from
your body
Arouses me in a way I have never felt before
Tiny beads of sweat form on your breasts
My tongue stands erect and ready for your sweetest
nectar
My lips are thirsty to drink your natural water
I wait for it to trickle down your chest,
Gaining momentum down the slope of your stomach
Coming to rest momentarily in the valley of your navel
The lips of your thirsty wings spread open knowing
what's coming
They are just as hungry as mine to be fed
The last bead of sweat trickles between your plump full
lips
Each lip will be licked and tongue kissed until my mouth
is tired
Or until you beg me to stop making you come
Whatever pleasure you desire is yours to have
I am here to please you because you are my sweet
addiction.
5/9/08…7:09pm

# One Last Come Before He Died

The heated scent of fucked pussy, wine, with the subtle fragrance of danger mixed together, filled the house with its concoction of night time passion even though it was the middle of the day. One sip of this love potion and the weak of heart could easily be inebriated. It took a man with a hard dick and even bigger balls to walk out of Caribbean Leroy's house upright and with most of his faculties still intact after dicking down his woman—in his bed.

When he met her that afternoon, it was the beginning of spring and the possibilities of new things filled the air. The afternoon air was filled with the aroma of flowers and new pussy just whispering his name seductively. Benjamin Stevens would never have guessed that helping a beautiful young woman carry her grocery bags would be the death of him. It wouldn't surprise anyone tomorrow morning when they read the obituary page that Benjamin had been found naked and dead in a married woman's bed and still erect inside of her. He had lived his life chasing every piece of pussy that smiled his way, so it seemed only right that he would die inside the confines of one.

Sometimes he wished he had eyes all over his body so he could see every single woman without missing anything. He loved being in Brooklyn during the spring and summer months and watching the world come back to life and celebrating the passing of winter's dreary demise.

It was a Saturday afternoon, and as he sipped on a glass of ice tea from his apartment window; he would occasionally watch a group of teenage girls and boys flirting with each other on the front steps of his building. It made him cringe to hear how the young men spoke to girls these days. There was no art or finesse to their language. The crudeness of their language was indicative of a society where everything is up for discussion and nothing is private. There was a classlessness that saddened him. Even though he was only thirty-five, Benjamin Stevens had always been an old soul. Maybe that was his problem, he couldn't be happy just being. He was always searching for the next best thing. The next thing always seemed to land him in a woman's bed. The lure of new pussy had always been his Achilles heel. Today, it would be the death of him.

The heads of the young men suddenly turned away from the girls and looked in one direction. Benjamin turned to see what they were all looking at. Even before he turned his head, he already knew that only one thing could capture the attention of young boys in the summertime. Their chests puffed out a few extra inches; one of them took off his shirt to show off his physique, but they all remained speechless as she walked by them and smiled. True beauty can leave you speechless and in awe. The young girls took mental notes on how to leave a man amazed and mute.

She was the reason why men cheated on their wives.

She was the reason why men would renounce everything just to slide between the comforts of her long legs and into the heaven of her tender pussy.

She was the reason why Benjamin Stevens would catch his death today.

His eyes followed the sway of her walk without blinking. Her body swung back and forth like a tree caught in the throes of a springtime breeze. Her skirt was the color of sunrise and barely enough material to cover the voluptuousness of her ass. It fluttered around her bare knees as if she was about to take flight into the afternoon sky. Every step she took, her high heels clicked rhythmically against the hot pavement and then she was gone, disappearing around the corner. In a flash, Benjamin picked up a shirt from the floor and ran outside with his shoes in his hands. He had to find her. The boys were all arguing that she had smiled at them and that she was their woman. The young women looked on in amusement as they began to realize the true power a woman can have over a man. Long after this moment, all of them would remember this day; a sort of an awakening of their womanhood. They would recognize her face the next day in the papers and would come to know her by her name and not just the pretty woman.

Benjamin ran in the direction of where she walked and it wasn't too hard to find her. The trail of her scent was still fresh in the air like freshly baked bread drawing a crowd, heads were still turned in her direction and the look in the eyes of the men was of naked lust. Benjamin snatched a red rose from a street vendor and promised to pay on his way back.

Benjamin was a handsome man and had no trouble talking to women, but something about her made him nervous. Maybe it was the surety of her walk or the bounce in her ass signaling that she could take on all comers. If he had allowed his nervousness to speak louder than his ego and turned around to walk back home, he would have lived many more years to keep chasing new pussy. Instead, he walked up to her, cleared his throat and spoke.

"I think you dropped your flower," he said with his best seductive smile. His teeth gleamed in the sunshine and created a beautiful contrast against his dark skin.

She stopped her stride and the air seemed to come crashing around her. She was even more beautiful up close as she smiled without any intent; but smile for a man and he assumes that he has gotten the green light to get into your panties.

"I didn't realize that I had dropped my flower," she said as she took it from his hand. The slight brush of her hand against his made Benjamin swoon. He knew he was in trouble with this one, but he couldn't know how much until it would be too late.

There was soulfulness in her brown eyes that drew him closer, and when she smiled he noticed the slight gap between her front teeth. He heard that women who had this gap could give a man pleasure beyond their wildest dreams. He was sure that the fullness of her lips could suck a dick like an angel in heaven singing the sweet praises of love and grace. Her long dreadlocks seemed to be more of a fashion statement than any sort of religious convictions, and he imagined running his hands through it as she moaned his name. He didn't even know here name and already he had her naked in bed and screaming profanities at God.

"What's your name beautiful lady?"

"Carry my bags and maybe I will tell you my name?"

She enjoyed flirting with men because she knew most of them would do anything she asked. Being beautiful made it hard to walk down the streets sometimes, but she knew that as long as there were men walking this earth, she would never want for anything. Her pussy was her ticket to the good life. Benjamin grabbed the two small bags and as he reached to take them from her; his eyes became transfixed on her breasts. Her nipples pressed hard against her tan blouse, and her dark full breasts peaked through the open buttons giving him a full view of what would soon be warm against his lips.

"Do you like what you see?" Her question startled Benjamin back to reality.

"Yes…yes very much so."

"You're a very naughty boy. I'm sure you just want to help me with my bags then get into my panties."

Benjamin felt emboldened and flirted right back with her. "Are you wearing any panties?"

She laughed a rich, full laugh that came from her heart and her breasts bounced up and down with it. He could tell that she liked him. He pretended to stop and tie his shoelaces just so he could get a full view of her ass again from the back. They looked like two full water balloons that he wanted to pop with some deep, sweet strokes to put her in flight. She knew that he was looking and gave him an eyeful as she bent over to pick up her fallen rose. A gust of wind gave her skirt wings and the roundness of her ass filled his gaze. As quickly as it came, the wind was gone and her skirt came back down to cover her ass. Their eyes met and they both knew what would be happening next. Her pussy was heavy with unreleased nectar juice and she was hungry to be fucked. She noticed the huge print in his pants and imagined what it would feel like in her hands, inside her pussy, in the warmth of her mouth, and the sweet dark tightness of her ass. Her body ached with want. Benjamin's dick throbbed in appreciation of her beauty and he mentally fucked her as they walked up the block.

She looked around anxiously as they entered her brownstone, but his excitement dismissed her nervousness as just a woman being a woman. If he was on his game, he would have noticed the two men trailing him from two blocks away. He would have sensed that danger was lurking in the air, but the only scent that was on Benjamin's mind was the aroma of her heated pussy on his face, lips and coating his dick with her honey. The front door to the brownstone creaked closed and Benjamin dropped the bags to the floor and pinned her against the red walls. His hands slid down to grasp the roundness of her ass and squeezed both cheeks tightly. Eagerly, he slipped his fingers between her legs which swung open like a front door and waves of her wet warmth saturated his fingers. She moaned into his mouth as their lips met roughly, and they kissed hard without any finesse. Gently he massaged the fullness of her crotch and used his fingers to encircle her protruding clit. Spasms of electric currents of arousal shot out like brilliant burst of light all over her body and her knees buckled, but he had her pinned against the wall for support. Pedestrians walked outside merely a few feet away oblivious to what was happening behind the closed front door of 1513 Passion Drive. The two men who were trailing them stopped at the front door and heard the familiar sounds of her moans, looked at each other and shook their heads before continuing to the *Two Plus Two* bar a few blocks away. Their boss, Caribbean Leroy, would not be pleased to know that his woman was about to be fucked by another man. The last man who thought he could enjoy Caribbean Leroy's pussy and walk away to brag about it walked away minus a dick and his balls stuffed in his mouth. They didn't kill him so he could spread the tale all around Brooklyn that Caribbean Leroy's woman was never to be touched. Benjamin Stevens never got that memo.

Benjamin knew that someone could walk down the stairs, open their door, or walk through the front of the building and catch them having relations, but he was so aroused that in the moment, he didn't care if anyone saw them. His fire ached to be wrapped inside the heat of her flames. Trickles of arousal dripped from his fingertips and he slipped one finger at a time between his lips to taste the essence of her arousal. He sighed deeply as he swallowed her and hungered for more. He ripped her blouse open and the fullness of her breasts spilled out like ripe mangoes falling softly to the earth from its branch. They were heavy with ache and he suckled each of them slowly as he pressed her back harder into the wall.

"Fuck me right here," she urged him as her legs spread open and he lifted her up by her ass. "Fuck this sweet black pussy."

Benjamin buried his face in the hollow of her neck and bit her deeply. She screamed as his teeth and dick sunk into her tender flesh simultaneously. She urged him to go deeper. She wanted him to find her buried treasure and expose its secrets to his dick and tongue. Every thrust brought him closer to hearing her scream like a banshee. He needed to hear her scream. He needed to know that he was touching something in her so deep that it was overwhelming all of her senses and sending her into passion overload.

Someone was trying to get into the building so they hurriedly picked up their clothes and the bags of groceries and ran down the hall to her apartment. The single red rose was forgotten on the step. They didn't bother to lock the door and went straight to her bedroom.

She threw herself on the bed, assumed the doggy style position, and spread her legs wide open to let him see the sweet darkness that was awaiting his invasion. The muscles in her ass contracted as both cheeks bounced up and down with an invitation that Benjamin planned on RSVPing immediately. His dick pulsed to life, the roundness of his brown head strained to be inside of her again. The long locks of her hair spread out evenly on the bed and he jumped on her like a jockey about to ride his horse. Before entering her again, he kissed both of her ass cheeks as if he were kissing her lips and her clit jumped to attention feeling neglected. He kissed every inch of her round, delicious ass and just when she thought that she could not take anymore; he held her firmly by the waist and bit into her deeply.

"Ohhhh Sssshittt," she moaned. She thrust her ass into his face to let him know she wanted him to bite her deeper. He bit her again, smacked both of her ass cheeks and her legs trembled as a spontaneous orgasm raged from her tight honey coated walls. He placed the full length of his manhood smoothly between the crack of her ass, and she maneuvered her body to let him slide inside of her aching pussy. His eyes closed, his back straightened, his balls tightened as she swallowed every inch of his ten inch dick. *This is what life is all about right here*, Benjamin thought to himself. He couldn't understand why men were gay when there was so much pussy waiting for them. He rationalized that there would just be more pussy waiting for him so he didn't have a problem with gays. Life was beautiful.

Caribbean Leroy listened to his men as they whispered to him what his woman was up to. He listened intently, finished up his Carib Beer and got up.

"I'm getting too old for this shit to be chasing after young pussy. Old pussy know how to act and take their foolishness someplace else, but these young gals today always want more and more. Leh we go teach she ass a lesson."

His accent always came out thicker when he was angry. Caribbean Leroy was a big, black ugly motherfucker, the color of night and teeth as white as snow. He stood 6'2", 300 lbs and a gut that made him look as if he was about to deliver at any minute. He was mockingly referred to as Biggie Smalls behind his back, the slain rapper from Brooklyn. He was in his mid-sixties and kept himself in reasonably good shape...except for his gut. He knew that this young girl, only twenty-two was too much for his old ass, but his pride wouldn't let him admit that age had finally caught up with him and it was time to stop chasing young trim. Not even Viagra could get his dick hard enough to fuck her, and he would lay in bed embarrassed sometimes and apologetic. "Just eat my pussy" she would order him with contempt in her voice. He wanted to slap this young cunt and put her in her place, but seeing her cry would hurt him more than it would hurt her. As far as he knew, he didn't have any kids. He knew now what his mother meant when she used to beat his ass as she professed it would hurt her more than it hurt him. He didn't know how that was possible. He was the one getting brutalized with mop sticks, wires, and anything she could lay her hands on. But now, with her, he knew what she meant. Seeing her cry one time was enough for him. If his men could see the pussy he had become behind closed doors, they would laugh in his face. Caribbean Leroy dressed the part of a pimp, always in a suit and hat and a cigar in his hand, but even though he looked the part; he was only a man, a lonely old man. He had immigrated to the States back in the 60's from Antigua and owned a string of bars around the neighborhood. Like most men his age, he had been through a string of women and it was only now that he was realizing how many good women had slipped through his fingers. He summoned his Caribbean Leroy persona and started to march up the street with his men following closely behind.

This was a first for Benjamin. His dick got harder with every stroke, and when she mounted him; she reached back and stroked his hardness in her right hand. He was about to come like a mountain spewing its lava, but she squeezed the base of his dick to control his ejaculation and only a 0.1 eruption was registered. Her body twisted into a 69 position and he was now lips to lips with a wet pussy in urgent need of licking. The heat of her breath ignited his pubic hair; she cupped his balls into the small of her palm and squeezed them gently as if she was testing the ripeness of grapes. Benjamin squirmed and moaned when she took his hardened manhood between her lips and sampled the remnants of his mini explosion. She wrapped her arms around his upper thighs and instinctively, he thrust upwards into the warmth of her lips and the depths of her hungry mouth. She gagged at the full size of his girth, but was up for the challenge as she swirled her tongue around his curved thickness. The veins protruding from his erection ran smoothly against her tongue, and she slid him deep into her thirsty throat. There were no words he could say to express the pleasure that was feeling, and he was cut off in mid-moan when she thrust her ass back into his face to taste her fevered arousal. Benjamin marveled at the plumpness of her lips and stuck his tongue into her sweet flower. He used the thumb on his right hand to prod her tight anus open. She shoved back hard on his thumb and it disappeared completely into her ass. The suddenness of having her tight hole filled caused her to stop sucking his dick and let out a cry of passion that filled the room.

"Pleasssse baby...give it to me," she almost begged. "Put that fat dick in my ass. Make me scream your fucking name! I need a real man to fuck this fat pussy!"

She quickly turned back around and mounted him. His erection looked like a rocket as it shot straight up into the air. He palmed her fleshy ass, spread his fingers open to hold her still, and she bent down lower to feed him a chocolate nipple. One nipple wasn't enough to satisfy Benjamin's hunger. He wanted both of them between his lips at the same time. No one had ever sucked both of her nipples at the same time, and the warmth of passion rolled over her like a whisper seductively caressing her ears.

"Say it again," he urged her in a throaty, horny voice. Hearing her say it excited him.

"Fuck me in my ass! Fill my ass with your pipe! Make me come hard baby!"

She didn't even know her name and she was calling him baby, but Benjamin didn't care. Her pussy knew his name and by the time he was done with her; his name would be engraved inside of her. With his fingers still spread across her ass, she sat upright as he gradually opened her tightest hole with his pulsating head to fill its darkness. It felt like his dick was being strangled as she used her hands to spread her ass open for him even more. Her whimpers of pleasure made his blood run hot and his strokes were slow and deliberate. She urged him to go faster and deeper as her darkness gave way to slivers of light. They were both lost to what they were feeling and didn't hear Caribbean Leroy and his men open the bedroom door.

The thick aroma of dick and pussy slapped Caribbean Leroy across his black face. It was an added insult that he had to inhale the scent of his woman's pussy being fucked by another man. He wanted to run to her and ask her why she would want to hurt him so deeply, but he felt the eyes of his men on him as they waited for him to make a move. He had never heard her scream so loud as they entered his house. It was like hearing an animal being brought out to slaughter as she bounced up and down on his dick. Caribbean Leroy wanted to look away from watching his woman get fucked by a man thirty years his junior, but it was a hypnotic thing to watch a dick slide in and out of a woman's ass—even if it was your woman's ass. She once told him that she thought it was nasty for a man to want to put his dick in a woman's ass. She said that nothing should go into it and it should be used only for its intended purpose. He had respected her wishes because he loved her. "Do you love me?" he asked her just last week. She pretended not to hear him and turned away from him to turn on the television. Caribbean Leroy was an old time player, and deep down inside of him, he knew that she was using him. He hoped that in time, she would see how much he loved her and they could have a good life together. That day would never come.

He pulled up a chair to the foot of the bed and set it down hard against the hardwood floor. His two men flanked him with their guns drawn and ready for him to give the word. The sound of the chair hitting the floor startled both of them back to the reality of the moment. Sweat drenched their bodies and stung Benjamin's eyes. He looked up to see three men staring menacingly at him. At first, he thought it was a robbery, but then he looked at her as she turned around and a flicker of recognition showed on her face.

"You having fun with my woman?" Caribbean Leroy said to Benjamin. His voice was steady but menacing. Underlying his menacing voice was a voice that wanted to cry from the pain that was ripping through his heart.

"Your woman? She never told me she had a man. I would never fuck another man's woman—you have to believe me," Benjamin said in a voice that betrayed how scared he really was at the moment.

"I got to do nothing pussyclot bwoy. All I got to do is eat and shit," Caribbean Leroy growled at him in his thick accent. "You...you are a bold face fucking liar. Men like you don't care who they fuck. You just happen to fuck the wrong man's pussy today."

Benjamin tried to remove her from atop of him, but she squeezed her ass muscles tighter around his erection and a low moan escaped his lips. She was still fucking him with just her ass muscles getting tighter and tighter around his erection. He exhaled slowly and tried to control himself from losing it and exploding inside of her ass. That's the last thing he wanted to do right now.

"Listen baby, I'm sorry but this guy means nothing to me. It won't happen again," she said almost nonchalantly as if she had picked up a stray dog on the street. "He followed me home and wouldn't go away like some fucking stray puppy dog." Her muscles gripped Benjamin tighter and he pulsated inside of her. *She was fucking crazy.*

"I don't even know her name," Benjamin offered to Caribbean Leroy as if that one tidbit of information should exonerate him from being inside of her ass.

"So lemme understand you correctly," Caribbean Leroy took a cigar from his pocket and gave one of his men to light it, "you come to a place without even knowing the name of the woman you fucking. It might just get you killed."

The way Caribbean Leroy stressed his last word made Benjamin realize that he was in some deep trouble. Deeper than the ass he was buried inside. He had been in some prickly predicaments before-but nothing like this. This would be one to tell the boys once he got out of it.

"Her name is Delores," Caribbean Leroy offered.

She didn't look like a Delores. She looked more like a Sugar or a Cinnamon. Benjamin shook his head to rid it of those thoughts. He had bigger problems now than her name.

Caribbean Leroy took a few puffs of his cigar and watched the circles float off into the air and disappear like magic before his eyes. He wished he had the common sense that God gave him to pick a woman who was beautiful inside and outside and not solely based on what Delores offered: big ass, tight pussy, full breasts, and lips that made your dick hard when she smiled at you. His erection stirred for a few seconds but quickly deflated as he watched her naked body with another man's dick impaled inside of her. He couldn't get hard to fuck her, but he could get hard seeing another man fuck his woman. *Ain't this some shit*! He crossed his legs slowly to hide his arousal, but his men, trained by Caribbean Leroy to look for the invisible; had already seen their Boss' third leg grow hard and then quickly fall asleep to take another long nap. They too had grown hard and wished they had gotten to sample the sweet pussy of Delores. Cold Beers was Caribbean Leroy's oldest associate, and he had never seen his Boss so pussy whipped for some pussy. His nose was open wider than a hooker getting double anal penetration. The old man had grown soft and Cold Beers was sure that he wasn't fucking Delores anymore. A young girl like that needs a man with a thick stiff dick to fuck her until she's about to lose her mind. Caribbean Leroy could barely walk a block without his asthma kicking in. Cold Beers eyed Delores discreetly from under the brim of his hat and mentally fucked her until she screamed his name.

The old man couldn't fuck. He had a narcoleptic dick. The first few times that that they did it and he couldn't get it up, she smiled and played the part of a good woman by telling him it was alright. Her pussy was aching to be fucked and her lips hungry to suck a young dick, but he had rescued her from that dead end job at Calabash over in Flatbush over a year ago. He had come in with his two henchmen Cold Beers and Fuck-Up like he owned the damn place. It turned out that he did.

"What can I get for you gentlemen today?" She said with complete disinterest in her voice. Her mind was on the Buju Banton reggae concert that night and she couldn't wait to wine her sweet waist. She knew she was fine and used it to her advantage every time she needed something from a man.

They used her and she used them.

They wanted her pussy and she wanted their money. It was just business.

Caribbean Leroy heard her voice and it sounded as sweet as sugarcane to him. It had been a long time since he had eaten sugarcane, but he imagined that every part of this young thing was just as sweet. He cleared his throat and ordered his usual salt fish, dumplings, green bananas and a glass of Sorrel. He watched her walk away and the thickness of her ass hypnotized him. He knew he was in trouble at that very second. He had to have her and by the end of the week, she was living in his house with an unlimited bank account.

Their first night together still played in Caribbean Leroy's mind as he sat there watching them in the bed that they had shared for the past year. He wondered now how many other men had been in his bed and cum all over his black silk sheets. She thought that he would be away on business in Baltimore today, but his appointment had been cancelled at the last moment. Eventually all cheaters get caught. When you least expect it and you've grown too comfortable in your deceit; the universe will right all wrongs and you will get your comeuppance. That first night, he had watched her undress slowly until she stood there naked with the soft light of the lamps caressing her dark skin. She was putting on a show for him to let him know that she was worth the money she had been spending quicker than a thirsty man drinking water. Her pink thongs lay in a heap at her feet and her 38D firm, youthful breasts swayed to its own inner rhythm as she approached him. Caribbean Leroy wanted to remain calm and play the part of the older man, but his emotions and thirst got the better of him. "Lemme taste that young pussy," he growled with lust in his voice. If there was one thing Caribbean Leroy could do well was eat pussy and by the time he had finished with Delores that night; her lips throbbed spontaneously every time she rolled over in bed. He had eaten her pussy for more than an hour and only fucked her for less than five minutes. Caribbean Leroy thought he was in heaven, but Delores knew that a young hot girl like herself would need more than a man's tongue to keep her satisfied. The very next day, she ventured to the Bronx to meet up with an ex-boyfriend from Jamaica who was hung like a horse and spread her open like a three lane highway. Caribbean Leroy assumed that her good mood that night was because of the pleasure he had given her the night before and all of his money that she was spending. And so it began.

Benjamin's dick had grown limp from fright as he watched the cold eyes of Caribbean Leroy and the guns that his men had drawn out. He prayed silently to God to get him out of this predicament. If God granted his wish, he would stop chasing pussy. A pussy chaser never stops chasing pussy. It's a part of your blood. It's who you are and even if you want to stop—*you can't*. All the men in his family were pussy chasers, so Benjamin was just following what he had seen and heard all his life.

"You look kinda scared young blood," Caribbean Leroy said to him without a trace of emotion in his voice.

Benjamin's mind raced as he tried to find a way out of this prickly situation. He hadn't even surveyed the apartment so he didn't know if there were any escape routes. The good thing was that they were on the first floor.

"I need to use the bathroom," he said meekly.

Caribbean Leroy held one finger, then two fingers.

Benjamin was confused and was about to put up one finger but thought better of it. He put up two fingers and the men laughed as he walked to the bathroom.

"I have a man outside—just in case your ass thinking about climbing out the window. He will put a bullet in that fat ass of yours."

Benjamin didn't think his ass was fat but it wasn't the time to be arguing with the man who held your life in his hands.

He closed the door behind him and peaked out the bathroom window. Two more of Caribbean Leroy's men were outside on the sidewalk and waved back to him. They were engrossed in a conversation about cricket and drinking Ting, a grapefruit flavored drink from Jamaica. Benjamin paced back and forth trying to come up with a plan, but he drew a blank. He splashed some cold water on his face and absently mindedly found a towel to wipe off his flaccid dick. He put his ear to the door and listened to Caribbean Leroy talk to Delores. Cold Beers and Fuck-Up had stepped out the room. The hurt in the old man's voice was undeniable.

"Delores, why you do this ting to me? Everything you want—you get—and still you want more."

It never crossed her mind that Caribbean Leroy might kill her, and Delores just took his show of force as nothing more than an act. She knew she had Caribbean Leroy whipped like a slave.

"Leroy, when was the last time you fucked me! All you want to do is eat my pussy. I need to be fucked and you're not man enough to do the job so I had to let this asshole come with me and do *your job*."

Benjamin, Cold Beers, and Fuck-Up were all listening to the conversation and shook their heads simultaneously in disbelief that this young girl had the hard clit to speak to Caribbean Leroy in that tone. They knew something that this young girl didn't know, but she should've known. Every man has his breaking point as to how much shit he is willing to take from a woman, and once he has crossed that street—there is no going back.

"You know I've tried everything. Even went to the Chinaman around the corner for some special herbs, but nothing has worked so far."

Benjamin almost felt sorry for the old man. He knew that he would be lost if his dick didn't work. He couldn't imagine going through life with a limp dick that was only good for pissing and playing dead. "So you want me to just wait around until your dick gets hard to fuck me! What the fuck am I supposed to do in the meantime? Masturbate everyday? I'm too young for that shit!"

Her words cut Caribbean Leroy deeper than any blade could have in a street fight. It hurt him more than the five times he had been shot and the doctors thought he wouldn't make it to another day. He had done things

299

for her that she did not even know about. He had paid off her parent's mortgage, paid for college for her two sisters and ensured that everyone in her family circle would be left alone by the hooligans on the block. For that, he got her disrespect and another man's dick up her ass.

"You're a stupid little girl. I should have left you right where I found you!"

Delores didn't know when to quit when she was ahead. "You know you wanted this young sweet pussy. I saw the way you looked at me when I served you that first day. If I was a piece of chicken, you would've eaten me right there." Her last comment made her laugh so loud that her breasts shook violently.

Caribbean Leroy called for his men to get the "pussy boy" from the bathroom. His eyes scanned Delores perfect body and he wished he was twenty years younger. He would've fucked the shit out of her and turned her out completely. But now, he was just an old man with nothing left but his pride.

Benjamin came back in and stood in the middle of the bedroom. He was unsure of what to do next. Delores was lying on the bed on her back as if she didn't have a care in the world. Caribbean Leroy strode to the bed and with his two huge black hands; he lifted Delores up by her dreadlocks and she swung back and forth like a rag doll. She was on her knees on the edge of the bed and his two hands wrapped around her throat to cut off her oxygen. He had never put his hands on her before and as she looked into his eyes for the first time-she saw the reflection of her death. Her words died in her throat and she swung her hands violently back and forth, but hitting him was like a butterfly trying to move a brick wall. Just when Delores thought she would blackout, Caribbean Leroy released her from his choke hold.

"You listening now," he growled at her.

She shook her head up and down to signal yes as she massaged her throat and coughed a few times. Her eyes met Benjamin's for a brief second and he was shaking like a leaf. This pussy clot boy would be no use to her. She would have to figure this out herself.

"Is man you want to fuck in my house! Come here boy!" Caribbean Leroy looked at Delores then signaled to Benjamin with a wave of his hand. Benjamin was too paralyzed to move so Fuck-Up and Cold Beers grabbed him around the elbow and brought him to their boss.

Caribbean Leroy's presence seemed to fill the room, and even though it was mid-afternoon, it felt darker as if death had settled in for the day. Benjamin felt like a child standing next to Caribbean Leroy. He didn't know where to look so he continued to look down at the floor.

"Look at me boy!" Caribbean Leroy called everybody boy, even grown men with children. It was his way of letting them know that they hadn't earned his respect.

Caribbean Leroy took two steps back from Benjamin as if he was going to walk away, and Benjamin took the opportunity to lust at Delores. He still wanted to fuck her and his dick stirred with interest. Before he could finish leering at her, the full force of Caribbean Leroy's giant black hand hit him across the face like the sound of thunder crackling through the sky. Caribbean Leroy slapped him so hard that he fell on to the bed right between Delores's open legs.

"Tis my pussy you want so much—take it then boy!" Caribbean Leroy ordered Benjamin. Benjamin wasn't sure what he wanted him to do so Cold Beers and Fuck-Up pressed their guns to his temple to make him comply. "The Bossman say to *yam*—so eat!" Cold Beers ordered Benjamin.

Benjamin began to slowly lick Delores' pussy and within a few licks, she was moist. It didn't take much to get her going. The whole thing was bizarre to him, but if it would keep him alive—he would do anything—he would even suck off all three of them if they ordered him to. Cold Beers had whispered to him before stepping away that Caribbean Leroy wanted him to make Delores come or else his brain would be splattered all over the bed. Fuck-Up whispered the same thing to Delores. Either they fuck like rabbits or else their bodies would be food for the fish in the Hudson River.

Caribbean Leroy sat back in his chair and watched the look of ecstasy come over Delores' face with every lick and tongue thrust inside of her pussy. She had never moaned this way for him. His face contorted into anger then sadness then acceptance.

Delores tried to control her moaning because she didn't want to piss off Caribbean Leroy even more, but there is something about knowing that you might die that gives you an extra rush of adrenaline. Her pussy was throbbing like crazy, her heart was beating way too fast and all she could think about was having Benjamin inside of her again. He was a pussyclot boy but he sure could fuck her pussy good. She was scared, but she was also horny. Her hips were gyrating in rhythm to Benjamin's deep tongue strokes in her pussy and her moans were louder now. Her pussy had grown wings, Benjamin's tongue was the pleasure that made her scream, and she was flying up in the clouds. He released her tender lips from his saturated lips and used the tip of his tongue to trace a trail of her sweetness from her belly button to her breasts. His lips found the ache in her breasts and sucked her erect nipples like a hungry baby sucking on a pacifier. He was into it now as his dick returned to its previous hardness and his curved thickness levitated at the entrance of her swollen heaven. The heat from her pussy whispered to his swollen head that she was hungry, but Benjamin held his ground still aware that Caribbean Leroy and his men were just a few feet away from them. But Delores was not to be denied; she wrapped her sinewy legs around his back, grabbed him by his ass and pulled the full length of his erection into her pussy. When pleasure calls your name it is hard to resist the lure of her seductive whisper, so Benjamin answered her mating call with his guttural moans of pleasure as he pierced the open wings of Delores' pussy.

Caribbean Leroy, Fuck-Up, and Cold Beers were transfixed watching Delores and Benjamin fuck. They weren't really fucking—it was more like sweet heavenly devouring. Before watching the show that was being performed before their eyes; these men believed themselves to be great lovers as do most men, but now, they envied the things that Benjamin was doing to Delores' body. His deep strokes inside of her tender lips were like watching a concert violinist at the height of his craft. It's too bad the motherfucker would have to die, they all thought, as her screams filled the room.

Delores' entire body shuddered as Benjamin's thickness expanded inside of her walls. Her body spoke to him and begged him to go faster…deeper—she wanted him to ram a hole through her if it would bring more pleasure. He obliged her cravings and fucked her like a crazy man. The familiar eruption of an orgasm careened through their bodies like a rocket taking off in the sky. They closed their eyes to better feel the pleasure circulating in their bodies and looking for a way to escape and give birth to its silent screams. Fuck-Up and Cold Beers approached the bed from both sides as Caribbean Leroy sat there with his eyes closed. He could not bear to watch what was about to happen. At least, she would die happy and in the throes of passion. That's all he ever wanted for her was to be happy.

Fuck-Up stifled his laughter as he watched Benjamin's "ugly face" the face that men get when they are about to come. It looked like he was constipated instead of experiencing great pleasure. Delores' body had reached its boiling point like a kettle whistling to let everyone know the water is hot. Benjamin felt her inner muscles pull him deeper into the quicksand of her pussy nectar and he released a flood of his own passion as she reached the zenith of her orgasm. Their moans merged together like an R & B duet team from the sixties as they traded sweet notes of passion. If they hadn't been so enthralled with their own voices; they would have heard Fuck-Up and Cold Beers getting ready to pull their triggers. The last thought that Benjamin Stevens had was that being inside of Delores was the closest he might ever get to heaven. In a few seconds, he would have a first class seat to heaven or hell. Delores' last thought was that she hoped that Caribbean Leroy would be so jealous of the dick down that Benjamin had given her that he would kill only Benjamin and not her.

Caribbean Leroy heard the simultaneous gunfire erupt and for a brief moment before the guns went off; he contemplated saving Delores' life, but there was no way he could keep the respect of his men and run his business. He ruled with fear. Men don't fear other men who are pussy whipped. Caribbean Leroy had seen many things in his sixty plus years and certain things are inevitable. There is always someone who will be a better lover than you, someone more dangerous, and there is always a sweeter pussy just waiting for the right dick to make it reach its full potential. Caribbean Leroy convinced himself that there would be another Delores as he took one last look at her dead body before leaving her apartment. On his way down the stairs, Caribbean Leroy noticed the single red rose on the floor by the front door of her building. He picked it up, inhaled deeply and closed his eyes to keep his tears from falling. He put the rose in his breast pocket and walked out into the afternoon.

It would be a long time before he forgot Delores St. Rose. There are some women that come into your life, and the minute they leave your side, their name is forgotten as quickly as the high from your last orgasm. Then there are some that live on in your heart and mind forever. Delores St. Rose would haunt Caribbean Leroy's dreams for the next twenty years of his life. On the day that he died, the last words he whispered before closing his eyes was her name.

1/26/09...6:11pm

# You Own Me

*"I do not want to be the leader. I refuse to be the leader. I want to live darkly and richly in my femaleness. I want a man lying over me, always over me. His will, his pleasure, his desire, his life, his work, his sexuality the touchstone, the command, my pivot. I don't mind working, holding my ground intellectually, artistically; but as a woman, oh, God, as a woman I want to be dominated. I don't mind being told to stand on my own feet, not to cling, be all that I am capable of doing, but I am going to be pursued, fucked, possessed by the will of a male at his time, his bidding."*

- Anaïs Nin

It had been almost a month since their last sexual encounter still shivers ran down her spine every time she replayed every nerve tingling detail, but to Serina it was more like a sensual religious experience. It confirmed to her everything that she knew about herself and awakened the submissive side of her, which had been lying dormant and unexplored for so many years. Serina always suspected that she would be open to it, but finding someone who could articulate what she wanted without her having to ask for it was the problem she faced until David Toussaint walked into her life.

Every single day that passed since David, who Serina now referred to as her Master, had first entered her life and planted his seed inside of her sweetest fruit, and every other orifice; Serina felt alive as if she had just awakened from a long self-induced coma. She loved the feeling that came with sexual liberation. During the course of the day, she would find herself daydreaming or just smiling to herself when thoughts of David came to mind. Her entire body would come to life as if someone had lit a fire to her. The experience, still eroticized in her mind and body, gave her chills just to think about him taking ownership of her. She still wasn't sure how he had done it, but why argue with the results. There was a glow about her which had not gone unnoticed by friends and co-workers.

Her friends had noticed the change in her and assumed that it was a man, but Serina enjoyed the secret life they shared of Master and slave. He owned her and it didn't feel cheap or make her feel weak that a man owned her mind, body, soul, and heart. In fact, it empowered her. It gave her confidence to tackle her everyday life with renewed vigor that she had not felt in a long time. Things were looking up for her.

Serina left work early for a scheduled hair appointment, but her stylist was backed-up with clients, so by the time she left the salon, she was running thirty minutes late to pick up her Master at JFK. She wanted everything to be perfect for their rendezvous because he demanded the best, and she always wanted to give him the best. She didn't want to disappoint him because it would mean that she wasn't being a good slave and thus expendable. He had become her breath, her air; she fell asleep to his image in her mind and thoughts of sucking his dick until he came repeatedly in her mouth. Serina was dick whipped and proud of it. Her pussy throbbed with anticipation knowing that in less than an hour; it would be filled with its Master's sweet black dick.

A slight shiver ran through her body as she thought about her Master punishing her severely for being late. She wondered what he would to do her if she were in fact late. The thought of his anger excited and scared her at the same time. A good slave does as she is told and it's not her place to push the boundaries of a slave/Master relationship. She feared losing him if she ever stepped out of line.

As she exited the beauty salon, Serina caught a glimpse of herself in the full-length mirror next to the door. The visual made her smile and she hoped her Master would like what he saw also. She had on black pumps, complimented by a tan skirt that reached just over her knees which allowed her to show off her smoothly shaven legs. Underneath she wore a pink thong that almost blended into her light skin. The crotch was Velcro and would give her Master easy access if he so desired. Serina subtlety ran her fingers across her skirt and pressed her fingers into the fleshy part of her pussy. The sensation made her moan softly as she imagined her Master ripping off her skirt separating her from her panties, and plunging his stiff dick deep inside of her swollen pussy lips. The thought of it made her flush with excitement and she felt exposed, but of course, no one was paying attention to her. They were all getting ready for their Friday night evenings on the town. She was getting ready to please her Master, to do whatever it was he needed her to do. She was here to serve him.

Serina wasn't a vain woman, but she loved how beautiful her hair looked when it was styled and looking pretty. It was long and brown and reached right above her shoulders. She always felt like a princess, like the ones in those romance novels she enjoyed reading as a child and later as a young adult. Her full lips and soft oval shaped eyes made her appear to be shy and gave away her secret that she was a sensual and passionate woman who enjoyed the act of making love. Every man who looked at her would instantly imagine her screaming his name and using her full lips for something other than kissing. Serina didn't want any of these men. All she wanted was to satisfy her Master's every wish. The cravings she felt for him were aches far beyond the physical. He fulfilled her in a way that no man had ever been able to before. For that kind of fulfillment, a woman would do anything she was told. Serina was no different. She was a pleaser and a giver. She would willingly give her Master anything he wanted, and if she couldn't do it—she would find a way to get it done.

She quickly checked her watch at the stoplight and immediately chastised herself for running late. Her Master wouldn't be pleased about being kept waiting. The thought of making her Master angry excited Serina because he would severely punish her for the slightest disobedience. She also did not want to disappoint him by being late. The dueling emotions raged in her body, and Serina didn't know which one she wanted to win.

The last time she had disobeyed her Master; he had unleashed the ferocity of his passion on her body that left her cowering and quivering on the edge of the bed. For the next few days, her entire body was sore, but it was the sort of pain that when remembered would bring a smile to her face.

Serina smiled so much that some of her friends thought that she was losing her damn mind. This was what she longed for all these years when she was married; a sense of sexual freedom that was unapologetic and untamed. Free to roam without harness; without having to explain to anyone why she enjoyed being a submissive slave to a man. Part of being a woman is having the freedom to choose the course of your sexuality. For too long, Serina had subjugated her will for another; a husband who was weak and undeserving of her. He was a good man, but he didn't possess the innate gift of overpowering her body and mind just by looking at her. Many times, Serina felt that she was the man in the relationship because he wasn't able to control her and dominate her in the way that she craved. She wanted that feeling of being overpowered so that when a man told her to lay still and she dared move—**even an inch**, he would punish her body and mind with sadistic pleasure that would make her ache for him even more. This is what she wanted, but she never received it from her ex-husband.

When David stared at Serina, her body would lose any desire to resist his charm. She was his to do his bidding. Finally, she was able to submit freely to a man who instinctively knew how to touch her body and leave her feeling as if she had been fucked and made love to by four or five dicks at the same time.

Her Master knew the secret to making love that most men, either didn't know or care to learn. To them it was all about the physical. They didn't understand that making love to the body was like taking a shower and only wetting the upper half of your body and the lower half is still dry. The full experience of a making love is to get her mind and body wet and make sure that every inch has been touched and made to feel loved. Making love is the same thing. You have to seduce the mind of a woman long before you can even think about penetrating her flesh. You have to mind fuck her and take her on a journey that will make her body ache for the physical, but the mental will be so real, so intense, that it will feel like the real thing. Before you even touch her enflamed skin and forever leave your imprint on her, her body will have already been primed and aroused just waiting to be touched. If a man can touch your mind and body with equal passion; then your heart is already his for the taking. He doesn't have to do anything except to look at you and he will know that you love him. Serina hoped that she wasn't so transparent to her Master as yet, but love is a feeling that when you breathe it from your soul, it becomes an entity that is its own person, with its own voice. It will not stay quiet even when you try to hide it. Serina's love lived in her eyes and glowed on her face.

A light rain had begun to fall as the light changed from red to green and then back to orange. Serina was so lost in thought that only the honking of the cars behind her snapped her back to her immediate reality. The succession of colors of the stoplight reminded her of a game she used to play as a child in school during recess: "Red Light Green Light One Two Three." The memory of her childhood brought a pained smile to her face. It was a life of strict adherence without any room for self-expression. She escaped into the fantasy world of books and movies and created her own persona. When you are a child, you submit to the will of your parents because you don't have any other choice. As an adult, you submit because you want to and can always walk away because you are now in control. Serina knew the truth. She had no control anymore. Her Master controlled her and she would have it no other way.

David was a man who prided himself on being on time even when tardiness was beyond his control; he didn't like the silent implication that he wasn't a man of his word. His flight into JFK was delayed by half an hour, and he was sure that Serina was already waiting for him. His lateness gave her the upper hand in their relationship because as her Master they both expected that everything go according to schedule. Any little hiccups could altar the balance of power.

"We will be landing at JFK in approximately five minutes," the pilot's voice crackled over the intercom. "We apologize for the delay and thank you for flying Delta Airlines. We appreciate your business."

"If you appreciate my business then get me here on time," David muttered to no one in particular. All he had was a carry on bag so he would not have to wait to clear customs. The flight attendant at the door gave him her best phony smile and he gave her one back.

Every step he took through the long winding corridor and onto the escalator was one step closer to pleasure; into the sweet depths of his slave, Serina. He deftly sidestepped passengers with children and other carry-on baggage that they were wheeling around without any consideration for people around them. He felt his body getting excited with each step he took that brought him closer to Serina. He ached to be inside of her and claim what was his. He wanted to fuck her into submission and remind her again that he was her Master and that he owned her. He hoped that she might challenge him so that he could get rough with her. He wanted to punish her. They both enjoyed this sort of intense sexual foreplay. On the escalator ride down to the sidewalk, he spotted her waiting for him and their first encounter came back to him in sharp colors of pleasure.

David had renamed her Serina because names starting with "S" were always more sensual when they whispered from your lips and being sung passionately into a woman's ears. Now that she was Serina, she inhabited the name as if she was born to it. They had met by accident at a Barnes and Noble bookstore in the city during one of his book tours for his recently published collection of erotic poetry, "Poetic Tongue". During the reading of one of his pieces "The Domination of Her Will," he glanced up and noticed her in the back row, seemingly in a trance. Every word pierced her deeply and she was visibly affected as he read this erotic piece. He would find out later that during the reading, she had become so aroused that she had a spontaneous orgasm. It was the first time something like that ever happened to her. David had to meet this woman so he approached her from behind in one of the aisles as she read *Sugar* by Bernice McFadden.

"How did you enjoy the prose?"

Serina was startled to hear a voice behind her feeling as if it was just inches away from her ears. She knew who it was even before she turned around. The lithe of his Caribbean accent fingered her earlobes and her skin felt as if it had been set on fire. She struggled to calm herself down before turning around to come face to face with David Toussaint.

In the two seconds it took Serina to turn around to face David, he had done a quick inspection of her to see if she was to his liking. She wore a simple black dress that clung to her body, but wasn't too tight as to draw any unwanted attention. She was a woman used to hiding her sexuality, and at first glance, she appeared to be demure, almost afraid to embrace the raw power of her beauty. David had noticed a few men giving her the eye as they walked by the aisle, but none of them approached her. She hadn't noticed the attention. When she finally turned around to face him, she was unable to look him in the eye. It was the classic sign of a submissive woman who was giving ground to a more dominant personality. David was intrigued by this shy beautiful flower

315

standing before him that was afraid to bloom to her full potential. When she finally managed to summon the courage to look at him, she pretended to be looking at a book behind his shoulders. It was in that first meeting that he knew that he had to have her. She was like an empty beautiful canvas of untapped sexuality. He wanted to paint her with every single passionate color he could conjure and watch her bloom into the beautiful woman that lived inside her heart. He wanted to paint a Masterpiece. She would be the perfect subject. He suspected she was willing, but he had to be sure.

He autographed a copy of his book for her and as they stood between the bookcases with the smell of new books, coffee, and raw passionate energy flowing between them; the air was heavy with their erotic thoughts. Serina's breath was heated with desire. Her eyes stared downwards as David's words of erotic sensuality caressed her mind, body, and soul. Every syllable, every word, felt like a match being lit on her skin. Serina wrapped her arms around her chest as David read a few of his poems to her attempting to exploit her amorous nature. He didn't have to try too hard. Serina was open to his touch. She yearned for a man to be a man and claim her body and mind, and order her to do his bidding. She ached to feel his words growing inside of her and settle inside of her soul.

David noticed her reaction as he read to her. She was lost in the moment, eyes closed and unaware of him watching her. Her head rocked back and forth slowly as she leaned against the bookshelf. She would sigh as he said certain words and exhale when phrases of being ravished and devoured crossed his lips. David took in the entire scene making mental notes to use later on when they made love. Her nipples pierced through her bra and called to David's lips to alleviate her pain. Serina was ready to let David release her deepest cravings. For the next few hours, they talked about her. They didn't talk about him. David got a good sense about her just by observing her. He knew what he had to do to make her submit. Over the next few days, through emails and phone conversations, Serina revealed herself to David. Her submissive personality once dormant slowly rose to the surface. She was ready to serve a Master. She was ready to be a slave. By the time they met for their first sexual encounter, the anticipation of what she expected would be hard to match. Her imagination had been working overtime and by the time David stepped through the doors of her apartment; she was so nervous that she was barely able to utter a word, but her body and mind were ready to submit fully to him. All he had to do was take what was already his.

The urge to be subservient overwhelmed Serina as she opened the door and David pushing her up against the wall to take control of the situation. The black nightgown she had worn for this special occasion lay on the floor within seconds. He ripped it off and it lay in tatters at her feet. She stood before him naked and blushing. She was embarrassed but aroused at being naked in his presence for the first time.

"You are beautiful," David whispered in her ears. He pulled her naked body into his arms and whispered something else into her ears. Serina nodded without hesitation. She was here to serve her Master.

She undressed him slowly and with his permission caressed his body. Within minutes, he stood before her naked with his erection waving around in the thickened sexual air. The magnitude of having her Master naked in front of her for the first time embarrassed Serina. She dared not look at his body because her emotions would spill over like a drink overflowing a glass. David seized the opportunity to begin training her and ordered her to step back and look at his body.

Slowly, Serina raised her eyes and filled it with the naked beauty of David Toussaint. Her reaction was instantaneous and unhidden. Her face turned a crimson red and her lips quivered with hunger as she fell in love with his eyes, nose, lips, chin, his hairy chest; and swinging slowly between his thick thighs was the most beautiful dick she had ever seen in her life. It called to her as it rose in strength and pointed directly at her.

"Come here, Serina."

"Yes, Master," Serina answered as if it was the most natural thing to call him Master and not David.

He whispered in her ears again and she dropped to her knees. The heat of his breath burned her ears, and her lips and mouth were on fire. She did what was asked of her as his manhood waved in front of her face and her head moved forward to taste what her body had been craving, but he pushed her to the ground and she fell back. Serina lay there confused and angry, but she quickly regained her composure. A slave does not defy her Master, and she wanted to completely submit to his will. If he wanted her on the floor then that is where she belonged. He knew best. He knew how far too push her to tap into her deepest sexual desires. She wanted her every thought and movement controlled in the bedroom.

David wanted to torture and tease her, and he wanted it as much as she did. He had to demonstrate from the outset that he was the dominant one. He had to lead the way so she would follow. Looking down at her on the floor, legs spread open and both sets of lips ready to please made his dick even harder. He got off on the power trip of owning her and controlling her. Sex within the parameters of the normal interaction didn't do anything for him. It was bland—boring. He needed this to get his blood flowing hot with passion. He needed her to inspire him in the bedroom.

Wordlessly, he signaled to her that she could get up and he cast his eyes down to his throbbing erection. He would allow her the pleasure of sucking his dick. "Thank you, Master."

For the next few minutes, Serina sucked, pulled, caressed and choked on every inch of David's erection. He held her head between his hands and at times would control how many inches she could have at one time. Serina was greedy and wanted it all. In a small act of defiance, she tried to take more than what her Master had offered her, and she felt the force of his anger for her defiance. He pulled her head back and as she looked up at him with innocent eyes; he slapped her twice across the right side of her face. They were controlled slaps meant to send a message, *Do as you're told!* It wasn't the first time a man hit Serina, but it was the first time it was done during the act of sexual pleasure. The suddenness of his violent outburst both shocked and excited her. It made her pussy tingle and her nipples got harder.

She wanted more but she dared not ask for it. They played a game of cat and mouse to see who would give in first. Serina, though inexperienced, had a talented mouth, lips, and tongue. She sucked her Master's dick as if she had a MDD (Master's Dick Degree) in oral pleasure. She wanted him to fill her throat so she could swallow him dry. He refused to give in to what she wanted, as was his intention, so she tried harder to please her Master. Just when she felt the veins in his dick pulsating and ready to erupt, he pulled away and stopped himself from exploding.

"I want you to bathe me. Go turn the shower on."

"Yes Master."

Serina got up to walk away but couldn't take her eyes off her Master's dick which was still hard and looked lonely without her lips curled around it. She wanted more but was still unsure of the rules of Master and slave.

"Can I have another taste, Master?"

Without waiting for her Master's response, Serina made a grave error, reached for his outstretched erection, and felt its warmth slide through her fingers. She dropped to her knees again to taste the sweet drops of his release. Her lips parted slowly, her tongue slid smoothly towards his glistening quenching liquid, and just as her eyes rolled back in their sockets to welcome his erection into its new home; her Master knelt down on one knee and grabbed her roughly by her jaw.

"Did I tell you to suck my dick? Did I give you permission to taste me?"

"No Master...I'm sorry."

"Slaves don't think. They just do what they are told. Get up!"

Her Master got up and walked over to the bed and motioned Serina to lie down across his lap.

Serina knew what was coming next. No one had ever done that to her before. She was fearful and excited. She silently hoped that her disobedience would result in this, but she knew that she had displeased her Master and that saddened her. A good slave always pleases her Master. Even as a child, she had learned this lesson well, to do as you're told or suffer the consequences. Her submission to authority had begun at an early age. She was well schooled in following directions.

Serina stretched out her entire body on her Master's lap and he tenderly ran his fingers from her feet to between her thighs and up her back. He did this a few times as her body trembled under his touch. As he did this, he whispered sweet words through her hair and it kissed her ears. She was in heaven. Every word that he said, she would nod yes.

"You are mine. You will do as I say. You are never to question my authority. I own you now. I am your Master and you are my slave. Your will is not your own. Your pussy is mine. Your lips are mine. Your ass is mine…every sweet orifice on your body is mine. Do you understand? You are here to serve me. I will fuck you when I want…how I want…and you will accept it without any question."

Every word from her Master's lips made Serina's clit throb and her pussy wetter. This is what she had always dreamed about and until recently had almost given up hope of it becoming a reality. Now that it was happening, she was only too happy to submit and give her body and mind completely to her Master. She couldn't help herself as her body began to spasm uncontrollably and she felt her orgasm building. That's when she felt the first waves of her Master exerting his control over her. His right hand came down on her naked flesh and sounded like a whip being snapped when hand met her soft naked flesh.

"Oh Master, please."

"Don't speak!"

"Yes Master," she whimpered.

He continued spanking her and Serina swallowed her tears, her cries, and numerous orgasms…and still— he continued to punish her. When he was finally finished spanking her, they were both drenched in sweat and Serina was unable sit down. She felt pain, but a pain she would gladly accept every time.

This was the beginning of their Master and slave relationship.

Serina didn't blink as she watched her Master descend down the escalator like a bronzed god descending from the skies. You are so beautiful she thought to herself, like an Adonis. The rain had stopped falling and she was thankful that her hair kept its body. She wanted to look perfect for her Master as she smoothed out her dress and ran her fingers through her brown hair. The evening that lay ahead would be filled with untold passion and Serina smiled at her good fortune. The lips of her already moist pussy rubbed together as if they were clapping lips cheering for her Master. They soon would be filled with the thickness of her Master. She hoped that he would water her already moist garden with every drop of sweet water from his dick. The sensation of having him come inside of her pussy and mouth was the ultimate sense of accomplishment for Serina. It was only then did she feel that she completely served her Master.

David stepped into the evening and the night became more beautiful. Serina wasn't aware that she was holding her breath until she released it and she felt a rush of oxygen flooding her lungs. The sight of this man did things to her that she never felt before. Every step he took closer to her was a step that he took deeper into her essence. She wanted to hold him there and keep him all to herself. She knew this was selfish, but the power of her desire and love outweighed all things rational. She wanted to merge her body and mind with his, to become one so that they would be indistinguishable.  She had images of them swimming together like fish in the ocean, swimming aimlessly with no direction, not a care in the world except the immediacy of satisfying their desires to feed on each other's mind and body.  Serina was in love.  She knew that she would not be able to keep it from her Master.  The words were stamped all over face so she assumed that he already knew, but just hadn't said anything as yet.

He was a few feet away from her and coming fast.  She was pleased that he wore the black pinstripe suit that she tailored for him.  He smiled when she presented it to him that day and it made her giddy to please him.  It was the same sort of intense giddiness she felt the day after their first encounter, and a permanent blush was painted on her light skin.  Surprisingly, he had called that day to check on her and hearing his words through the receiver was like having his hands, fingers, tongue, lips, and dick inside of her simultaneously.  As Serina squirmed in her chair, she put one hand between her thighs to try and stem the flood of an impending orgasm.  It was too late.  When he claimed her again as his, she moaned with joy and her clit pulsated without shame.  She relaxed, leaned back in her chair and allowed her orgasm to consume her.  No one in the office heard her quiet moans as her orgasm sustained its life far beyond the birth of a normal orgasm.  It was the first time she came without being physically touched, but he had touched her in ways that not even her Master could imagine or comprehend.

There are some experiences that defy logic and to try to capture them in words would be wholly insufficient.

He was here.

Everything around her cease to exist: cabs honking trying to get passengers, airplanes flying overhead, or passengers struggling with their baggage. The only thing that mattered to Serina was that her Master was here.

"Hello Serina."

She kept her head down as she approached him. All she saw was the gray pavement and his black shoes when she stood right in front of him. Goosebumps lined her exposed arms like thousands of little brown dots. She was in his space and inhaled the scent of his cologne. It surged through her like electricity running through wire. She wanted to be in his arms, but she had to wait for his permission.

"Hello Master."

He touched her under her chin with the lightest of touches and his touch directed her to look into his eyes. He knew the power he had over her and wanted to exercise his dominance. He knew she wanted a kiss, a hug, but to deny her would only intensify the pleasure later on. No words were exchanged. It was an exchange of sexual energy that didn't need to be verbalized. If he had asked her to drop to her knees at that instant—Serina would have complied. He walked to the passenger side of the car and left his bag on the sidewalk. Serina picked it up and deposited it in the backseat.

She slid into the driver's seat and her dress rode up her thighs leaving her legs exposed. Even though she could not see his eyes, she knew that he was watching her. The intensity of his stare felt like heat piercing her skin and caressing her thighs. Her pussy was on fire like a burning brushfire in California and he had not even laid a finger on her yet. How is it possible that one person can have such power over another human being? It reminded Serina of the scene from "Malcolm X" when Denzel Washington had all the men from the nation of Islam ready to act on his signal. A police officer said to no one in particular, "No man should have that much power." David had all the power and she wanted to give him more.

The hotel wasn't that far from the airport, and they would be there in less than fifteen minutes. David had other plans for Serina. As she pulled out of the parking lot, he turned to face her from across from the passenger's seat and ran his hands up her thighs until he touched the warmth of her pussy lips. She was never to wear any underwear or bra unless he told her to wear them. His hands felt strong, sure of what it wanted to do and knowing what turned Serina on. She stared straight ahead as his eyes bore into her, and she tried to concentrate on the traffic ahead. He used his fingers to spread her legs further apart and slid them one by one inside of her moistness without any resistance. She was wet and ready to be fucked.

"I know you're hungry, Serina," he teased her as he fed her the warm juices from her pussy that dripped on his fingertips then licked his own fingers.

"Thank you Master," she purred as she sucked his fingers while keeping her eyes on the road. Traffic had come to a stop. There was an accident up ahead. They were boxed-in with nowhere to go.

He was moving around in his seat. Undoing his pants, opening his jacket and revealing to her the sweetest dick her eyes had ever seen.

"Come here," he ordered her. "Suck your Master's dick."

Serina didn't have to be told twice. She quickly undid her seatbelt and reached for his erection which was swaying back and forth like a seductive dream that she had to taste. The veins of his erection looked like roots growing from a tree; each one pulsating and vital with the ability to give life. That's how she felt as her tongue traced up and down the full length of her Master's dick. With every encounter, she felt more alive and secure in the knowledge that she had found herself. She no longer felt as if she was wandering in the dark in search of answers. The light was now on. The answers were right here pulsating between her lips. Every time they were together, she discovered secrets about herself that up until now had been a mystery to her. The answer for her was absolute servitude to her Master.

The full length of his erection could not be contained in the smallness of her sweet mouth, and he used his hands to hold her head still as the rest of his manhood slipped inside the wetness of her throat.

"Don't stop until I tell you to," he ordered as he eased back into his seat and fucked her mouth. Every thrust felt like a jackhammer exploding between Serina's lips and making her teeth ache with the force of his penetration. He would fill her throat with his thickness and held her head down until she had no more oxygen; then he would pull her back up by her neck and slap her a few times across her face with this dick. Every time he did this, Serina would keep her mouth open hoping that his dick would slip back into its wet home. A minute without her Master's dick between her lips was sixty seconds too long without pleasure. His dick was her air. It gave her life.

The traffic ahead began to move, but Serina didn't stop sucking until her master allowed her to stop and continue to drive. A few irate drivers honked their horns behind them and gave Serina dirty looks as they drove by. She serenely smiled back at them. They arrived at the hotel without further incident and went straight to their hotel room. The elevator ride up to the fifth floor was packed with adults and teenagers. Her Master leaned against the wall and drew Serina into his body. She felt safe like a little girl who knew that her man would always take of her. He reached for her right hand and allowed her to touch his erection through the material of his pants. Serina closed her eyes for the entire ride up, and every vibration of the ride up to their hotel room caused her to moan softly as she massaged his thickness. She wanted to drop to her knees and allow him to drain his liquid sweetness down her throat. Before the room door was even closed, Serina had slipped out of her dress and ached to drop to her knees to suck her Master's dick. She knew better. She didn't want to take a chance that he would deny her the pleasure of sucking and licking his entire body for the evening as punishment for thinking on her own.

"Master, can I run you a bath and wash you down?"

"Yes. That would be nice."

Every word of approval from her Master was like oxygen giving Serina a breath of fresh air to invigorate her soul. She clung to every word; and later on in the evening after he left; she would replay those words searching for the inflection in his tone as she tried to decipher the true depths of his approval.

He checked his phone messages while Serina ran the shower. He liked it hot, but not too hot. She got in to test it before letting him get in. Everything had to be just right.

"Are you ready to take a shower, Master?"

She was disappointed that he had undressed himself, but the full impact of his naked body eased her disappointment. He looked like a stallion prancing around the hotel room. A Mandingo warrior about to launch his spear into her sweet nectar fruit. He had one those football player balloon asses that just stood there in defiance of gravity. Serina had the urge to smack his ass the same he had smacked hers, but she dared not cross the invisible line of Master and slave.

"Master?"

"No."

He knew what she wanted even before she asked. He always seemed to know what she needed. Her lips trembled with hunger as she watched his dick sway rhythmically between his legs as if dancing to its own music.

Serina held her breath when he entered the shower, and slowly exhaled as his entire body got wet. She reached for the washrag and soap over her head, and proceeded to lather his body completely. He stepped into the water allowing it to soak his back. He stood there quiet, unmoving as Serina dropped to her knees to wash his feet, working her way up to his dangling erection which glistened like a sword and seemingly begged for her lips. She washed his hairy chest with her bare hands and felt the curls of his chest hairs sliding between her fingers. Without a word, he turned around and she washed his arms, worked the rag around his entire back, and then slowly washed his ass. Deliberately, she dropped to her knees and inhaled the scent of soap, and for an extra second, she allowed herself the pleasure of feeling the heat emitting from the crack of his ass to kiss her face. She wanted to spread his cheeks and bury her tongue in his darkness. She yearned to taste the secret that lay hidden in his unexplored anus. Only a man secure in his inherent manhood would be secure enough to let her try such a thing. She would have to wait for such a treat.

David walked back into the bedroom still wet, and a trail of water followed him along with Serina's eyes. She was ready to use her tongue like a towel and dry him off on his command. To her delight, he granted her wish as he laid his entire body horizontally across the bed. Serina enjoyed the scene of him laying there for a second and allowed it to seep into her mind so she could vividly recollect it later. He looked like a delicious chocolate buffet adorned with goodies, just waiting for her tongue to sample everything and everywhere on his body. She was hungry. A month is too long to go without the thing you crave for the most—to suck, lick, swallow and feel deep inside of your mind, body and pussy.

His eyes were closed as if he was dreaming. He looked peaceful. Serenely beautiful. His erection lay on his stomach—thick and long. It was curved like a boomerang. The only place Serina wanted it to come back to was between the fullness of all four of her lips. Her body quivered with anticipation as she got on the bed and prepared to feel the supremacy of thick-headed manhood piercing the tight moist folds of her sweet pussy. She would submit to him only if he took her by force. Serina yearned for a man to overpower her with the sheer force of his manhood. She wanted a man to be blessed equally with sensitivity and a will to dominate his woman. Too many times in her life, she had been left unfulfilled and wondered what the hell had just happened to her night of passion. David walked softly, but behind closed doors, he wielded the power of his manhood with the confidence that Serina's pussy throbbed for incessantly.

His eyes were still closed as if playing a cat and mouse game with her. She wanted to be caught. She wanted him to fuck what he owned without showing any mercy. Maybe she would have to push him a bit more to awaken the beast that she knew lived right below the surface. There is a beast in every man. Some men wear it in their words and actions, and others like David; it is simmering right below the surface, ready to explode. Serina wanted to find that right chemistry to make him use her body like a piñata. An idea came to her, but she didn't know if she would be brave enough to pull it off. Her thighs straddled his upper body and the heat of his erection thumped softly against her lower back. He reached up to her face and stroked her cheeks tenderly. Serina closed her eyes and lost herself in the tender moment. She reached behind her back and grasped the full thickness of his erection in her hand, and guided it to the center of the heat emitting from between her thighs. The heat and hardness of his erection slid effortlessly between her swollen lips, and she cried out with pleasure. He controlled how many inches she would receive by grabbing her around the waist and the nape of her neck, to control the depth of his penetration. She wanted every thick inch of it, but he teased her by stopping at the exact moment when he knew that another inch would make her cry out with the passion of a woman who was getting deliciously dicked down.

"Please Master," Serina begged as he continued not give her what she wanted. "Hurt me. Make your pussy cry for you. Fuck what is yours."

"Shut up! I will fuck you how I want to fuck you. Do you understand?"

"Yes Master," Serina said reluctantly. This was the opening she needed to goad him. She didn't want to overstep her bounds, but she ached to feel the physicality and brutality of his passion, lashes administered to her body. She chose her words carefully. It was now or never.

"I thought you were my Master," she cooed as she rode his dick. "Maybe I should be your master," Serina laughed girlishly in order to distract his attention away from her combative words. If he truly was the man, the Master, that she had envisioned; he would respond with the fierceness of the male ego being called to battle.

His left hand slowly tightened around her throat. Air was a commodity she would not have much of soon.

It was happening.

Serina closed her eyes in readiness for anything and everything her Master had in store for her. She wanted him to punish her for her disobedience to his will.

His hands tightened. His body grew tense beneath her coiled like a snake about to strike. He drew her head right along his and whispered in her ear, "You asked for it."

His erection throbbed hard inside of her heated pussy and his fingers dug deep into her waist. Without any foreplay, he launched himself upward deep inside of her tightness. The suddenness of his aerial assault caught Serina by surprise and her body bucked upwards as if she was riding a mechanical bull. He continued pounding her so deeply and fiercely that Serina didn't have time to process her thoughts or catch her breath. Her screams echoed through the small room and bounced back to her ears.

"This is what happens when you challenge me," her Master said throatily as he kept one hand on her waist and lifted the left one to wrap around her throat. "I own you. Don't you ever tell me what to do!"

All Serina could do was nod yes as she bounced up and down viciously on his erection, and could barely breath with his hand wrapped around her throat. With each penetration, it closed tighter until she thought that she would black out. Her pussy ached for more and her Master gave her what she desired.

He used his left hand to make her body more upright then removed it from her waist. Her back arched backwards slightly and she braced herself for the inevitable. The feel of his open hand slamming against the softness of her right cheek shook something loose inside of Serina. This is what she wanted. She needed to be disciplined. Slaps rained down from his right hand to both sides of her face and he continued to punish her pussy and face repeatedly without any mercy. The simultaneous pounding and vicious slaps ignited Serina's body with a fire that demanded to be fed. She was in her glory. "Fuck me Master! This pussy is yours baby! There is nothing I won't do for you! I am here to serve only you!"

The words streamed from her mouth between whimpers and tears as her body shook violently with the ferocity of his passion assaulting her body. It was a level of physical passion that few would understand. She had always craved it in silence, afraid that the men before her Master would think she was some kind of freak or pervert. He however understood. He embraced her desires as being valid and did not think that she was less of a woman for feeling this way. She was what he needed. She was what he craved to make him feel alive. They understood the complexities of passion and love. They were both separate emotions careening down a one-way street without any brakes. The crash was inevitable. The façade of control is an illusion, and once we come to the realization that feelings, like love and passion, adhere only to its own rules, can we free ourselves to bask in the true beauty of love and passion without any restraints.

There was nothing left for Serina's body to do except to submit to the passion that enveloped it. The shackles of her former life as an unfulfilled wife seemed to be racing by her with every penetration and every slap that stung her face. She wanted to make up for lost time. She wanted to steal back all the years she had lost. She wished that her Master could fuck her for every lousy day of her marriage. She wanted the dignity she had lost every time her husband told her that it was her fault when he came in under a minute. It was her fault that he was unsatisfied. He made her feel like less than a woman. If only he could see her now. If he could see how a real man fucked a woman. If he could see the ecstasy of passion etched on her face as her Master fucked his pussy. Serina relived all these emotions as her body convulsed, the muscles in her pussy tightened, and she came so hard that tears flowed freely down her face.

"I'm not done with you yet. After tonight, you will never challenge me again. On your knees...NOW!"

Serina gently removed herself from her Master's still stiff erection and did as she was told. He sat on the side of the bed, grabbed her by her long hair, and forced the full length of his erection down her throat. She gagged and struggled for breath. He held her head and continued to fuck her mouth. Tears and saliva mingled together as one. He removed himself fully from her mouth and slapped her again. He did it repeatedly until he was satisfied.

"Have you had enough?"

There was only one answer she wanted to give him.

"No. I want more Master."

He stood up and looked down at his slave. The woman he now owned. A feeling of power, entitlement, swept over David and it felt like a hurricane washing ashore. He had punished her as he had never done to another woman, and still, she wanted more. A good Master gives his slave what she wants.

He crouched slightly over and slapped her hard across her face with his erection. His dick was heavy as it smacked her cheeks and brushed past her lips. Serina looked up at her Master with love in her eyes. He had permission to do anything he wanted to her. She was his with no questions asked. He held her by the back of her neck and used his other hand to open her mouth wider. He didn't have to do that. Serina was ready and willing to give him anything he wanted without him ever having to ask for it. The heat of his erection brushed across her lips and Serina wrapped her long tongue around its girth and tried to pull it deep inside of her mouth. Her Master had other plans for her.

"You will learn the true meaning of being a slave," he said softly to her. His voice wasn't menacing but it was strong and filled with passion. It made Serina tremble inside with desire.

"Yes, Master. Do anything you want to me," Serina said with surety. "I am yours. You own me."

Before the words barely escaped her lips, David forced the full length of his thick shaft down Serina's throat. She gagged at suddenly being unable to breath and struggled for air but David deprived her of it. For a brief moment, Serina thought that she would pass out, but then he withdrew himself completely from her throat. Serina gasped and it suddenly hit her that her life was in her Master's hands. He had the power give her pleasure, pain, happiness, and anything else he wanted to. Knowing that Serina could never get enough of sucking his dick, David turned to walk away and heard her whimper softly. His dick stiffened again and he turned around to face her.

"You want more?"

She nodded yes.

"Show me how much you want it. Crawl to me."

Serina got down on all fours and crawled towards David. He backed away and let her crawl to him. She kissed his feet and slowly worked her way up between his thighs. The sensation of Serina's wet tongue sent tremors rocketing through his entire body, but he had more work to do before allowing himself to fully let go and let the moment wash over him.

He bent down and whispered in her ears, "Get on the bed and lay down on your stomach." Without looking at him, Serina did what she was told.

She could feel her pussy pulsating between her thighs as if there was a time bomb inside of it, and at any moment, it would explode. Her heart was beating just as fast as she waited for her Master to have his way with her again. This is who she was; a woman who loved to please and she found the right man to indulge her fantasies. Serina could not get enough of him—he was intoxicating. She wore her passion as if it was her skin. It made her feel like a woman who was being ravished, devoured, made love to and fucked to within an inch of her life. Then she felt his breath and words caressing her ears with passion that did not scream, but was quiet and just as intense. He was mind fucking her. "This is my pussy. I will fuck you when and how I want to—at anytime I want to. No other man will touch my pussy or kiss your lips. If I ever hear of you doing anything to disrespect or give away what is mine—you will pay dearly. Do you understand?" Serina nodded without saying a word. "I am your Master. You are my slave. You will not question your orders. You will just do as you're told." He slapped her again and Serina absorbed the full impact of it and came again.

David held her by her waist and lifted her ass into the air. Serina looked as if she was ready to be fucked again. He used his hands to pry her legs open a little wider and stepped back to admire his work. The first smack of his right hand against her ass caught her by surprise and Serina screamed with sweet pain. She had never been spanked before in her life. The severity of his spanking her was so swift and hard that she could actually feel her ass throbbing with pain. Serina would have problems sitting down for the next week, but in the midst of pleasure, the future is irrelevant. He stopped for a minute, bent down, kissed each cheek tenderly and then bit into her so deeply that it felt like he had literally bitten away a chunk of her ass.

"Awwwwww fuck baby," Serina whimpered. "What are you doing to me baby? You make me so crazy for you that I can't control myself."

"That's how I always want you —hungry and thirsty for me."

David got up on the bed behind Serina and slipped a finger into the tightness of her ass, and used her wetness to lubricate her tight hole. Serina groaned in appreciation of having him inside of her. He slipped the thickness of his fat dick head gently into her ass and Serina moaned with desire. She struggled to accommodate his many inches as he slipped deeper and deeper inside of her until she thought that she might actually pass out, but then they hit a groove. Every stroke hit her just right and she bucked her ass backwards as she urged him to fuck her deeper. He reached between her thighs and started to manipulate her clit and it drove Serina crazier. Her ass was being fucked. Her clit was being stroked. She felt the ticking time bomb of an orgasm about to explode. She tried to slow down his penetration, but he knew that her orgasm would be gushing out within seconds. His strokes became harder and deeper and Serina felt as if she was hallucinating with pleasure as she came so hard that her entire body shook with her release.

She lay quietly on the bed for a few seconds and the passion of the moment overwhelmed her senses. Her tears were soft at first and then became increasingly louder. Serina wasn't sure why she was crying, but then realized she was crying for the woman in her that had been lost all these years and made to feel less than she was. She was crying for the woman who had been unleashed and made to feel more beautiful and more passionate than she had ever been in her life. Her tears were a reminder to her that she was still alive and able to feel what it was like to be touched to the core of her being. She was being touched, kissed, fucked, made to feel special, and made love to all at the same time. Her body and mind were overflowing with sensual ecstasy. "Thank you," she whispered.

David stepped into the bedroom and cleaned off his still erect dick with a warm rag.

"Come here."

Hearing his command jumpstarted Serina's body and she crawled to the edge of the bed where her Master stood waiting for her. She knew what he wanted as she stared hungrily at his waving hypnotic dick. It looked so beautiful like a separate entity from his body. It was as if it was its own life form—a separate entity. The sheer beauty of her Master's dick stole Serina's breath away and she was unashamed in her thoughts. She wanted it all to herself. She wanted to be the one to receive all its pleasures. She wanted to be the one who sucked him until he was empty. She wanted to be everything to him. She wanted him more than anything she had ever wanted in her life, but was satisfied with what he was able to give her.

His dick was hot as it slid across her lips. It felt like the first taste of a hot drink that she would swallow. The sensation of his thickness against her lips and tongue was a feeling that went beyond words for Serina. The sheer thrill of it shocked her system like a car battery receiving a jolt. It brought her a special joy to feel his strength throbbing between her lips, and knowing that she would be the one to swallow the sweet fruit of his passion. She took a peak up at his face and saw the contortion of his facial muscles as he grew inside of her. Serina used her hands to stroke him to full length and tasted the first drop of the warmth of his juices. Her throat was hungry for it but she knew that she could not rush him. He would fill her throat when he was ready. Her Master did nothing before he was ready.

David grabbed a handful of Serina's hair and pulled it hard as he forced himself down her throat again. There was something special about the extra softness of her full lips, the way she looked at him and how hungry she was to drink him that made his erection throb even harder. He gently caressed her face as his erection went back and forth between her lips. There is something extra special about a woman who willingly serves her man without him ever having to ask. She does it from a sense of desire not of duty because she wants him to be happy, and in turn, she too is happy.

Serina felt her Master's throbbing head expanding inside of her mouth and she prepared for an explosion. His muscles became tense, his breathing shallower, and he pump-fucked her face faster. She titled her head slightly back and cradled the base of his dick as his warm cum flowed freely from his head and down her throat. She continued to suck him and drain every bit of strength from his body. Her thirst was unquenchable and Serina made sure that not a drop of her Master's precious cum spilled on the sheets below her. She slowly removed his still erect dick from her lips and rubbed it all around her face as if it was a rag and she was washing her face.

"Oh God," was all she could murmur as she took him in her mouth again. "I can't get enough of you. What have you done to me?"

Silently he laid down on the bed and motioned for her to get on top of him again. Serina eagerly grabbed his dick and stuffed it inside of her as he held her by the waist, and torpedoed his erection inside of her. He grabbed her by her hair and pulled her neck down to his face. Slowly he licked her neck and she moaned. Then he bit her savagely as he fucked her deeply for over a minute without stopping. Tears of passion streamed down Serina's face again and waves of tiny orgasms spasm throughout her body. It was surreal the way a body can feel when it is being touched in the right way. Everything becomes intensified beyond your imagination. She laid on his chest limp and exhausted. His dick was still inside of her moving slowly and without thought.

"Thank you, Master," she breathed into the hairs on his chest.

He stroked her hair gently without saying a word and they both closed their eyes to revel in the passion they had just created. It could only get better with time. Serina smiled as she closed her eyes. She had met her match; a man who was willing to put her pleasure before his and still get everything from her, and more than she had ever given. She couldn't wait to see what else he had in store for her.

11/02/08...3:26pm

# Submission

For your pleasure
I am always willing to surrender
Take what is rightfully yours
I have given you all that I am
Your will is seared into my consciousness
Everything I am is for your pleasure
I give it all to you without a second thought
Only you know how to feed my mind what it needs
In the absence of You, my hunger feeds on itself
Leaving me more empty than ever before
For only You,
Will my body and mind completely submit without fail
In the throes of our passion
I don't recall who I am
Nor does it even matter
I am born again in the image of your creation
Molded to satisfy your every want and desire
To your will I fully submit
At your feet I lay naked and ready
Waiting to be filled with your strength
Ready to do your every bidding
Eagerly awaiting every orifice on my body to be filled
To submit fully goes against my very nature
I am not myself anymore
I freely admit to being under your influence
For you…anything For you…everything.
2-08-08…6:40pm

*Read on for a preview of Dean Jéan-Pierre's next collection of erotic short stories*

## Moist

### *Good Girl*

For him, I want to be a good girl. His safe place to come to escape the world when everything seems to be going wrong and no one understands him—except me. I will anticipate his every desire even before he can articulate what he wants and needs from me. The minute he walks through the door, he will know that his façade of impenetrability is not needed with me in this place of love we have created together. In my presence, he is free to be himself without reservation and naked as the day he was born without any embarrassment or judgment from me.

I see him as he is—a man who needs me to feed him my strength and my love. Even when he does not ask for it, I know that the strength of my passion will give him wings to soar higher than he knows he can fly. I will believe in him even when he does not believe in himself.

My smile greets his energy when he enters the bedroom and he cannot help but exhale and allow me to love him like the King that he is. He relaxes and allows me to embrace his body and I feel the strength of his heart, his love, beating against my breasts.

Tomorrow, he will love me like the Queen that I am, but right now, it is all about him and what he needs to make him feel special and appreciated. Every man needs that special attention so when he goes back into the world, he will know that at least one person in the world loves him unequivocally.

He wraps his long strong arms around my waist and pulls me into his body. His scent is a mixture of Eternity, sweat and the heat of summer permeating from his body. It overpowers my senses, leaving me weak and in need of his kisses to restore my strength.

He is my Kryptonite.

I am weak and vulnerable for his touch, for his kisses and the intensity of our lovemaking is so overwhelming that even when he is not with me; I can feel his touch caressing my body into a fever, keeping me warm, until I am back in his arms again.

I am his good girl. I am whatever he wants me to be without any stipulation or reciprocation. Love, when it runs deep and true, does not adhere to the principles of behavior that make us afraid to share our deepest self.

He is my Master without commanding my obedience. A true Master does not command by his words, but by the sheer force of his aura demands my complete submission. His words are silently powerful and in the breath of one sentence, he can inspire both fear and love in me. To displease or disappoint him, makes me feel unworthy of his love. He is deserving of my absolute best, not because he is my Master, but because without him in my life—I cease to be who I am—who I was meant to be.  His love, my love, enhances everything that lives within the circle of our love.  Without him in it, nothing works quite as well.

Even when clothed, I feel naked in his presence.  My clothes are on fire.  My skin burns for his touch.  When he finally touches me, kisses me, I will hold my breath so I can stop time to let the moment find its own rhythm and live forever.  His lips find the hollow of my shoulders and he fills that empty space with his beautiful fire kisses.  My feet are still on the carpet but in his arms; I am flying to our place, the place that only he can take me on the wings of our love and passion.

I am so wet that it feels as if I have gone swimming in the ocean.  He takes his time building my passion to a crescendo.  He will not allow me to climax too fast.  He thoroughly enjoys torturing me unmercifully until I beg for it like a whore, his whore.  I am every woman to him: his lover, friend, whore, slut, confidante and his Queen.  Words cannot fully describe what I am to him and what he is to me.  Whatever he needs and wants me to be--I will be that woman for him.  Love is a strange and demanding master.  We are not free to choose who we fall in love with, but falling in love gives us the freedom to be ourselves and find the person who lives within us all.  With him, I know who I am.  I know where I belong.  Even in my submission, I am free because it is my choice to submit to only him.